Other books by Kendra E. Ardnek:

The Ankulen
The Seven Drawers
The Worth of a King
A Twist of Adventure

The Rizkaland Legends
Water Princess, Fire Prince
Lady Dragon, Tela Du
Love and Memory

The Bookania Quests
Sew, It's a Quest
Do You Take This Quest?
My Kingdom for a Quest
Honor: A Quest In
Hair We Go Again
The Merchant of Menace
Snow Quest Like Home (Coming Soon!)

The Austen Fairy Tale
Rose Petals & Snowflakes
Crown & Cinder
Emmazel
Snowfield Palace
Thornrose Estate (Coming Soon!)
A Little Persuaded (Coming Soon!)

When the Snow Queen invades Mansfield Park

Snowfield Palace

The Austen Fairy Tales — 4

Kendra E. Ardnek

Copyright © 2022 Kendra E. Roden

All rights reserved.

ISBN: 9798370743832

Dedication

For Avyana and Rosalind. Because blood isn't the only thing that makes family.

Who's Who?

Ginny: Fanny / Gerta
Kaimund: Edmund / Kai
Lady Bethim: Lady Bertram
Lord Bethim: Lord Bertram
Mayblossom: Mrs. Grant
Sir Graham: Mr. Grant
Maia: Mary Crawford / The Snow queen
Hans: Henry Crawford
Lady Nora: Aunt Norris
Rina: Maria / The Princess
Lord Reynard: Mr. Rushworth / The Prince
Calla: Julia
Robert: Thomas Bertram
Will: William / Mr. Yates / The Robbermaiden
Suzy: Suzy Price

1

There once were two girls, daughters of merchants, sisters in all but blood. Seldom was there an argument between them as children, and they were quite inseparable. But children grow, and time has a way of dissolving even the best of friendships.

Their fathers were quite successful, and with success comes ambition. As the girls came of age, their fathers sought to use their marriages to ally with the nobility. As both maidens were fair indeed and their fathers were wealthy, their hands were well-sought, and soon their fathers accepted two offers.

The girls were to marry brothers, two lords of considerable influence. The girls would live together as sisters, and there was nothing they could want more—

Save that Anastasia, the younger, had fallen in love with a footman. No matter how appealing the circumstance, she couldn't bear to betray her heart, so she and her lover made plans to escape together.

But before she left the life she knew and her father's chosen future, Anastasia met with her best friend one last time to explain it all.

Elsabet had known about the footman but had thought her friend would do her duty and abandon him. As such, she was quite horrified to learn of the scheme.

"Oh! But you can't!" she cried in alarm. "You gave your

word, and it's all arranged. Your father—"

"My father gave my word, despite all of my protests." Anastasia shook her head, resolute. "But *I* had given it to my Jack, and I *shan't* abandon him for anything."

"But we are to be sisters!" Elsabet reached forward to grab Anastasia's hands. "If you run away, then I – I fear that I shall never see you again."

"Don't be silly!" cried Anastasia. "We're only getting married. We—"

"No, *you're* being silly!" Elsabet shook her head. "If you do this, your father will disown you, and you will live as a peasant. I am to join the nobility – if you abandon me now, we will be forever separated by our walks of life. And the life you'll live! Have you even thought about how difficult it will be to live as a peasant – when you *could* be a lady?"

Anastasia just shook her head. "It's easy for you to make this choice, Elsabet – you're to marry the older brother, who is handsome and healthy, while *my* would-be husband is sickly. You love none other, so you can bestow your hand at liberty, while my heart is already taken. How can I abandon love for riches? It is a choice between miseries, and my mind is already made up."

Elsabet gripped her friend's hands tighter, eyes desperately wide. Then she broke away and spun around to grab a silk rose from her table.

"Take this," she instructed. "If you're ever in trouble that I can help, then send this to me, and I'll – I'll do what I can." She took a long, frustrated breath. "But it might not be much."

Anastasia eased into a slow smile as she accepted the rose. "Thank you, my friend, but I pray that I shall never need it."

"As do I," said Elsabet. She hesitated a moment, and then threw her arms around Anastasia and held her tight. "Oh, but I shall miss you, friend. Sister."

"And I shall miss you," said Anastasia. "It is a cruel fate that we should be so torn apart, but what can we do?"

Elsabet had opinions about that, but they had already been said, so she held her silence as her friend slipped through the window and into the night.

That was the last time the two friends saw each other.

~

Eleven years passed. Elsabet obediently married the lord her father had chosen and settled into her new life as Lady Bethim in Snowfield Palace. His intended gone, Lord Bethim's brother, Lord Fillip, eventually married a lower-ranking noblewoman named Lady Nora, and the whole embarrassment with Anastasia was forgotten by all but her former friend.

Lady Bethim was soon distracted by the arrival of a son, Kaimund, not two years later, and then daughters, Rina and Calla in the years that followed. Calla's birth was particularly hard, and she never really recovered, leaving her tired and sickly afterward. Lady Nora remained childless but eventually took in her brother's second son as a ward. He was of an age with Kaimund, and they hoped for a friendship between the two boys, but Robert proved a reckless young man and Kaimund too cautious for his schemes.

Theirs was a quiet, orderly life. Robert sometimes caused trouble, but Lady Nora always laughed it off as harmless boyhood fun. Kaimund was everything a father could ask for: dutiful, intelligent, and dependable. The two daughters were more troublesome, but they always gave a proper appearance when required.

It was thirteen years before Lady Bethim had to remember her promise. Thirteen years before a girl of seven appeared on the doorstep of Snowfield Palace, clutching the red silk rose to her chest.

The child was ushered inside and into the kitchens at once, for it was the coldest, darkest day of winter, and no child should have been left on a doorstep in that storm. It took an hour, a bowl of hot soup, and a mug of warm milk before she overcame her timidity, told Cook her name – Ginny – and asked her to take the rose to Lady Bethim.

It was a strange request, and Cook almost ignored it, but the girl's eyes were so wide and earnest that she sent the rose with a page boy.

Lady Bethim fainted upon seeing it. When she recovered, she demanded to know where it had been found. Everyone was shocked at her passion when she usually had such a quiet disposition. When she heard about the child, she insisted she be brought at once.

So, Ginny was brought before the lady and stood trembling at the foot of the sofa. What a small, frail thing she was, with her pale hair bound in two braids and her blue eyes wide, especially compared to Rina and Calla, who were playing on the other side of the room.

Lady Bethim sat up and held out her hand. "Dear child, where did you get this rose?"

Ginny stared at the hand, shaking her head.

"Come now, dear." Lady Bethim gave Ginny her best smile. "Don't be frightened. I'm here to help you. You – you have Anastasia's eyes. Is she your mother? Are you Anastasia's little girl? How is my old friend?"

The child burst into tears.

"Anastasia?" said Lady Nora sharply, from where she sat at embroidery at the other side of the room. "Wasn't that the silly friend you used to have? The one who thought herself too good for my Fillip? Fool girl! He was too good for *her!*"

"Anastasia always thought with her heart first, poor thing," Lady Bethim declared with a sigh. "I couldn't convince her to see sense, hard as I tried."

Ginny continued to cry. Not loudly – indeed, she seemed to be trying to stay as quiet as possible, wiping away the tears with her sleeve as they fell, and her breath came in muffled gasps.

"Ma-mama has go-gone where Daddy is and won't–won't be back, Will says," she finally stuttered out. "Will can't–can't take care of me, too, and–and said that if–if I gave Lady Bethim the r-rose, then she–she would!"

"Oh, you poor thing!" cried Lady Bethim.

"It's just like that Anastasia to shirk her responsibilities," said Lady Nora. "Shove her waif on you." She gave a sniff, pulling her thread taunt. "But it won't do to toss the child back out into the cold. Send her back to Cook and see if use can be found for her. She can turn the spit if nothing else, I'm sure."

Ginny started to cry harder. The tears came faster, the gasps harder to quiet, and her shoulders were shaking.

"Oh, *do* be quiet, child." Lady Nora shook her head, exasperated. "Don't make a fool of yourself, like your mother."

"Poor Anastasia…" muttered Lady Bethim, then her gaze drifted to her daughters. "Don't you think that Rina and Calla could use a companion their age?"

"They have each other," said Lady Nora. "And if they need another, they can do so much better than this creature." She sniffed. "Looks like a street rat, she does. Half-starved and dressed in rags like this. Just *think* of all the horrid manners she must have."

"Oh, poor Anastasia," Lady Bethim repeated. "Poor, poor child. Come here, let's dry those tears and lift that chin. It's going to be all right. Like Will said, we'll take care of you."

"And look who's thinking with her heart now!" cried Lady Nora, throwing down her embroidery hoop. "I don't know how they do things in the backward circles you grew up in, but your husband will have words to say about this!"

Lady Bethim blinked, then seized Ginny's hand and stood. "Yes, of course! I should tell Lord Bethim. Poor thing – poor, *poor* Anastasia."

Lady Nora shook her head as Lady Bethim led Ginny away. Her sister-in-law would have to learn sometime. Commoners should never mix with nobility – what *was* the world coming to?

But, to Lady Nora's great horror, Lord Bethim was more than happy to take on another ward. He thought her a charming little thing, and Lady Bethim rarely asked for anything. Lord Bethim was one of those men who substituted gifts for true affection, and this was a very *small* child.

"Besides," he said. "She might have been my brother's child, and he has no children of his own. Perhaps Austere sent her as an answer to Nora's prayers."

Lady Nora wanted nothing to do with Ginny. No, if Lady Bethim wanted to take in a vagrant off the street, then she would be the one responsible. Rina and Calla protested sharing their room with another, so Ginny was given a smaller room almost within the servants' quarters. It was a cozy space, but it still felt enormous to her, and she cried herself to sleep most nights.

Ginny didn't complain – how could she when everyone told her how lucky she was to have been plucked from the streets? Yes, she had a roof over her head, a decently warm bed, and good food each day, but she was a very small, frightened child in a large, strange place.

She drifted through, clinging to corners and the edges of rooms in an attempt to go unnoticed. When she was noticed, she tried to obey whatever was asked of her as quickly as possible. After all, frightening as it was to live in such a large, imposing place, the threat of being rejected and turned out on the street filled her with dread. She didn't know where to find Will again – the only other person who would care for her – and she certainly didn't know how to survive on her own. No, she would never give her benefactors cause to regret their charity.

And so the years passed. Ginny quietly found a place in the Bethim household, though she never quite felt like she fit. She spent most of her time at Lady Bethim's side, as she was the easiest to please, and avoided Lady Nora, who could never be satisfied.

She never became the companion for Rina and Calla that Lady Bethim hoped for, but she did form a close friendship with Kaimund, beginning one day when he found her crying in the gardens under a short clump of evergreen shrubs at the end of a walk. He asked her what was the matter, and heard the story in halting gasps – Lady Nora had scolded her particularly harshly for idleness and had sent her outside for exercise. It was a warm day, she never handled the heat well, and the evergreen had been the best shade she could find.

"Come with me," he instructed, holding out a hand to her.

She accepted it hesitantly and allowed him to guide her down the paths to a beautiful, hidden arbor of roses, complete with a small, bubbling brook.

"Don't tell anyone," he said, "but sometimes I wish I could be a gardener instead of the son of a lord. Getting to spend my time tending Austere's creation – that would be my dream. Alas, but it isn't my lot. People are his creation, too, though, so it's just as noble to tend them as well, don't you think?"

Ginny gave a silent nod, not sure what to say to a confession like that.

"But this is my part of the garden," Kaimund continued. "The gardeners tend it for me when I can't, which is often, but I do as much as possible. My sisters don't know of it, and I'd never tell Robert, but you're gentle, and I know you'll take care of it. When you need a place to hide, you can come here. It's the coolest part of the garden."

"Thank you," she whispered. "I'd like that."

"Then it's settled." He patted her hand. "This garden is yours whenever you need it."

Ginny's cheeks were already warm from the heat, for which she was glad – there was no way for Kaimund to see her blush as the first sparks of love lit in the heart of the nine-year-old girl.

Ginny's nineteenth year was when everything changed.

Things hadn't exactly been a constant up until then, true enough. When she was twelve, the youngest Bethim brother, Sir Graham, finally married. His bride was the foreign Princess Mayblossom, and it was a strange affair, to be certain – a love match, even! – but the Bethims had been happy to ally themselves with royalty.

When Ginny was seventeen, the sickly Lord Fillip passed into the Ever After, leaving Lady Nora a widow. Without her husband to care for, she became twice the meddlesome busybody she'd been before, much to Ginny's misery. Lady Nora's temper had always been short, but as a widow, it was practically nonexistent.

But neither change truly disrupted the order of Snowfield Palace. Princess Mayblossom and Sir Graham were in her country almost as often as they were at Snowfield, and she was the quiet sort and easy to please. And Lady Nora was, well, she was Lady Nora.

Ginny liked Princess Mayblossom, for she often had stories

to tell of her childhood in the North Country and the mysterious Forest, where her aunt ruled as the Gardener. Rina and Calla found those stories dull, so Ginny gradually became Princess Mayblossom's companion as frequently as she was Lady Bethim's – when Princess Mayblossom was at Snowfield, at least.

And so it happened one day that Princess Mayblossom and Ginny were walking through the garden in the cool of the evening. Ginny had just escaped a very stern scolding from Lady Nora, so she was especially quiet as they walked.

"It's sad, you know," Princess Mayblossom commented once she finally got Ginny to confess to the confrontation. "A woman can be so insecure when her status depends on the whims of the men around her. Nora's family is struggling, despite their status, and she wasn't able to produce a child to irrevocably tie her to the Bethims. It was Fillip's fault, far more than her own, if you ask me, and Lord Bethim would never turn her away, but she's still scared and uncertain. Since she sees you as small and inferior, she considers you something she can control."

"What can I do, then?" asked Ginny.

"Keep that cheerful spirit of yours, for one," Princess Mayblossom recommended. "And pray for her. Only Austere can truly heal her heart."

Ginny nodded. "I know. I wish I could do enough to make her happy, though."

"That shall never happen," said Princess Mayblossom. "She sees the world through the lens of her fears and bitterness, so nothing will ever be good enough for her. Especially not you. Like anyone else, the only person you can really control is yourself – in the way you view the world and how you respond to the things that happen to you, for good or ill. My Aunt Elin always says that if you seek out the best in people, they very often show it to you, eventually. And even if they don't, then it's on them."

"It can be hard to see any good in someone like Lady Nora," said Ginny.

"She's a tough one." Princess Mayblossom reached for Ginny's hand and squeezed it. "But she's part of Austere's creation, and that's reason enough. Show her a gracious spirit and pray. Eventually, Austere might prick her conscience and begin a change." She gave a long sigh. "Nora would have given anything for children of her own, while I…"

When Princess Mayblossom left the thought dangling, Ginny swallowed and asked, "While you what?"

Princess Mayblossom shook her head. "I have nothing against children – indeed, I loved helping both my aunts and stepmother while my cousins and half-siblings were small." She gave another sigh. "But the truth is that I'm terrified of pregnancy. Well, mostly the childbirth part of it."

"I've heard that it can be difficult," Ginny timidly squeezed Princess Mayblossom's hand back.

"Both my mother and grandmother died in childbirth." Princess Mayblossom took a deep breath as they turned down another path. "It's only natural that I fear that I'll follow the same fate – irrational though that fear might be. Graham loves me just the same, with or without children. Still…"

"I'm sorry," said Ginny, unsure how else to answer the princess.

"There's nothing you can do about it – but I do appreciate the listening ear." Princess Mayblossom tilted her head to the side. "And it's not even a looming fear. Aunt Emmazel makes me a potion to prevent pregnancy. Which Graham knows about, don't worry. He would prefer to have me here with him than to risk my life for the chance of children, if that is my fear. It's just … some days … and especially lately…" She shook her head. "Everyone is hiding some form of pain, Ginny. Remember that. And everyone responds to their pain in different ways. That's why you have to treat everyone with grace."

Ginny swallowed and nodded. "I'll try."

~

And she did try. It still wasn't easy, but there already was so little that Ginny could do but comply with every whim in the Bethim household. Not unless she was willing to risk her place in it.

It was three months after her conversation with Princess Mayblossom that Rina and the princess each made an announcement that together changed the course of life for the Bethim household irrevocably.

Rina was a beautiful young lady of twenty, and as the eldest Bethim daughter, her hand was eagerly sought – much to Calla's jealousy. She had been refusing to pick a favorite – to her father's consternation. He wished to see her settled, but arranged marriages had fallen out of fashion.

But that night, as everyone gathered for dinner, Rina suddenly stood, raised her glass, and declared, "I have chosen my husband!"

"Finally!" cried Calla. "Now, the rest can leave you alone, and I shall have *my* chance."

Rina rolled her eyes. "You're barely eighteen – you didn't need any of their attention until now, anyway."

"Who is your husband-to-be, dear?" asked Lady Bethim.

"I do hope you were wise about it and made the *best* choice," said Lady Nora. "The number of young ladies marrying beneath their stations these days is shocking. It never would have happened in my day, I tell you."

Rina rolled her eyes again but more subtly so Lady Nora wouldn't notice. "Of course, Aunt. What is the world coming to? Father *quite* approves of my choice, don't worry. It's all properly arranged, and the wedding is set for six months from now. Lord Reynard is the gentleman, and as the Duke of Suthers, not even *you* can find flaws in him."

Lady Nora sniffed. "Ah, an excellent choice. I always knew you were a prudent young woman, Rina, and you have done well for yourself! There are few rivals to Suthers in status, not in this part of the country, and I can't wait to call upon you in your new domain."

"Lord Reynard," said Calla, her nose wrinkling. "Isn't he the dull fellow nearly in his thirties? I swear, but if he says even three words to me, I feel that I'll fall asleep! Or laugh. He says the most ridiculous things, at times. Why, last week, he complimented me on my dress at least three times, a different name each time, and not once was it the right one. Tell me, does he remember *your* name, Rina."

"He won't need to, once he gives her his," said Lady Nora before Rina could properly open her mouth to answer. "Young women these days and their need for *conversation*. Calla, your sister knows that a woman's best chance of happiness is stability – a foundation under her feet and a roof over her head. Lord Reynard is as stable a fellow as ever there was. Once they're married and she's given him a son or two, she'll want for nothing."

"Oh, yes, stability, the *most* romantic trait of all," muttered Calla.

"He's handsome enough – and *I've* always preferred mature men," said Rina, her cheeks flushing red. "It will not be an intolerable affair."

"I should say not!" cried Lady Nora with a huff. "Perhaps Mayblossom's aunt will be able to give you a potion or two to ensure that an heir comes *sooner* rather than later, if you know what I mean. Though … they haven't seemed to help her at all, so take that as you will."

Rina's blush deepened. "I'll … keep that in mind."

"Emmazel's potions are seldom ineffective," said Princess Mayblossom, heat blooming in her own cheeks. "And if I had ever asked her for *that* sort of potion, she would have given it to me, but I … preferred to not rush."

"You've lost the prime of your youth in your patience," said Lady Nora, shaking her head. "But who am I to criticize your Highness?"

Sir Graham reached for Princess Mayblossom's hand as she leaned against him. Ginny swallowed. She knew how difficult the situation was for the princess, but not how she could help. Maybe it was best to let Princess Mayblossom's husband handle the situation.

"Kaimund is my brother's heir, and I have no need for one

of my own," he said. "I put no pressure on Mayblossom."

Lady Nora sniffed. "Well, to each their own."

Princess Mayblossom took a deep breath and straightened. "We … are actually expecting the arrival of our first next winter, if all goes well."

Ginny nearly choked on the spoonful of soup she had just put in her mouth, earning a disgruntled side-eye from Lady Nora.

"Congratulations," said Lord Bethim, nodding in approval. "I expect that you plan to settle down now that you're starting a family of your own."

"That remains to be seen," said Sir Graham, squeezing Princess Mayblossom's hand tighter. "This has been quite unexpected for us."

"You must be *so* excited, my dear," said Lady Nora, her gaze narrow.

"Of course," said Princess Mayblossom, but her smile was tense, and she excused herself from the table not long after, Sir Graham going with her.

"Well!" said Lady Nora, shaking her head. "This is certainly going to be an interesting year, won't it be?"

Murmurs of agreement rippled around the table, but if only they had known the half of it then!

Ginny excused herself from the table as soon as she thought it acceptable and slipped down the halls, curiosity burning within her. She didn't *dare* intrude upon the princess, and yet…

Poor Mayblossom! After so long avoiding this and now! She must be terrified right now! She'd certainly seemed so at the table, especially in response to Lady Nora's cruel jabs.

Ginny found herself standing in front of the door to Princess Mayblossom's rooms, shifting her weight from one foot to the other as she considered whether or not to knock. Would Princess Mayblossom want her right now? She'd confided in Ginny before, and Ginny certainly knew more than her fair share about Lady Nora's critical comments.

But she had her husband right now, didn't she? Wouldn't he be enough? Princess Mayblossom didn't need Ginny there to gossip.

Ginny sent up a silent prayer for wisdom and then knocked at the door before she finished. Her breath caught at the impulsiveness. Her mind screamed at her to run, but her feet seemed frozen to the floor.

Then the door opened, and there was Sir Graham, blinking at her in confusion. "Miss Ginny. Is everything all right?"

"I—" Ginny's breath came out in a panicked squeak.

"If that's Ginny, then you can send her in," came Princess Mayblossom's voice from behind him. "She … knew about things and is probably worried about me."

"Very well," said Sir Graham, and he stepped out of the way so Ginny could enter.

Princess Mayblossom lay on a sofa already in her nightdress, with a hand covering her eyes.

"It's sweet of you to check in on me," she said, lowering her hand to offer an encouraging smile. "I'm fine, you know. It's just … saying it aloud made it real. Now that everyone knows, I can put it out of my mind again. For now."

"What happened!" Ginny demanded, rushing to Princess Mayblossom's bedside. Then she swallowed. "I mean, you just said that your aunt's potions always work, so…"

"They can fail quite easily if a person stops taking them." Princess Mayblossom gave a rueful laugh. "Which is what I did over two months ago."

"Why?" breathed Ginny. "You said…"

Sir Graham gave a disapproving grunt but said nothing, and the princess sent him a placating smile.

"I was a fool, I know." She sighed. "It seemed so simple at the time – to stop meddling and leave it all up to Austere, but now I have to live with the decision. I've had three panic attacks already today. Might have to also ask Aunt Emmazel if she has anything for anxiety that wouldn't hurt the baby." She reached for Ginny's hand and squeezed it. "The truth of the matter is that I've always wanted to be a mother, fears aside. I blame my half-siblings and cousins – they're all grown up now, and I realized that I'm thirty years old and not getting any younger. So I stopped taking the potion – it tasted awful, anyway – and left it up to Austere. As I already said."

"We could have taken in a child. Or something," said Sir Graham.

"I know, but we hadn't yet." Princess Mayblossom swallowed. "We do travel a lot, and the Bethims have already taken in both Robert and you, Ginny dear, and I doubt they want another."

"I'm sorry," said Ginny.

"Oh, no, don't be!" Princess Mayblossom squeezed Ginny's hand. "I never would want you to lose your home for my sake. No, this is not your fault at all. I'm only a mess because I just found out for sure yesterday. It's new. That's all. Aunt Elin assures me that I'm healthy and don't have to follow my mother's fate. And Aunt Emmazel has given me a whole set of potions to take to ensure my health and the baby's." She sighed. "Don't worry about me. I'm in very good hands." She leaned back. "And that goes for you doubly, husband of mine. I need everyone around me as positive as possible. Distract me from my impending doom. Believe so hard that I will live that I can't even consider the alternative."

Sir Graham gave another grunt and then walked around Ginny to press a kiss to the top of his wife's head. "Anything you need, my dear." He glanced at Ginny. "I do think she needs her rest now, if you will…"

"Oh, Graham! None of that!" Princess Mayblossom batted playfully at him, then shook her head. "You have done me a world of good already, just by listening, Ginny."

"I *should* be going, though," said Ginny, nodding as she awkwardly stood. "I'll … I'll be praying. And if you need anything I can do … I'll try."

"Thank you," said Princess Mayblossom. "You're a good soul. Really."

Ginny gave her a small smile as she slipped out of the room, and she paused on the other side of the door to catch her breath—

But there was Lady Nora, standing with her arms folded

over her chest. "What do you think you're doing, young lady?"

Ginny squeaked and ran, not stopping until she reached the sanctuary of her bedroom.

The disaster of that year might still have
been averted, but Lord Bethim and Sir
Graham received a summons to attend
the king in the capitol with no indication of when they might
come home again. They left the very next day.

With the men gone, all attention was given to Princess
Mayblossom and Rina. Rina drank it up, but it did nothing to
help Princess Mayblossom's nerves. In fact, between both
Lady Bethim and Lady Nora, the princess was a trembling
mess by the end of the week.

Lady Bethim, for her part, had been overjoyed for one of
her sisters-in-law to finally join her in motherhood and regaled
Mayblossom with stories of her own pregnancies and every
little thing that had gone wrong with each. Princess
Mayblossom listened silently, wringing her hands, growing
paler with each account.

Ginny tried to rescue the princess, suggesting that she was
tired and needed to be taken to her room for a nap. Lady
Bethim, with her own weak constitution, believed the excuse
and shooed Princess Mayblossom away. Lady Nora, however,
with her critical, narrow eyes, intercepted Ginny as she
escorted the princess out of the room and insisted on doing
such a duty herself.

And routinely after that, Lady Nora insisted on being the
one to attend Princess Mayblossom at all times. She feared

losing her place in the household now that she was the only wife to have not produced children. Clearly, she thought that if she was indispensable to the princess, then she was secure. However, her attitude and energy only increased Princess Mayblossom's agitation. Ginny tried to do what she could to relieve the situation, but standing up to Lady Nora's stern glare was hard.

By the end of a week, it was so bad that Ginny found the princess crying in the corner of the dining room. She tried to reassure her, but then Lady Nora was there, glaring. Ginny ran, as Lady Nora stepped forward to *reassure* Princess Mayblossom herself.

Reassurance that more closely resembled a scolding.

Ginny found herself in the garden, and a thought occurred to her that made her breath catch. *She* couldn't help Princess Mayblossom, but perhaps she could contact someone who could.

She rushed through the paths. When Princess Mayblossom married Sir Graham, she'd planted a hazel tree in a corner of the garden that had a magical connection to the Forest where her aunts ruled. She could use it to travel to and from the Forest, but no one else could, not even her husband.

But Ginny could at least *try*. Princess Mayblossom needed help. Swallowing, she brushed her fingers against the bark of the hazel tree. What now? How was she to reach the Gardener? Did she need to speak aloud? Would this even work? Oh, but Princess Mayblossom desperately needed her aunt right now—

The world shifted, and there stood the Gardener beside the hazel tree with her, hands folded tightly in front of her, a frown creasing her brow. Ginny's breath caught, and she took a step back as she stared up at the strange woman. She'd seen the Gardener before, yes, but only ever at a distance.

She seemed young unless one looked into her eyes. A rose vine grew from her head, tangling through her curls, and her dress was made of leaves and rose petals.

"What's wrong with Mayblossom," she demanded. "Is it the baby?"

Ginny opened and shut her mouth, but all that came out was a squeak.

The Gardener's frown grew, but then she schooled her face into a smile, and her voice softened as she continued.

"I'm not going to hurt you, dear – Ginny, isn't it? I'm not in the habit of shooting messengers." The Gardener took a deep breath. "I'm glad you were able to reach me – you must have had a parent from the Forest, for you don't seem to have any Sensitive magic at all. Now, why does Mayblossom need me?"

And the story spilled out of Ginny in halting sentences. She didn't tell everything – she had her own secrets to keep, after all – but she somehow made sure that the Gardener knew that Princess Mayblossom was struggling to keep her spirits up in the face of Lady Nora's "care" and that Ginny herself was powerless to intercede.

The Gardener nodded solemnly as she finished. "I feared as much, especially when she told me that Graham was called away. Poor thing – this whole affair has been messy all around. I told her she should stay in the Forest with me, but she wants to stay as close to Graham as possible – which I entirely understand. But rest assured – I will do what I can for her. Mayblossom is as dear to me as either of my own children, and I will *not* see her spirits trampled by the likes of Nora. Not at this delicate time."

With that, she pressed a kiss to the top of Ginny's head, then turned and swept out of the garden, the scent of roses lingering after her.

Ginny's stomach twisted into knots as she stood alone again. Princess Mayblossom would be taken care of; she knew that for sure. But would Lady Nora suspect that Ginny had been the one to meddle? Would she punish her as revenge?

She would, wouldn't she?

Swallowing, Ginny fled again, this time to Kaimund's corner of the garden. The roses weren't blooming yet, but the buds held promise. She sat down on the bench and buried her face in her hands as she fought to catch her breath.

She'd done the right thing, she reassured herself. It didn't matter what happened to her. Princess Mayblossom would get the help she needed. Ginny had borne Lady Nora's ire her whole life – it was the price of her life at Snowfield Palace. She would survive.

"Ah, Ginny. I'd hoped I would find you here."

Her hands fell from her eyes, and she looked up with a smile as Kaimund stood before her. He quietly circled around the spring and sat down on the bench beside her. "Is everything all right? Aunt Nora didn't scold you again, did she?"

Ginny bit her lip and shrugged. "It's just dreadful, watching her with the princess. Doesn't she realize that she's just making it harder for her?"

Kaimund sighed. "Who knows what Aunt Nora realizes. But don't worry. Aunt Mayblossom's aunt just showed up for a surprise visit to check on her and has banished Aunt Nora from Aunt Mayblossom's rooms. It was quite unexpected, but I can't say that I'm not sorry."

"Poor Princess Mayblossom," Ginny muttered.

"And her aunt will take care of her." Kaimund reached for Ginny's hand and squeezed it. "But if you think that Aunt Nora isn't good for Aunt Mayblossom, then I will do what I can to keep her focused on Rina's wedding. She gets along with Rina better than anyone else, you know."

"I know." Ginny's smile tightened. "But that will leave Princess Mayblossom with your mother, and your mother's stories about Calla's birth scare her. She—" She swallowed. Would it be a breach of the princess's trust to confide in Kaimund? He would be able to help, wouldn't he? But if she wanted him to know, then she would have told him herself. Right?

She gave another shrug. "Her mother and grandmother both died in childbirth, you know." It couldn't be wrong to tell him a known fact and let him piece it together himself. Or, at least, it was better.

"They did, didn't they?" Kaimund thoughtfully tilted his head to the side. "Oh, I see. Mother's stories would upset her, wouldn't they?"

Ginny nodded. "Exactly."

Kaimund gave a long sigh and then tugged one of Ginny's braids. "Well, I don't know what to do about my mother, but the Gardener is here now. She'll take care of Aunt Mayblossom. Aunt Nora might act like a force of nature, but the Gardener *is* one, you know."

A small laugh escaped Ginny, and she fidgeted with the braid he'd held. "She is, isn't she? But she can't be here all of the time. She has the Forest to take care of, you know."

"She'll figure it out – you don't have to worry about Aunt Mayblossom, though it's just like you to do so." He stood, took her hand again, and pulled her to her feet. "Now, come along. We can't keep hiding out here, frightful as it is to step into Aunt Nora's line of fire. I'll do what I can about her, and you can try to distract my mother."

"If Lady Nora isn't there, I think I can manage Lady Bethim." Ginny squeezed Kaimund's hand before letting go of it. "Thank you."

~

Kaimund did his best to keep Lady Nora away from Princess Mayblossom, really he did, but she was incredibly stubborn and determined to run the household the way she liked. The Gardener came nearly daily, but even she admitted that it wasn't a permanent solution. The Forest needed her, and it was a strain on Emmazel for her to come and go so often.

Emmazel herself came one day to deliver a new set of potions for Princess Mayblossom and engage in a hissing match with Lady Nora. Ginny hung back while Emmazel was there, for she seemed even more frightful than the Gardener, even without thorns. And Lady Nora's mood was truly foul when she left, and Ginny was the sufferer for it.

It took a week for them to determine a solution, and two weeks after that, Princess Mayblossom's younger half-siblings arrived. Princess Maia was to keep her sister company, and though she was only the same age as Rina, she had the status and spirit to stand up to Lady Nora and knew how to comfort her sister. Her older brother, Prince Hans, had insisted on accompanying her.

Ginny wasn't required to join the rest of the Bethim household to greet the prince and princess when they arrived. In fact, Lady Nora strongly recommended that she make herself scarce.

So she did, watching instead from the sitting room window as the carriage pulled up to the palace doorstep. The door opened, and a dark-haired young man sprang out, gave everyone a winsome smile, and then turned to hand out a beautiful young woman paler than Ginny herself. Her hair was nearly *white*, and while her brother was fair himself, her hand was nearly translucent within his.

Princess Maia was a Frost, like her mother. Ginny knew that already from Princess Mayblossom's stories, but it was different now that she actually saw her. A real Frost…

It called up echoes of memory that Ginny hadn't thought of in years.

Princess Maia rushed forward to hug her sister while Prince Hans exchanged greetings with the rest of the Bethim family, bowing deeply before Rina and Calla before he moved on to shake hands with Kaimund. Ginny's stomach twisted at the sight – at the way that Rina's and Calla's cheeks flushed at the attention.

Prince Hans was a charming young man. Ginny could recognize that well enough. Not necessarily *handsome*, not in her mind, not with him standing next to Kaimund, who was tall, and honest, and kind. Prince Hans was shorter than Kaimund by a whole handswidth, and there was nothing honest or kind about his smile at all. It was … dangerous. An unspoken request for the viewer to risk her heart, with no promise of safety. A false openness that revealed nothing true.

Ginny had never disliked anyone so thoroughly on sight, and she had met most of Rina's crowd of suitors.

Princess Maia was quite unlike both her brother and sister, processing neither Princess Mayblossom's quiet, yet open kindness, nor Prince Hans' friendly intrigue. She smiled only when she hugged her sister – and that smile was real enough – but her lips pressed back into a firm line when she pulled back to address the others. Not a smile. Not a frown. Just a cool expression of placid watchfulness. Like she was a frozen lake with ice blue eyes that missed nothing.

Ginny couldn't hear the conversation from her window. She could really only judge them by their appearance and mannerisms, which she knew was unfair. But there was also a lot to learn from appearances.

She decided that she would sooner trust Princess Maia than Prince Hans – though she felt terrible thinking that she would dislike any of Princess Mayblossom's relations. She certainly didn't like the glint in Lady Nora's eyes as she watched the prince and princess, then leaned over to whisper in Calla's ear.

She liked it even less when they all entered the house—

Princess Maia on Kaimund's arm.

Ginny pulled away from the window, knuckles pressed against her teeth as she tried to swallow down the icy knots in her stomach. It meant nothing, she tried to tell herself. Princess Maia was the guest of honor, and Kaimund the master of the house in the absence of his father and uncle. It was his duty to escort her inside…

But—

Princess Maia was beautiful – in her cold, solemn way. And Ginny had noticed the way that Kaimund stared at her. The way that he would never look at Ginny herself.

It didn't matter. It couldn't. She'd always known that Kaimund would never be hers – that he was destined for one of his own status. Hers would only be stolen moments.

But she had never expected it to hurt so much to watch it happen – as though icy shards slashed across her heart.

Kaimund sought her out hours later. He told her he'd been worried about her disappearance and asked why she hadn't been there to greet North's younger prince and princess. Ginny just shook her head and tried to stammer out an answer, but his face lit with understanding as soon as she said Lady Nora's name.

"Ah, sweet Ginny," he said, taking her hand in both of his and squeezing it tight. "Aunt Nora will never accept that you're as worthy as any member in the Bethim household – and Maia asked about you specifically. I had to tell her that you weren't feeling well." He took a deep breath and leaned in. "It seems that you made quite the impression on the Gardener."

Ginny squeaked, but with her hand in his, the world felt … more right than it had been before. But he still wasn't hers and never would be.

No matter how much she loved him.

"What did … did Lady Nora hear…"

"Maia and I were quite in confidence at the moment," Kaimund assured her. "She knows your vulnerable position in our household and commends you for what you've done for her sister." He dropped her hand. "Did you really summon the Gardener when she told us the visit was a surprise?"

Ginny bit her lip and nodded. "Princess Mayblossom

needed more than any of us were able to do. I had to do what I could – I didn't think it would work, but I couldn't think of what else to do. I had to try."

"And it's good that you did," he said. "So, thank you. Aunt Mayblossom feels better already, and the new faces will change everything for the better."

Ginny swallowed, dropping her gaze from his smile to her hands. "And … what do you think of our guests?"

It was best to hear it now, before she could let any more seeds of hope take root in her heart. Kaimund might be her dearest friend in all the world, but he was so far beyond her reach … and she had to remember that.

"Hans is the same fellow he's always been – a personality so much larger than himself." Kaimund gave a laugh. "Maia, though. She … she's grown up since I last saw her. She's … beautiful."

"She's a princess," said Ginny, glancing up at him through her lashes.

"Yes," he said. "But she wants to meet you. Her mother was of no consequence before marrying King James. She knows better than to place too much value on a title."

And he slipped her hand into the crook of his elbow – where Princess Maia's had rested not hours before – and led her out of the room. The knots in her stomach tightened with each step.

Everything had changed. Ginny couldn't help feeling that everything had slipped through her fingers – but there wasn't a thing that she would have done differently.

And what did she matter in the grand scheme of things? She had done her duty and had helped the people she cared about. She would do that a thousand times over with no regrets, but why did her heart have to break into so many pieces?

As they neared the sitting room where the others were gathered, Ginny gave Kaimund's arm a last squeeze before she slipped her hand free and dropped it to her side. Kaimund glanced down at her with a frown but said nothing as he pushed open the door to the room.

Maia sat on a sofa next to her sister, talking. Lady Bethim reclined on another couch, softly snoring. Prince Hans stood in a corner, regaling Rina and Calla with a story that held them both enraptured. Meanwhile, Lady Nora, as always, presided over it all from her armchair, her eye sharp as she worked at her embroidery.

Princess Maia, though, was Ginny's and Kaimund's focus as they stepped into the room. Her expression had been engaged enough as she'd talked to Princess Mayblossom, but now it turned placid again, her lips pressed into a line.

"This is Ginny," Kaimund proudly declared, directing Ginny to stand in front of the princesses.

Princess Mayblossom grinned broadly and leaned closer to her sister. "And a dear girl she is, too. I hope you're feeling better now, Ginny."

"Yes," said Ginny, glancing across the room to Lady Nora, and then she dipped into a curtsy. "It's an honor to meet you, your Highness."

Princess Maia's lips twisted briefly into a semblance of a smile. "The honor is all mine, I assure you."

Princess Mayblossom shifted over and patted the space on her other side. "Sit down, dear – your hovering is enough to set a body's nerves on edge."

Ginny swallowed and sat down quickly and quietly. Arguing would only make a scene. And thankfully, Lady Nora's attention was solidly on Rina and Calla. She was safe with the princesses. For now.

"Did you and your brother have a good trip, your Highness?" she asked, trying to be polite. She wanted to stay silent, but Princess Mayblossom seemed determined to include her. The least she could do was keep it focused on Princess Maia where it belonged.

"It was fair for what it was," said Princess Maia. "Travel is always more hassle than it's worth – if you want my opinion – and Hans and I, tragically, do not have enough Forest magic in our blood for us to use the hazel trees like Blana can. We just didn't spend enough time with Aunt Elin, growing up, no matter how we would beg and cajole Father, while Aunt Elin is practically Blana's mother."

"Blana?" Ginny repeated.

"It's how Maia would say my name when she was learning to talk," Princess Mayblossom explained. "She would have grown out of it, but Hans started calling me by it, and then Father, too, and now here we are." She gave a sigh that indicated long-suffering, but the smile she cast toward Princess Maia spoke a different story."

"Mayblossom is just *too* long a name," declared Princess Maia, waving off her sister. "We had to cut it short somehow, just as we do Aunt Elin and Aunt Mari. Now, as I was saying, the natural solution would have been for Blana to come and stay with us — as her family, we *would* have taken care of her — but, no, she insists on staying in her husband's household, so here Hans and I are!" She shook her head with a tsk of her tongue.

"It means the world to have you here, despite all of the troubles," said Princess Mayblossom, squeezing her sister's hand. "Thank you."

"It's a fair trade for all the troubles I've given you, growing up, I'm sure," said Princess Maia. "But I won't lie — for as near as Snowfield Palace is to the border between Howsill and the North Country, the mountains separating our countries makes travel between infuriating — though I'm sure you know all about that, Blana. They're impossible to cross, so we must take the long way around, through the Forest."

"Things will be so much nicer when the pass can be made through the mountains," said Princess Mayblossom. "And that's why Graham is away in the capitol right now. To help finish negotiations. Ember is ready to send a team of their best Dwarven, and I can't wait for it."

Ginny bit her lip and nodded — as though she understood any of the politics of the situation. She'd only heard the rumors that passed through the servants' quarters and what interested or worried Lady Bethim.

But she did know that the pass was needed. When the

Gardener's grandmother ruled the Forest, she had prevented anyone from leaving the Forest if the entered it, which effectively isolated both Howsill and the North Country. Farra, Ember, and Binfield, on the other side of the Forest, had faired better, since they shared open borders with each other, but Howsill and North were both surrounded by mountains on the sides not bordering the Forest.

Having a pass cut through the mountains between the countries would mean that if something ever went wrong with the Forest again, at least North and Howsill would have each other.

"It will be good for Bethim territory," said Kaimund. "Since Howsill's end will be on our land, we'll have control of it."

Ginny nodded again.

"And the responsibility," said Princess Mayblossom. "While I would swear on my life that North means Howsill no harm, it is still a hole in the natural defenses that have stood between our countries for so long. If ever a threat comes to Howsill from us, then you will stand as the first defense."

"A responsibility that we don't take lightly," said Kaimund.

"Politics," said Princess Maia. "The greatest barrier to convenience."

"The more people involved in a decision, the harder It is to keep them all happy and cared for," said Princess Mayblossom. "Politics is the art of maximizing the happy parties."

"Or catering to the most powerful," said Kaimund.

"Unfortunately," said Princess Mayblossom.

"When I marry, I want there to be no politics involved in it at all," Princess Maia declared. "Father wants us all to marry for love, you know, and I don't want politics to mar any part of it."

"You're a princess, dear," said her sister. "Politics are part of your very existence. Focus on the love and see where that takes you."

Princess Maia made a noise in the back of her throat that wasn't *quite* ladylike, Ginny thought. But, then, she knew from Rina and Calla that *real* ladies were rarely as *ladylike* as they were supposed to be. "Well, no marriage that will take me so far away from mother and father, certainly. I don't know how you can do it, Blana."

Princess Mayblossom tilted her head back and laughed. "It's called love, dear."

~

Ginny sat on the sofa next to Princess Mayblossom, entirely forgotten by the conversation, for at least an hour before the party broke up so everyone could prepare for supper. She rushed quickly to her room to catch her breath and sort through her thoughts.

Unfortunately, they were a scattered mess that refused to listen to order. Princess Maia was good for her sister – that much was certain. But was she good for Kaimund? Ginny was sure that Prince Hans was good for no one at all.

Quickly she washed her face and redid her braids. Then she gathered her courage and stepped back out of the room.

She had to pass Rina and Calla's room to get to the dining hall, and she heard arguing before reaching them. The sisters spilled out of their room, Calla still shouting at Rina. Ginny pulled back so they wouldn't notice her.

"You're *engaged,* Rina!" Calla declared. "You need to stop flirting with every eligible man we meet. Your choice is *made.* It's my turn now!"

Rina waved her sister away – clearly rolling her eyes, even though her back was to Ginny, so she couldn't see. "My dear sister, if you can't catch a man's attention on your own, that's hardly my problem, now is it?"

"You're engaged! You shouldn't be flirting!"

"You're a spoilsport." Rina shook her head. "No harm will come of this, I promise. Prince Hans is our guest, and I *must* be polite. Now, Calla, you're only eighteen. You can hardly expect to be an expert in these matters already. You're pretty enough – and once I'm married and you're older, I'm sure you'll have figured it out. Perhaps if you didn't make such a pig of yourself at mealtimes?"

"You are *horrible,* Rina!" shouted Calla, loud enough that Ginny winced.

"Don't blame me for your own failings, sister dear," Rina said. "I'm just trying to help you. You want a husband? Well, good husbands don't want silly wives who do nothing but complain about the world not going their way and who are the size of horses. You can't expect me to fix your life for you."

"I don't want you to fix anything! I want you to stop acting like every handsome man we meet is yours. You're engaged!"

"And he knows that, don't you worry." Rina laughed at her sister. "And if you can't compete against a woman already engaged, then I am truly sorry for you."

"But not sorry enough to *do* anything about it," Calla muttered. "Maybe I don't need your help. Maybe I can win Prince Hans all on my own."

"And I wish you *all* the luck for that, dear," said Rina.

"And *you're* going to be stuck with Reynard forever," Calla further declared. "I'm the one who should feel sorry for you."

They reached the dining hall, so the sisters fell silent. Calla fluttered her eyelashes at Prince Hans far too aggressively as they entered, while Rina just gave him a coy smile and complimented his waistcoat. Prince Hans, in turn, gave each a compliment on their dresses.

Ginny's stomach felt even heavier as she took her place at the table. Prince Hans was trouble.

But Princess Mayblossom needed the comfort of her family. And you could hardly judge the future based on the events of one day. Surely, things would settle once their visitors weren't so novel.

Ginny tried to put her worries away as she picked at her food. She had no real appetite, but Lady Nora's sharp glances kept her from abandoning her plate entirely. Everything would be all right, she tried to convince herself. She didn't need to imagine anything that wasn't there.

But as the dinner party broke up, Kaimund caught Ginny by the elbow in the hallway. "So, what did you think?"

Her heart missed a painful beat as she watched everyone

else disappear down the hall. "I—" she breathed. "Of what?"

"Of Maia," he quickly answered, sounding breathless. "Oh, Ginny, what do you think of her? Is she not the most perfect creature in existence? Or am I blind? Tell me quickly, for you are my dearest friend in all the world, and I trust your judgment more than anyone else's."

Ginny's chest warmed at his confidence, but *oh,* had it been about anything besides Princess Maia!

"I think," she said, her mouth dry. "I think she is very good to have come all this way to help her sister when travel is clearly so distasteful to her." That was a true enough compliment.

"True, very true," said Kaimund, nodding. "She *is* good, is she not?"

Ginny took a deep breath, feeling that he was pulled further away from her with every word. "I think she's almost everything a princess should be," she continued. "But she's also … very reserved. I don't feel I know her well enough *yet* to make any real judgments about her character."

That was the truth as well. She swallowed, unsure of what else she could say. Why couldn't he have asked her advice on *anything* else?

"Well, I hope that the two of you will soon be friends," Kaimund concluded, nodding. "In fact, it's my dearest wish in all the world."

5 Ginny felt embarrassed *for* the sisters, as she watched Rina and Calla flirt with Prince Hans. Rina was engaged! And Calla had no sense of reservation, behaving far too forwardly for a lady.

But it was still easier to watch them than the alternative. Princess Maia sat on the other side of the room, playing a silver harp, while Kaimund sat near her, utterly enraptured. It was beautiful music, a haunting melody of ice and snow, but Ginny felt that Kaimund slipped further away from her with each note.

So, instead, she watched the impending disaster that was Rina, Calla, and Prince Hans.

Princess Mayblossom was asleep – the baby was making her very ill that morning – and Lady Bethim languished on the couch on the other side of Princess Maia – the music had been meant to soothe her nerves. Lady Nora, as usual, oversaw the room from her armchair as she did her embroidery.

Ginny wished that Lady Nora would do *something* about the girls. Surely *she* could see that it was nothing but trouble? But, no, Rina could do no wrong in Lady Nora's eyes, and if Calla could secure a royal match, then who cared about the means? Prince Hans seemed a willing suitor. And Ginny dared not bring Lady Nora's attention on herself by arguing otherwise.

Lord Reynard was coming to call today. Surely *his* presence would make Rina behave!

Ginny worked faster at her knitting – a simple, mindless ribbed scarf. She wished that she had a more demanding project to distract her from the chaos before her. Except that she didn't have the focus for anything more than the regular switch between knit and purl stitches.

Oh, why couldn't Lord Reynard arrive soon? The minutes ticked by, torturously slow. Ginny's needles moved faster and faster in her attempt to speed up time, but that did nothing.

Prince Maia's song ended, and she stepped away from the harp with a firm announcement that her fingers needed a rest. Lady Bethim gave a loud sigh, so Kaimund rushed over to attend to her. Princess Maia, for her part, walked across the room to sit next to Ginny.

"How industrious you are, dear!" she declared. "My mother despaired of ever teaching me how to knit. I had no inclination to learn anything practical, alas!"

"I could never hope to play the harp the way you can." Ginny bit her lip as she had purled the last three stitches and had to undo them.

"I like the harp," said Princess Maia, turning to stare at the instrument. "There's something calming about the precision of music, and freeing about the creativity."

"Knitting is like that, too," Ginny muttered.

"I think I understand that," said Princess Maia, tilting her head to the side. "Oh, now you make me wish that I'd had the inclination to learn – ah, but here we are."

Ginny nearly missed another stitch. She swallowed. "Well, I don't think it's ever really too late to learn. If you want to learn."

"True – but I think I shall spare you the embarrassment of teaching me. Perhaps that would be a good way to distract Blana." Princess Maia tilted her head to the side thoughtfully. "Oh, the things one does for family. Do you have any brothers or sisters, Ginny?"

The needles paused as the chill of memory rushed through Ginny. "Yes," she whispered. "But I don't remember much.

Will … Will couldn't take care of me. That's why I'm here."

"I'm sorry." Princess Maia reached over and squeezed Ginny's shoulder. "There's nothing like family. Though, if your brother is a thing like mine, perhaps you've been better off without him."

Ginny dropped the knitting needles to her lap and rubbed at her temples, frowning. "But…"

Princess Maia withdrew her hand. "Oh, I love my brother dearly enough," she explained, "but I think even you can see how much trouble he is. Father spoiled him, I'm afraid, and he plays a prince charming far too well. I don't see the appeal myself. I'm his sister, true enough, but I'm afraid I just can't take a girl seriously if they're taken in by him." She glanced towards Rina and Calla, and a puffing sigh passed her lips. "It's all a game to him – he leaves a trail of broken hearts behind him. Father says that he'll settle once he finds the right one, but I don't know."

"Rina is *engaged*," said Ginny.

"Then she's one of the lucky ones," said Princess Maia. "She'll have somewhere to fall."

Ginny shook her head and raised her knitting needles, resuming the project with a quiet ferocity. "Unless she gets herself caught in a scandal."

"Hans means no harm," Princess Maia insisted, but there was the slightest tremble to her voice. "I have not yet heard that a couple has broken up over him. Despite all of his other flaws, he is careful, at least."

Ginny swallowed but felt slightly reassured. Still…

"I should go and check on Blana," the princess announced before she stood and turned to hold out a hand to Ginny. "Would you like to come with me? I fear that you and I are the only sane souls under this roof, and I desperately need a companion."

Ginny blinked, her eye straying to Kaimund. "But what about…" Her cheeks grew warm as she trailed off.

"What about Kaimund?" Princess Maia's eyebrow arched. "Ah, Kaimund. I see; yes, of course. Well, I'm afraid that young

Lord Bethim must be the one subject that you and I must never broach. Keep your opinions, and I'll keep mine, and all will be happy. Are you coming with me?"

Nodding in confusion, Ginny put her knitting away in her basket and followed the princess out of the room. She noticed Kaimund smiling after them as they left, and she gave him a thin smile back.

He wanted her to be friends with Princess Maia. Maybe that wouldn't be as difficult as she'd feared.

Princess Mayblossom was awake when they reached the room, eating an oatmeal gruel that was one of the few things she could keep down. She smiled weakly as Princess Maia sat down on the bed next to her.

"Babies are more trouble than they're worth," she said. "Remind me again why I wanted this?"

Princess Maia took a deep breath and rubbed her sister's back. "Because you love your Graham."

"Right," said Princess Mayblossom. She ate a final spoonful of gruel and then set the bowl aside to pick up her mug of herbal tea. "Has our guest already come and gone yet? I was hoping to meet Rina's Reynard. This is his first visit since their engagement, and he's never stood out to me before."

"He hadn't arrived yet when we left to come check on you," said Ginny. "But it isn't an easy journey between Sothers and Snowfield. He's likely encountered unexpected delays, that's all."

Princess Mayblossom nodded. "Of course."

"Are you ready to get dressed, Blana?" asked Princess Maia. "I don't think it's appropriate for you to meet a young man in your nightdress, even in your state."

"No, it wouldn't be," said Princess Mayblossom, finishing her tea. "Call my maid for me, will you?" She stood, resting a hand against her stomach, muttering about needing to take out the waists of her dresses soon.

Princess Maia took a deep breath and sought Ginny's gaze. Ginny automatically pasted on an encouraging smile.

Complaining about immediate struggles kept Princess

Mayblossom from thinking about the end of the whole affair. But Ginny could see Princess Maia's nerves fraying already, the same as her own.

Could *they* survive the remaining six and a half months before the baby was born?

Princess Maia smiled back – a thin, tired smile, but a smile nonetheless. Then she stood to help her sister, and Ginny peeled away from the doorway to give her own assistance.

Reasonably later, they escorted Princess Mayblossom through the halls back to the others – and found that Lord Reynard had arrived in their absence. Ginny slid back to her vacated sofa to resume her scarf. No one took notice of her.

Lord Reynard was an unremarkable man. Not dashingly handsome, but not hideous either. His voice wasn't unpleasant, but neither was it compelling. He had a non-descript but not off-putting face, his height was average, and he had average brown hair that was cropped short and neatly combed.

However, he wore a very fine waistcoat. As the Duke of Sothers, he was a very rich man, and that fact alone made him notable.

Rina sat at his side on the couch as he was explaining himself to Lady Nora. But there was no ... draw between them. No connection. They sat together, not touching, and not just because of propriety. There were no longing looks. No pensive sighs. No secret smiles.

As Lord Reynard talked, Rina's eyes were on Prince Hans.

Ginny's stomach twisted. Oh, this was going to end *badly*.

~

By the time Lord Reynard left, Prince Hans had secured an invitation for the entire household to visit Sothers in two weeks' time. It wasn't a bad idea – it would be Rina's home in just a few months. Even the fact that it had been Prince Hans' idea was innocent enough. After all, he was a crown prince and the most influential person in the room.

Still.

Princess Maia and Kaimund continued to be Ginny's

biggest source of confusion. Individually – well, Kaimund had always been her dearest friend, and she had found in Princess Maia an unexpected ally. But together, ah, but when they were together!

The cracks in Ginny's heart grew wider each time she saw them. The way Kaimund looked at the princess with his heart in his eyes. The way he would never look at Ginny herself…

But he deserved someone of his own station, not an orphan who had lived on his family's charity her whole life. She just didn't know how she was going to watch them be so happy together. And she had nowhere else to go.

Maybe she should give thought to her future instead of drifting through life on charity.

She didn't want to think of the future. Not if it might be one without Kaimund.

Maybe Princess Mayblossom would be able to help her. After the baby was born. Ginny could hold out that long. She could pretend until then.

The first truly warm days of the year were upon them, and Ginny paced the garden with restless abandon. She'd had enough of watching Kaimund with Princess Maia and had retreated to consider things on her own.

What was she going to do? What could she do?

Her breath caught as she saw Lady Nora tending some flowers ahead of her. Ginny hesitated, frozen for a moment, then spun around and ran.

Without thinking, she found herself speeding down the paths to her sanctuary. Lady Nora never visited Kaimund's corner of the garden. She didn't even know about it.

Ginny would be safe there. She—

She heard voices as she neared the hidden alcove. Her steps stalled, and she fought to control her breath as she crept forward the last few feet.

Kaimund was already in his garden. That was natural enough – it was his garden, after all. But he wasn't alone. Princess Maia was with him.

Ginny took a step back, her heart racing as she shook her

head.

She shouldn't feel this weight of betrayal. She knew that. The garden belonged to Kaimund, and he had the right to share it with whomever he liked. But until now, he had only ever shared it with Ginny. It had been *their* secret. The piece of him that she held and no one else could touch.

Now that was gone. Now he had shared it with Princess Maia. Now someone else had seen that hidden part of him.

And Princess Maia had a right to see that hidden part if he was courting her. But it meant that this was real. Kaimund *was* slipping away from Ginny.

"This is the coolest part of the garden," he was saying. The words that he had said to Ginny, so many years ago, at the beginning of their friendship. "You can come here whenever you need to, I know—"

Ginny turned and fled again. She couldn't stand there and listen to him give everything to the princess that she'd held alone for so long. Why did this have to be real?

"Ginny! What are you doing! Do you really think that Lord Bethim feeds and clothes you to let you wander around like an idle waif? Come here and help me cut these roses for some arrangements. They're at their prime, and if we wait any longer, then they will fade and it will be a waste. This isn't a task to be left to the servants."

Ginny was too numb to protest, too scared to flee again. No, she did as Lady Nora bid, thankful for a task that could keep her from thinking. She said nothing, cutting the roses that Lady Nora wanted, and if the thorns cut her hands, then that was just physical pain to distract from the cracks in her heart.

The sun beat down on her as the day grew warmer, and the heat mixed uncomfortably with Ginny's turmoil. By the time Lady Nora was satisfied and they hauled the roses inside, she felt too ill for thoughts, and she collapsed on a couch while Lady Nora recruited Calla's help with arranging the roses.

She didn't know if she slept or not, or how long she stared up at the ceiling. She only became aware of the world again as a cold hand rested against her forehead.

Ginny sucked in a sharp breath as she focused on Princess Maia's face, hovering over her with a worried frown.

"What happened, dear?" she asked as Ginny blinked back into reality. "Are you feeling all right?"

Ginny opened her mouth to answer and then shook her head, her heart too heavy for words.

"Here," said Princess Maia, helping Ginny to sit up and putting a cup in her hands. "Drink this. You're severely overheated."

"I've never seen her this bad, though she's always struggled with heat," said Kaimund.

Ginny took a long draught of ice-cold water and took a deep breath as her headache subsided and her stomach settled. But her heart hurt more again.

"I was helping Lady Nora in the garden," she whispered, closing her eyes. "She found me, and I – I couldn't get away. I couldn't … hide."

"Oh, Ginny." Kaimund's hand rested on her shoulder. "I'm sorry – I didn't think. I … you need to take care of yourself. You know you can use my garden whenever you need it, whether I'm there or not. Even if … even if I'm not alone."

Ginny took another sip of water and nodded. She'd been a silly fool, of course.

But how could she have interrupted?

6 Ginny almost didn't get to go to Sothers. In hindsight, she wished she hadn't.

She *was* going to stay behind with Princess Mayblossom and Lady Bethim to keep them both company and prevent either of them from having a nervous breakdown.

But, then, at the last moment, Princess Mayblossom announced that she was going to spend the day in the Forest with her aunt. Lady Nora, for her part, woke with a headache that prevented her from traveling. So she would stay home with Lady Bethim while Ginny would go to Sothers as an escort.

Prince Hans and Kaimund rode alongside the carriage while Ginny sat inside, next to Princess Maia, Rina and Calla across from them, quietly bickering with each other. As they always did when away from Prince Hans.

Princess Maia watched placidly, not interrupting them. Ginny wished she would. Why didn't the princess save them so much embarrassment and tell them that her brother only toyed with their hearts?

But, no, she just watched silently, her hands folded carefully in her lap, ignoring the world around her.

So, Ginny did the same. Or tried to. She fidgeted far more than she liked, but Rina and Calla were too distracted to notice, and Princess Maia, well, she simply ignored everything.

Ginny fixed her gaze out the window. This was the first time she had left Snowfield Palace since she'd arrived there at the age of seven. It felt strange to realize, but there had never been a reason for her to go anywhere before. She had been needed to stay behind with Lady Bethim. Why would they take the charity ward with them to events such as balls and weddings? It had been too much trouble.

But here she was now. And she didn't know what to do. To leave Snowfield Palace had been to leave safety.

It was only for today, she reminded herself. Tonight, she would be home again, and all would be right. It was good for her to stretch her boundaries. She wasn't a child anymore. She couldn't expect Snowfield Palace to be her sanctuary forever.

But where else was she to go?

No, best to not think about that.

A nervous hour or so later, they finally arrived at Sothers. Ginny bit her lip as the carriage rolled to a stop. Rina and Calla finally fell silent, and Princess Maia blinked back into reality. The door opened, and there was Lord Reynard, there to greet Rina and offer her his arm. Her manner turned cool as she accepted it and stepped out of the carriage.

Kaimund and Prince Hans were there, too, to escort Princess Maia and Calla, respectively. Leaving Ginny to wander alone behind them.

Lady Merita, Lord Reynard's mother, fell into step beside her as they entered the house, the woman seeming eager for a companion of her own during the tour.

"Oh, don't they make a fine pair, dear!" she announced. "You know, I've been so worried about my Reynard ever since he lost his father last year. I'm glad he's found the right girl to settle down with. Rina is such a good girl, very pretty, and from a very good family. He couldn't have done better for himself, no, indeed."

Ginny swallowed. "It … is a good match, yes."

Lady Merita beamed, reaching over to pat Ginny's arm. "I'm so pleased that your family agrees. No, I quite insist that she couldn't have done better for herself – though a mother can be blind, you know! I quite look forward to seeing her take my place as the mistress of the house. I'm not as young as I used to be, and it's time for me to pass the reins on to young blood."

"I think Rina will enjoy being mistress of her own home," said Ginny. "I wish her, and all of you, the best."

And, really, she did. She wanted Rina to be happy.

"Do you, dear? Ah, then they will be happy indeed if they have your wishes upon them." Lady Merita patted her arm again. "You seem like a good soul, though I confess that I've not seen you around before. Reynard said that Rina would be arriving with her aunt's relations, a prince and princess. Are you connected to them?"

Ginny glanced down. She wasn't used to explaining her place in the Bethim household. No one took notice of her, and someone else was always there to answer when they did. Snidely, if it was Rina or Lady Nora, less so if it was Kaimund or Lady Bethim. Ginny would then be looked upon with revulsion or pity, making her wish to melt into her own skin either way.

But to introduce herself? Did she dare? How did she wish to be seen?

"I'm Rina and Calla's companion," she said. "My mother was Lady Bethim's best friend in their youth, and they took me in as a ward when I was seven."

"Ah." Lady Merita nodded. "They're good people, the Bethims."

Then she patted Ginny's arm a final time before she hurried on to catch up with her son and Rina. Ginny hugged her arms around herself. Should she have told Lady Merita about her worries for Rina's affection? Was that her place?

Or was she really worrying about nothing?

What did she really know about love and romance and marriage? Not a single thing.

She had lagged behind the others, so now she sped her steps to catch up. Kaimund glanced over his shoulder and gave her a smile.

"Don't fall behind, Ginny dear," he said. "It'd be dreadful for you to get lost in this place."

"Oh, yes, it would, indeed," cried Princess Maia, and she slipped from Kaimund's arm so she could dash back and hook her arm through Ginny's. "But we won't let that happen, now will we?"

Ginny gave a nervous smile back.

"I was just saying how lucky Rina is to have found a husband who will keep her so close to home," Princess Maia rambled on. "I find it such a tragedy when marriage splits a family apart."

"I suppose you never have forgiven us for stealing your sister away from you," Kaimund mused, falling back to walk on Ginny's other side.

"I was thirteen," Princess Maia stated. "It shattered my world."

"Yet she and Uncle Graham have spent almost as much of their marriage in the North Country as they have at Snowfield Palace," said Kaimund.

"It still wasn't the same." Princess Maia tilted her head to the side. "As I said, I was thirteen, and suddenly everything had changed. Blana tries to tell me that it was worse for her when Aunt Mari and Aunt Elin got married when she was eight, but that just goes on to prove my point. Marriage disrupts everything."

"And yet people seek it out – it's how the world keeps going," said Ginny. "My … my mother gave up everything for love. It didn't end well for her." She ended in the barest whisper.

Princess Maia squeezed Ginny's hand. "I'm sorry, dear."

"What if marriage would bring you closer to your sister?" Kaimund suggested. "Would that be a suitable arrangement?"

Ginny and Princess Maia both stiffened, and Ginny's heart sank further. Why, oh, why did he have to be thinking of marriage so soon? The eternity it took Princess Maia to answer only worsened the matter.

"I think," she finally, slowly said, "that if I *must* leave my home, then that will be the best scenario. But still not ideal."

"Well." Kaimund gave an awkward cough. "I hope you someday find an ideal situation. Or, at least, well, we all just want our future happiness, you know."

Ginny glanced down at her feet, but she couldn't fall back, with Princess Maia's arm hooked through hers. Why did she have to be between them right now?

"Of course," Princess Maia muttered. She took a deep breath. "Kaimund, you are sweet, but you're also my sister's nephew, and I just don't know how I feel about that. And I'm here in Howsill to provide companionship to my sister, not to indulge in romance myself. It's not something I want to rush into. I have to guard my heart. I'm a Frost, after all."

Kaimund gave a long sigh and said nothing more. Ginny's heart twisted. On one hand, hearing that Princess Maia was disinterested in Kaimund's suit meant he could be Ginny's for a little while longer. But on the other, why *wouldn't* she love him? He was the best man in all of existence!

Was *Ginny* somehow too blind to see something terribly wrong with her best friend?

How *dare* Princess Maia tread so carelessly on his heart!

"No," Princess Maia muttered, pulling Ginny closer. "Kaimund is a subject that you and I must never discuss."

~

Sothers was a grand house, and Ginny's legs already ached by the time she saw the half of it. Rina seemed pleased with the place, at least, exclaiming over artwork and praising cleverly designed rooms.

Formality was lost after a while, and the ladies walked among the party unaided by the gentlemen's arms.

Princess Maia stayed stubbornly at Ginny's side, much to Ginny's confusion. Meanwhile, Lady Merita had found Rina's ear and was no doubt gushing on about her joy at finally gaining a daughter. Calla lurked a step behind her sister, scowling at everything.

Kaimund, thankfully, had abandoned his attempt to woo

Princess Maia and now walked alongside Prince Hans and Lord Reynard, talking about … whatever it was that men talked about.

Eventually, the tour led outside, where they wound through the garden, which were *almost* as extensive as the house itself. The day was warm, and Ginny and Princess Maia soon lagged behind the others.

"I ought to have you come back to the North Country with us, when we return home," said Princess Maia, after a while. "It's warmer than it used to be, now that Aunt Elin rules the Forest, but it's still far better than this. Oh, but at least we aren't in Ember. That country is true torture to a Frost. I don't know how Anthony can stand living there, but he is only a Zephyr. And he spends a lot of time at sea. Do you think any of the others would notice if we stopped to rest on that bench up ahead? Would they care?"

"We don't want to get lost," Ginny pointed out.

Princess Maia glanced back over her shoulder and shrugged. "We have a clear sightline back to the house. We'll be fine, even if no one comes looking for us."

With that, she threw herself onto the bench, raising an eyebrow as though to dare Ginny to protest. Ginny stared after the others for a moment more before she swallowed and sat down next to the princess.

"We'll be fine," said Princess Maia, patting Ginny's arm. "But they're moving too fast for us, and we have to take care of ourselves. Contrary to popular belief, the weaker a Frost is, the harder heat is for them."

"What?" Ginny straightened, blinking.

"A Frost's body is built to be cold," Princess Maia explained. "But a weak Frost has little internal ice to combat external heat. You scarcely have any ice at all in your blood, so it's no wonder that you overheat so easily."

Ginny frowned down at her hands. "You think that I'm a Frost? Like you?"

"One can generally recognize their own," said Princess Maia. "I wasn't sure until you overheated in the garden, but

Aunt Elin thought you were one, so I've been watching." She took a deep breath. "I'm not the strongest Frost, not compared to Aunt Mari, so I know how hard it can be – but to have scarcely any magic at all!"

Ginny gave a weak smile and nodded, then frowned as Lord Reynard marched past them in a retreat back to the house. He paused and turned to face them, an expression somewhere between confusion and relief passing briefly across his face before he nodded.

"There you girls are. Good. You're not lost."

"It's a warm day, and we didn't think we could walk any further without resting!" Princess Maia answered him brightly. "Don't worry about us – we found a tree to shade us, and we will recover shortly."

"Good," Lord Reynard repeated, nodding again. "I'm returning to get a key from the house. I should have had it on me – should have thought that they would want to see that part of the garden. It's hardly the *best* part of it. But Rina wants to see it, so see it she shall."

And then he continued on without another word. Ginny frowned after him, then in the direction he had come from.

"Why would Rina want to see a garden?" she asked, not expecting an answer. "She's never *particularly* interested in any gardens."

"I think she's mostly interested in having her way in her future home," said Princess Maia. "Testing her power over her future husband. He seems to have proved himself quite biddable."

Ginny wrinkled her nose. Would that make Rina happy? Would she stop making a fool of herself with Prince Hans?

"How are you feeling now?" asked Princess Maia, standing suddenly. "Do you think that we should go and catch up with the others so we can see this remarkable garden for ourselves?"

Ginny shrugged and followed the princess. Sothers *did* have beautiful gardens – though Ginny greatly preferred Snowfield Palace's grounds. After all, Snowfield had Kaimund's garden, even if the specialness of a shared secret was gone.

Princess Maia walked with confident footsteps, her head held high. The privilege of royalty to never feel that they don't belong. Even in the garden of a duke in a foreign land.

They soon found Kaimund, who grinned in relief as he saw them, exclaiming with joy that they were found. Princess Maia simply shook her head and repeated the same excuse she had given Lord Reynard.

Kaimund frowned. "You should have told us you needed to rest. I was worried when we realized that you were both missing."

"And you don't trust Ginny and me to take care of each other?" asked Princess Maia, tilting her head to the side. "We were fine, I promise."

"We didn't mean to worry anyone," said Ginny, dropping her gaze.

"Nor did we want to spoil anyone's fun," said Princess Maia.

Kaimund took a deep breath and shook his head. "Well, you're both here now. That's what matters."

Ginny gave a weak smile before her gaze drifted down the path. "What about the others?" she asked. "We saw Lord Reynard returning to get a key, but what about your sisters? And Lady Merita?"

"I think some of them might also be looking for the two of you," said Kaimund, turning to head back down the path, motioning for them to follow. "I left them at the garden gate, so I don't know."

"Don't fret about it," said Princess Maia, placing a hand on his arm. "It's just like you to worry, and of *course* you would come looking for us. It's just the way you are."

It didn't take much longer for them to reach the garden gate where Kaimund had left the others, but only Rina and Prince Hans remained at the gate, examining the fence that barred them from the garden.

"Oh, good, you found them!" cried Rina, glancing over her shoulder. "Now I think you'll have to form a search party for Calla and Lady Merita! Oh, but I *told* them that all Kaimund had to do was retrace our steps. And now they're gone, too!" She gave an exaggerated sigh and shook her head.

"I'll go look for them, too," Kaimund offered, and he headed off in the direction that Rina indicated.

"You know, I really think that this gate will open if one just lifts it enough," Prince Hans announced, when he was gone.

"Shouldn't we still wait for Lord Reynard to bring the key?" asked Ginny, casting a frown back down the path. "Surely he'll return soon?"

"Ah, but what would be the fun in that?" Prince Hans asked. Then he put his shoulder against the gate, and it swung open with minimal effort. "Shall we?" he asked, waving a hand towards the revealed path.

"You are being presumptuous, Hans," said Princess Maia, folding her arms over her chest. "You know your rank doesn't mean you can do whatever you want no matter where you go."

"It's harmless fun," said Prince Hans, shrugging. "We have permission to go this way already. I'm just speeding things along."

"And I'm to be the mistress of this place soon, and I think it's fine," Rina declared and traipsed down the path. Prince Hans followed after her with a smirk and not another word.

Princess Maia sighed and gave Ginny a longsuffering glance. "I guess I have to go make sure that they stay escorted. You don't mind being left behind to explain to people as they catch up? No? You're a dear, Ginny!" Then she disappeared down the path.

Ginny's breath quickened as she realized that she'd been left alone. What was Rina thinking?

Oh, but Prince Hans was trouble!

Lord Reynard returned after a while and stared down the path in confusion as Ginny dutifully explained. He fidgeted with the key and muttered something about talking to the servants about fixing the gate before he followed.

Then Kaimund returned with Calla and Lady Merita. Calla stamped her foot in frustration when she realized that Rina had been spending time with Prince Hans alone and then quickly rushed after them.

Altogether, Ginny considered the day a total disaster.

7

Lord Reynard began visiting more often after that. Ginny wondered if he felt threatened by Prince Hans; if so, that might have been the one good thing to come of their visit to Sothers. He couldn't come every day, but he did arrive at Snowfield Palace at least twice a week, usually with a gift for Rina. Lady Nora fawned over him, and Rina *seemed* to be warming to her betrothed. Ginny began to have hope that they would be happy together, after all.

Lady Nora's nephew, Robert, had been enlisted in the king's guard for the last year, and it was a week after their trip to Sothers that she received a letter from him saying that he would be returning home for his first furlough, and that he would be bringing a new friend who had no family of his own to stay with.

Everything was thrown into a new frenzy as they prepared for his arrival. Ginny thought it rather extreme – this *was* his home, after all, and he was just as much a ward as she was – but it gave Lady Nora something to focus on, and anything she could focus on that wasn't Princess Mayblossom was good. Right?

Two weeks after his letter, Robert arrived, in the flesh, late one afternoon, the mysterious friend riding alongside him. They'd given no warning of *exactly* when they would arrive – far be it from Robert to be so decorous as to give an *exact* date in his letter – and so it sent the sitting room into quite a frenzy when he bounded into the room.

Lady Nora threw her embroidery to the side with a cry of delight and rushed forward to throw her arms around her beloved nephew. She made him sit down and demanded that he tell them all about his journey.

But Robert just laughed and shook his head as he complied. "Ah, Aunt Nora. Don't you realize how tiring it is to tell of travel? I made it home, our horses never lost their shoes, we only had to dispatch one band of desperate thieves, and bears only stole our breakfast once. All trivial matters, really. Hardly worth telling. Come now, don't you think it's far better manners for me to present my friend to the family?"

Ginny's gaze drifted to the pale young man with sharp, boyish features hovering in the doorway. An icy hand wrapped around her heart at his ice-blue eyes and nearly-white hair. He stared directly at her, lips pressed into a hard line, as though he wanted to say something but didn't dare. She squirmed under the attention.

"Oh, yes, dear," cried Lady Nora, nodding eagerly. "Do introduce us to your friend. He must be a good young man, to have won your loyalty."

"The very best," said Robert. He stood, sauntered over, and clapped the young man on the shoulder. "This is Will, who has saved my life more times than I can count, and for that, we have taken an eternal vow of brotherhood."

"Will," Ginny whispered as the pieces of memory clicked into place. She sprung from her seat and rushed to him. His arms folded around her, and he held her tight.

"Ginny," he whispered hoarsely in her ear. "You're all grown up."

"Wait," said Robert. "You're Ginny's Will?"

Will stiffened, pulled back out of the hug, and lifted his chin, nostrils flaring defiantly. "What of it if I am?"

But Robert just slapped Will on the back again, laughing heartily. "You should have told me sooner! Ah, but you are doubly family now if you're Ginny's brother."

Will's shoulders relaxed, and he tugged one of Ginny's braids. "Ah, but then you might have told her and ruined all of the surprise."

Lady Nora gave a harumph and retreated back to her armchair. "So, you're the one who left her on our doorstep all those years ago?"

"Well, I was only ten, myself," Will answered, hugging Ginny close again. "After our mother's death, I barely knew how I was going to take care of myself, and I wasn't going to ask for charity for both of us. After everything we'd been through … she didn't deserve to live the life that I led. She's too soft."

"And where was your father in all of this?" asked Lady Nora with another harumph.

"I wish I knew." Will shrugged. "The last Mother saw of him was before Ginny was born. She swore that he had to be dead for him to abandon her like he did, but I couldn't tell you, myself. I only know that I've never been able to track him back down. And that I was left alone in the world at the age of ten, with only a seven-year-old sister, who I loved more than life, but I didn't know how to keep alive."

"We've been happy to have her," said Kaimund, his smile disarming. "My mother was glad to fulfill the promise she made to your mother, all those years before. It's only terrible that it followed such a tragedy."

"Yes, well," said Lady Nora, "I suppose ten-year-old boys can't be expected to make the best decisions when they're in situations like that. Robert, you said that this young man saved your life?"

"Time and again," Robert confirmed, all solemnity. "Some are figurative enough – such as when he covered my backside when I wasn't where I was supposed to be. But, this last winter, he and I had a mission for the king, and we were caught in a truly frightful storm. I thought we were dead men, but Will here kept his head the whole time and saw us safely back to the outpost, where we could thaw out and live to travel another day."

"I've had to live through many a cold night, through my life," said Will, directing Ginny to a couch where they sat down. "I've learned to keep my wits about me. And, besides," he glanced down at Ginny, "our father was a Zephyr, and while I didn't inherit his wind, I do still have the immunity to the cold. So I did what I had to do for my fellow soldier."

"And since you saved my life, you now have my undying loyalty," Robert declared. "And since you *keep* saving it, I can only assume that you return my friendship."

"Given that your family has provided my sister a home for the last twelve years, it's the least I could do," said Will, squeezing Ginny closer. "I didn't know who you were until after that blizzard – I would have done the same for any other comrade – but when I found out what family you belonged to, I knew that I had to stick by you no matter what."

"And here I thought it was my winsome personality." Robert shook his head.

"You're good for trouble, I'll give you that," said Will, a smile twisting his lips. "But I had my own debt to pay."

~

Ginny stayed silent through it all, while Will and Robert told tales of their exploits among the guards. She had her brother again. Her own flesh and blood. A person to whom she belonged and who loved her unconditionally. She had seen the torture that was their years of separation in Will's eyes. Now, all was right. *Lady Nora* had declared that he had a home here at Snowfield Palace.

And yet, some jagged piece of memory didn't quite fit. Something was wrong, but she couldn't grasp it. It melted in the churning storm of her past every time she tried.

Will was here. That was what mattered.

But, at length, Lady Nora announced that Robert and Will had to be tired after their journey and shooed them away to their rooms. Will kept hold of Ginny's hand as they left, pulling her after him with a declaration that they needed to talk alone.

The room prepared for Will was far nicer than Ginny's own.

Of *course,* Lady Nora would give preference to her nephew's friend. Ginny didn't mind. She liked the coziness of her room.

"Answer me honestly – have they treated you well?" Will demanded as he closed the door behind them. "I don't like the way that woman looks at you."

Ginny tried to swallow down the lump that formed in her throat, but it stuck fast. Tears welled in the corners of her eyes.

"Hey." Will's voice turned hoarse again, and he wrapped Ginny in another tight hug. "Has it been that bad? Oh, Ginny! I did what I had to do, but there hasn't been a moment that I haven't thought about you. Worried about you—"

"I've been fine!" Ginny quickly insisted. She tried to stop her tears, but they flowed stubbornly down her cheeks and into Will's shirt. "Lady Nora was the one to marry Lord Fillip when Mother didn't. She doesn't like me because she never had any children of her own, but almost everyone else has been kind. I've had a home, have never been hungry, have always had clothes – even if they're Rina's and Calla's cast-off's – and I was educated. I've worried about *you*! All alone! You've had no one!"

"Oh, sweet Ginny," breathed Will. "I told you then that I'd be all right. And I have been. One way or another. And here we are, together again. Oh, how I've missed you!"

"You're alive," Ginny whispered. "You're really alive."

"Yes, I am," Will whispered back. "And, Austere willing, I'll be able to take care of you myself, now."

Ginny relaxed into the hug, the pain of the last twelve years melting away as she cried. Will held her tight and held her close, rubbing her back and indulging in a few tears of his own.

Slowly, surely, the sobs subsided, and Ginny pulled back, wiping her lingering tears away. "It's good to have you here. Were you really all right, all this time?"

Will gave a long sigh and shrugged. "It wasn't always easy. I faced a lot of hungry nights alone on the streets, but I always found a way. Until I was old enough to join the guards, giving me a monthly income and guaranteed meals, most days at least. And when I went with Robert on that mission, and he waxed sentimental about his family when he thought he was going to die, he mentioned your name, and I knew I had found my way back to you. Ah, but Austere has watched over us both, hasn't he?"

Ginny nodded, giving a weak smile. "Robert told you about me?"

"Not much – mostly just your name and the fact that you were another ward of the Bethim household." Will tilted his head to the side and directed Ginny to some chairs where they could sit. "He mentioned you a few more times but never *told* me anything about you. And I didn't know how to probe for more information without making him suspicious." He took a deep breath. "I didn't know what you might have told him about me, and I – I didn't want to take risks."

"Well, you're here now. I've been fine, as I've said." Ginny glanced down. "They've taken care of me. And maybe I don't always feel like I belong here, but I have been thankful for it. And Kaimund … Lady Bethim … Princess Mayblossom…" she trailed off with a sigh. "Not everyone in the Bethim household is Lady Nora. Most merely ignore me, at worst."

Will pressed his lips together. "All right. You look well. Quiet and timid, certainly, but you always were those things. That's why I knew you would never survive on the streets." He shook his head, then his gaze turned distant. "Gin, what have you told these people about me? What do they know?"

"Not a lot." Ginny shrugged. "Why?"

"Oh, you know." Will leaned back with a shrug of his own, running a hand through his hair. "A fellow wants to know what reputation proceeds him. You're my little sister, so, you know, I'd like to know what you've said."

Ginny frowned, rubbing her temples. "I never said much. I don't remember much. No one was ever interested, and I didn't like to dwell on the past. They know your name and that you're the one who left me on the doorstep, but I think that's all I've *ever* said. They know you're my brother, though."

"They know I'm your *brother*?" Will repeated.

Ginny's frown deepened at the emphasis and the odd way

Will's voice rose when he said it. But she nodded. "Yes. They know you're my brother. You *are* my brother, right? I don't remember much of life before, but I was sure…"

That niggling piece that didn't quite fit jabbed painfully.

Will stared at Ginny for a long, heartrending moment and then broke into a grin before reaching over to tug Ginny's braid. "Of course, I'm your brother, Silly Ginny. The best big brother in all the world. Sorry I've been away for so long."

"You did what you had to do." Ginny smiled again as she released a breath of relief.

"Yes," said Will. "I'm sorry. But here we are."

8 Ginny scarcely slept that night. Her brother was here. Actually here. After so many nights alone, she had family. Her real flesh and blood.

She felt that if she slipped into sleep, she'd only wake the next day to find that it had all been a cruel dream. It had felt surreal enough.

Could Will *really* have found Robert, of all people, and befriended him? Could he really be under this very roof? Was he actually here now?

The niggling whisper of *wrongness* told her that it had to be a dream. What was that broken piece of memory that didn't fit?

But, eventually, sleep took her. When she woke the next morning, a knock was at her door as she was finishing her routine. It was Will.

He really was here!

"Dearest sister of mine," he said with a mock bow. "Will you kindly allow me to make up for the years of abandonment by escorting you to breakfast?"

Ginny laughed and took her brother's arm. "As though it wasn't already forgiven the moment you walked through the door yesterday."

"You're too good for this world, Ginevra." Will frowned as he leaned into her room. "Is this really where they keep you?

It's scarcely more than a closet!"

"Large rooms scared me when I was seven." A shiver ran down Ginny's spine at his use of her full name. She hadn't heard it in twelve years. "It's my space. I don't mind that it's small. *I'm* small." She pulled him away from her room, shutting the door behind them.

"Very well, if you insist." Will shrugged as he led her away from the room. "Now, a man knows when he deserves the condemnation of the women in his life. But I shall accept your forgiveness, just the same."

"I can't believe you're really here."

"I can't, either," Will agreed. "All those years of surviving and suffering, and now we're together again. The Eyce siblings against the world."

"Ice?" Ginny repeated.

"I had to give a last name when I signed up to the guards," Will explained. "I couldn't remember either Mother's or Father's family names, but William Eyce had a nice enough ring to it. Not *ice*, it's spelled differently, but the same idea."

"Pryce," Ginny whispered. "Lady Bethim says that Mother's family name was Pryce."

"Ah! Then I came close enough." Will nodded in satisfaction. "I tried to find our grandfather, you know. After Mother's death. But not knowing what his name was made it difficult."

"Our grandfather was ruined when Mother ran away from marriage to Lord Fillip," Ginny explained. "He moved away to another country, and I think he must be dead now, or else Lady Nora would have found a way to send me to him."

"I see," said Will. "Tragic, that." He was silent for a moment more, his expression thoughtful. "Ginny, who was the Frost at dinner last night?"

Ginny swallowed. "That would be Princess Maia from the North Country. Her older sister is married to Lord Bethim's youngest brother, and she and their brother, Prince Hans, are currently visiting."

"Ah." Will was silent for another thoughtful moment and

then continued. "I don't like the way she was staring at me last night. I don't think I trust her."

"She—" Ginny didn't know how to explain her conflicting thoughts about Princess Maia. Finally, she shrugged. "She's a complicated person, I've discovered. I think I would even call her a friend if it weren't for..." She swallowed again. "Well, she's a princess, you know. Who am I to call *her* a friend?"

Will stopped and turned to face Ginny, his brow knitting in concern. "You're the sweetest creature in all of existence. You're worthy of the friendship of any princess you want."

Ginny took a sharp breath and shrugged. "That's not the way the world works, unfortunately. But I try to be a good friend to *her*."

Will's jaw worked, but any response he might have given was interrupted by Robert, who had just found them in the hall and immediately claimed his friend's attention. Ginny fell into the background, watching as Will and Robert talked and laughed. She heard her name, but her heart was too full to truly process anything they said.

"So, who would have guessed that Robert would have befriended your brother, of all people."

Ginny gasped as she found Kaimund at her side, as he took her hand and placed it on his arm. "I—"

"I'm glad he's here," he said, grinning down at her. "You've been alone for too long. And now you have him."

Ginny nodded. "I've missed him."

"As you should have," said Kaimund. "He's missed you, too. I can tell."

They reached the breakfast room, and Ginny quietly slipped into the chair next to her brother. Will gave her an encouraging smile but remained engaged in his conversation with Robert.

She still couldn't believe that this was real. That this was the turn her life had taken.

Will and Robert eagerly recounted more of their exploits among the guards while everyone ate. Ginny shuddered at many of the tales they told, hating to think that Will might have been in such danger.

"I did see Uncle Bethim and Uncle Graham before I left the capital," Robert suddenly announced. "That reminds me, and I should have mentioned this sooner, I know. They send their love and all that rot. The negotiations are going well but slow. Princess Giana of Ember has arrived with the Dwarven who will build the pass, but some council members remain unconvinced that this will benefit Howsill. More question the value of it being on Bethim land. Politics, you know."

There was a long sigh from Princess Mayblossom. "Politics," she repeated. "Well, I look forward to seeing Giana again. She's always good fun. I expect that she will stay with us while the Dwarven build?"

"I believe that's the plan," said Robert. "Ah, but it will be a lark to escape through those mountains whenever we want."

"Not *whenever* you want," said Lady Nora, shaking her head. "We have to be responsible about this. Even the hazel trees are subject to the Gardener's judgment, and even Mayblossom can't travel entirely at her own whim."

Robert leaned closer to Will and whispered something that Ginny *just* overheard. "Ah, but I do look forward to slipping through when the pass is finished. Are you with me?"

"It does sound like an interesting challenge," said Will, tilting his head to the side. "I've always been interested in the North Country. Do you think you can handle the cold?"

Ginny nearly choked on a bite of porridge.

"Are you all right, Ginny-dear?" asked Will, slapping her on the back.

"I'm fine." Ginny took a long drink of water to get her coughing under control.

"Good," said Will. "I would hate to lose you like this when I only just found you again."

Ginny gave a wincing smile.

"Don't make a scene of yourself, child," said Lady Nora, turning a sharp glare upon her. Ginny shrank back in her seat.

~

"You ... you don't have to *sneak* into the North Country,"

Ginny told Will, as soon as they were away from the table. "Princess Maia has given me an invitation to visit her after her sister's baby is born. I – I *think* she's serious."

Will tilted his head to the side as he considered Ginny and then tugged one of her braids. "I'll keep that idea in mind. But remember, I don't trust Princess Maia just yet, so I don't know how I feel about you accepting favors from her."

Ginny raised her chin and took a step back. "Will, with all due respect, you've been gone for the last twelve years of my life, and whatever Lady Nora might say, I'm not a child anymore. I might not know much about the world, but I know enough to decide my own friendships."

Will opened and shut his mouth and then sighed, his shoulders drooping. "I'm sorry. I … I didn't get to be the big brother to you I was supposed to be. I'm just trying to make up for lost time, but I guess it's too late."

"No, Will…" Ginny shook her head. "It's not too late, I promise. You are my brother, and that *has* to count for something. We've just had … very different lives, and it's going to take time."

Will's gaze turned distant, and he slowly nodded. "I guess you're right. How did you get so wise, Gin?"

Ginny's cheeks warmed, and she ducked her head. "Oh, I can be the biggest fool, I promise," she said, and then she ducked past him and into the sitting room.

"Ah, there you are, Will!" Robert cried as Will followed her. "I was just telling Aunt Nora about the mirror you won in that bet some weeks back. Ah, but that was an interesting game! He's having it shipped here with the rest of our things, and you'll all be able to see it for yourselves. A delightful thing it is, too. No ordinary mirror at all! The thing is magic, I tell you."

"The Mirror of Thurt," said Will, nodding solemnly. "Ah, but that was a find – it's worth a fortune and good fun besides."

"We look forward to seeing it," said Lady Nora, clapping her hands together. "A real magic mirror! Will wonders never cease these days?"

Ginny frowned at the thought of Will *gambling*. And magic mirrors were a dreadful business.

"Oh, but that's a long face if I've ever seen one," declared Princess Mayblossom as she sat on the couch next to her. "What's bothering you?"

Ginny gave a long sigh, and her shoulders drooped. "Will and I argued. And … I'm worried about him. He seems to be mixed up in things that just aren't right!"

"I see." Princess Mayblossom gave a long sigh as she reached over and laid a hand on Ginny's shoulder. "Well, I've never known a pair of siblings who have always gotten along. Why, Aunt Elin and Aunt Mari can be truly frightful when they engage in a shouting match. And Maia and I argued just this morning about the dress I'm wearing. *I* think I look like a snowdrift in it, but she insists that it's fine." She laughed and ran a hand over her stomach, which was noticeably round these days. "You and Will have had such different lives. You're bound to clash sometime."

"I know," Ginny whispered. "It's just so … new, you know. It doesn't seem strong enough for arguing yet. And the things he seems to be involved in worry me. I mean, he's friends with *Robert,* of all people, and they don't seem to be positive influences on each other."

"Yet it's that very friendship that has brought him back into your life," Princess Mayblossom reminded her. "I do know that the best things in life never come easily. Like babies."

Ginny sighed and nodded. "I know that. I do. Still, I feel that the fact that he's grown up alone has broken something in him, and I don't know how to help him."

"You can pray," Princess Mayblossom suggested. "You can always pray. Austere is the only one who can *actually* fix people."

"Of course." But Ginny still sighed. "I still feel like there should be something that I can do. Or say. Or … something."

"Stand firm in your beliefs, don't compromise your morals, but extend grace to the people around you." Princess Mayblossom's gaze turned distant. "Because none of us are perfect, and we all require grace, one way or another. And I can tell you that your brother loves and has missed you dearly."

"I know. And I've missed him. I just … want to help him."

"And I'm sure you will," said Princess Mayblossom. "He now has you to live for, at least. And having a woman to live for – even if it's a sister – goes far to plant a man's feet on the ground." She shifted and suddenly went stiff, taking a sharp gasp.

"Princess Mayblossom?" Ginny sat up straight, frowning in concern. "What's wrong? Is it the baby? Oh!"

"I—" Princess Mayblossom fell back against the cushions and squeezed her eyes shut. "No, nothing's wrong," she whispered. "I just felt the baby move, and it startled me. That's all."

"Oh," said Ginny. "But that's a good thing, right?"

"So they tell me."

9 Robert's and Will's luggage arrived two days later, including the mirror, wrapped in a thick cloth.

"It's powerful magic," Will stated, all serious, as it was brought in. "And it must be guarded and handled carefully. No one must glance upon it casually."

"Oh, but what *does* it do?" asked Calla, rolling her eyes at the theatrics. "You keep going on about its magic, but you haven't told us what the magic *is*."

"Ah, but that's just it!" Will declared, perching on the railing of the stairwell. "No one can *agree* what the Mirror of Thurt does. Some look upon it and see themselves horribly disfigured. Some see themselves altered to perfection. Some can hardly recognize themselves when they look into it, while others can't see a single change. My personal opinion? It shows you the real you. The person you really are inside."

"And who would want to see that?" sneered Rina. "It sounds like a dreadful bore."

"We can all stand to learn more about ourselves," said Will, leaping up a few steps. "But we shall be careful. No one shall see anyone else's reflection, only their own. Perhaps we should build some sort of alcove for it. Perform a ritual. Ah! But this is a good time!"

With that, he finished disappearing up the stairs.

Calla gave a growl of frustration and stormed away. Rina

rolled her eyes and went a different direction, and the rest of the group dispersed.

"This shall be interesting," said Princess Maia, who was somehow standing next to Ginny, though she hadn't noticed her approach. "You know, I think your brother might be hiding something, hm? What do you think, Ginny? Is that demand for secrecy really out of consideration, or is he trying to *keep* something from all of us?"

Ginny frowned and took a step away from Princess Maia. "If he's hiding something, then that's his right. Everyone has secrets."

"But some are more dangerous than others."

Ginny took a sharp breath and shook her head. "I don't think I like what you're implying."

Princess Maia turned to Ginny, her head tilting to the side. "Oh, but I was thinking about my mother and Aunt Mari. Back when they had to conceal the fact that they were Frosts. To be a member of our kind used to be a death sentence in the North Country. You probably would have been fine, but anyone stronger feared for their lives."

"Oh." But Ginny still shook her head. "But what secret might Will be hiding of *that* magnitude? Magic isn't considered evil anymore – not even in the North Country."

"True enough."

Ginny glanced at Princess Maia out of the corner of her eye. "I ... don't think that you and I should be discussing my brother."

"Very well," said Princess Maia, her eyebrow arched. "But I'm watching him. Something doesn't add up about him, and I care too much about you to watch you get taken in by an imposter."

"He's not an imposter," Ginny protested. "He knows enough things that no one else would have ever bothered to learn. He's who he says he is."

Princess Maia pressed her lips together. "Perhaps so."

But was he? What was that shard of memory that wouldn't fit? What would it change? And his hesitation before he had confirmed their relation had been so odd! Maybe he wasn't her brother? But he was her Will. She knew that much.

Oh! That she could remember more!

"Come," said Princess Maia, pulling Ginny away from the stairwell. "It's a lovely day outside, and we should get some fresh air before the light is gone, now that it's cool enough for us to enjoy it."

But Ginny tore away from the princess and rushed up the stairs after Will.

She hesitated when she reached his room. What was she going to say to him? How was she supposed to admit a lack of trust?

Because she suddenly knew with sudden certainty that whatever lies he told, they were somehow her fault. He'd asked what the Bethims knew about him. She'd never called him her brother, growing up, not until he'd walked through that door with Robert and had stood before her in the flesh. She had only ever called him by his name, and everyone else had assumed.

And now he was trapped in the lie she hadn't meant to tell. Guilt knotted within her. How could she make this right?

Yet, what was the truth? Try as she might, she just couldn't make sense of her jagged, scattered pieces of memory. That *was* her Will. She knew at least that much for sure.

She knocked and held her breath as she waited for him to answer. It took several seconds, but then he was there, brushing the hair out of his face, grinning as he saw her.

"Ah, Gin, can't resist the mystery of the Mirror of Thurt, can you?" he said. "Few can. But don't you worry – as my little sister, you'll naturally be the first to see it. Come inside."

Ginny bit the inside of her cheek as he pulled her into the room, and her heart pounded in her chest. His little sister. Those words rang so true, and yet—

And yet.

"The mirror shows who you really are, you said?" she asked, fixing her gaze on the frame that now leaned against the wall before her. It was still covered with cloth, but that cloth was now askew, as though it'd been hastily replaced. "You're sure of this?"

"It's my best guess," said Will. "But no one really knows. Whoever this Thurt was who made it, his secrets have been lost to time."

"What do you see when you look into it?"

Will's breath caught. "Ah, but that's a delicate question, isn't it, Gin?"

"I'm sorry." Ginny glanced up at him. "I just … sometimes feel like I barely know you. We've been parted for so long!"

"I know." Will gave a long sigh, and then his grin was back. "Well, if you *must* know, I see myself dripping in jewels and dressed in clothing far finer than any mere soldier could afford. And I'm at least three inches taller, so clearly, I'm due at least one more growth spurt, and I won't be forever condemned to be the shortest guard in Howsill."

"And you think that's your true self?" asked Ginny.

"I'm the grandson of a formerly *very* successful merchant," said Will. "*Clearly,* it's my true self to be rich and successful. I've made it this far, clawing my way up from nothing. It's only a matter of time."

Ginny's frown grew. That *didn't* ring true, but who was she to argue? It was only a theory, after all.

"Ah, but you need to see the mirror for yourself," Will declared, darting away from her. He took a position beside the frame and tugged the cloth aside. "I won't look with you – I'll respect your privacy and let you tell me what the mirror reveals. Unless you want to keep that to yourself, in which case, I shall completely respect that, too."

The mirror stood before Ginny uncovered. The frame was black and intricately wrought. The silver surface rippled and churned, showing a shifting version of the room. A shudder ran down Ginny's spine, and she rubbed her arm.

Dared she approach? Did she really want to see the person she really was? Was anyone ever really prepared for such knowledge?

She took one step forward and then another. Then she was upon the mirror. The breath stuck in her throat. She reached out, not quite touching the swirling surface.

"Nothing," she whispered.

Will snapped to attention, tilting his head to the side as he stared at her. "You look the same as ever, eh? I should have known that someone as good as you would live so honestly."

"Yeah." Ginny swallowed and backed away from the mirror, hugging herself. "Nothing changed."

But the lie tasted horrible on her tongue. Because she saw *nothing*. She wasn't there. Just the swirling room.

She looked up at Will, swallowed, and then fled the room.

~

Everyone else eagerly speculated what the mirror might show them. They could talk of nothing else – all while Ginny hung back, trying to guess what her own vision had meant.

Maybe nothing at all, she tried to tell herself. Will's statement that it showed a person's true self was nothing but a guess. Given what he said he saw, it had to be. Unless that wasn't what he saw at all. Had he *lied* to her about what he'd seen in the mirror? Why?

But, then, she had lied, too. Not intentionally, but she had. Maybe what Will had seen was just as horrible as nothingness, and he was sparing her feelings the way she spared his.

Oh, that mirror was the worst thing to ever exist.

Maybe if she confessed to Will what she had really seen, he would tell her the truth, too? But the words caught in her throat every time she tried to say them.

They told no one that she had seen the mirror already. Not when there was nothing worth telling, and it would only make Rina and Calla jealous.

Lord Reynard came for his next visit and was brought into the scheme. He thought it great fun, and immediately agreed to join them.

Robert and Kaimund agreed to use Lord Bethim's office to build the alcove, and Lady Nora gave instructions to the servants. It wasn't to be *too* elaborate of a construction. Just a small, artificial cave with a curtain at the entrance and candles inside.

Ginny thought that the whole affair was overblown and ridiculous. She tried to say as much, too, but everyone laughed and told her that it was "all just good fun."

Will took her aside.

"Just because your reflection showed nothing doesn't mean the others will be similarly disappointed." He patted Ginny's shoulder. "Let them have their fun. It's good for a person to see themself for who they really are. Not everyone is as honest as you."

Ginny opened her mouth to protest but then shut it and shook her head. He didn't know what she'd really seen. She should tell him.

But she couldn't.

Kaimund, at least, seemed to share her trepidation. Yet even he dismissed her concern.

"Everyone is determined to see this mirror," he said. "And it's a decision they have to make on their own. The mirror is here, whether or not you and I like it. Everyone wants to know their true self – or whatever it is that one sees in the mirror. Let them enjoy themselves – it even has Aunt Mayblossom distracted, and you know how important that is."

Ginny bit her lip and nodded. "I know. Still…"

"We each are only looking upon our own reflections," Kaimund stated. He shrugged. "It's good to know one's self, and if the mirror can help with that, it would be good, yes?"

"But what if it isn't? What if someone looks in the mirror and sees something horrible?"

"Then we thank Austere that we have received such a warning and then endeavor to change our ways before it's too late."

"But…" Ginny gave a long sigh. "I still don't like it."

"Afraid of what you will see when you look at yourself?" Kaimund tugged one of her braids. "Ah, Ginny – you, of all people, have nothing to fear. And you won't be forced to look if you would rather not. Besides, it's your brother's mirror. I would think that you would support his endeavor."

So, really, what could she do?

And then the matter grew worse over the course of a single picnic.

Lord Reynard was there that day, and they were all taking advantage of the beautiful sun and a charming hill on the edge of Snowfield Palace's grounds. And, of course, the topic of the conversation was the Mirror of Thurt.

"It seems a waste that each of us is only going to see ourselves," Rina declared with sudden vehemence. "This is an opportunity to get to know one *another* better!"

Will, who had been lounging beside Ginny, sat up straight. "Ah, but can friendships survive when secrets are revealed? 'Tis a foolish plan, I say. Let's each look upon our own reflection and no more."

"We could each make our own choice," said Prince Hans. "Once we've seen our own reflection, we can then offer to let those closest to us look as well."

"It would have to be a mutual offer," said Robert. "After all, we would see both reflections simultaneously."

"True enough," said Prince Hans. "And if we look at our own reflection first, we can decide if it's something we're comfortably sharing."

"And then face the assumption that we are truly horrible people if we choose to not share?" asked Princess Maia. "No, I agree with Will. Each of us should view our own reflection and no one else's."

"Already frightened of what you might see, are you, Maia?" asked Prince Hans, laughing. "You betray yourself. But, come, no one has to know if your refusal to share is because of your own image or if you simply don't want to be burdened with the knowledge of someone else."

"It is my mirror," said Will.

"It is," said Kaimund. "We should abide by the rules he sets."

Ginny shrunk back, nibbling on a muffin, praying that Kaimund, Princess Maia, and Will would prevail.

"Ah, come now, Will," said Robert. "Would you really be

so stingy? It's all in good fun, and no one will have to share if they don't have to. No assumptions will be made."

"You *can't* promise that," said Kaimund.

"And now you make us wonder what the three of you have to hide," said Prince Hans. He leaned back and tilted his head to the side as he stared at his sister. "I wish I could vouch for you, but you're a closed book. Alas, but I have no idea who you truly are. My own sister!"

Princess Maia rolled her eyes and gave a heavy sigh. "You are being horrid again, Hans. People have a right to privacy, and *that* is exactly why we don't want to see each others' reflections. You know, I begin to wonder if Ginny might have the best idea of all of us, not wanting to look at all."

Ginny almost dropped her muffin.

"Perhaps she does," Prince Hans agreed. "But I fear that the rest of us lack her self-control to resist our curiosity. Oh, to be as good as Miss Ginny!"

"Oh, to be as *boring* as Ginny," said Rina with a sniff. "Oh, Reynard, do tell them that they're all being ridiculous and that it's all good fun."

"An excellent diversion, to be certain," said Lord Reynard.

Rina nodded in satisfaction as though Lord Reynard had spoken the most solemn proverb in existence.

"Ginny can make her own judgments the same as any of us," said Will. "But it's my mirror, and I say that each of us should only look at our own reflections."

And with that, he stood and marched away. Ginny swallowed as she glanced toward Princess Maia, who frowned. *Was* Will hiding his reflection? Was it otherwise than he'd told Ginny?

Maybe …

Oh, but this mirror was a horrid affair.

"Well, we still have a week before we're looking in the mirror," Rina said, taking a long sip of her drink. "We have time to cajole him. He can't be stubborn forever."

"Or we have time to convince him to not let us look at all," said Calla. "Oh, *please* don't push it! I don't want to give it up!

It's been the most interesting thing to have ever happened here in Snowfield Palace!"

"Don't worry, Calla dear," said Prince Hans. "We won't push him too far. He'll come around. He's a good sort, you know. But too used to holding all his cards against his chest, and he doesn't understand why anyone else would want to bare themselves to the world. Maia's the same way, and she doesn't even have a terrible childhood to excuse her. Just give him time."

Princess Maia sent her brother a glare, then quietly stood and excused herself, following in the same direction Will had gone.

10

Ginny sat frozen as she considered everything that had happened.

Princess Maia thought that Will was hiding something. Will didn't trust Princess Maia. What would they do to each other? What would they say?

Quickly, she stuffed the rest of her muffin into her mouth, then she stood and rushed after them.

Will should have left the mirror at the capital! He should never have gambled for it! Oh, why did everyone have to treat this like a game? It wasn't!

She reached the bottom of the hill, and the air already felt colder. Her heart leapt into her throat. Had Will *attacked* Princess Maia, forcing her to defend herself? The last thing he needed was the assault of a foreign princess on his record. He would lose his place in the guards, and then what would happen to him? What would happen to Ginny herself? They'd only *just* found each other again, and Ginny didn't feel that she'd been able to get to know her brother by *half,* yet.

There was still the matter of *if* he really was her brother. How was she supposed to get answers if he was gone?

The ground beneath Ginny's feet crunched, and she looked down to see frost coating everything. A few more steps, and she found Princess Maia and Will standing in the middle of the frozen patch, staring wordlessly at each other.

Ginny swallowed, her stomach sinking.

"What's going on here?"

She twisted around. Kaimund had also followed a few steps behind her.

Will's eyes widened as his gaze went from Princess Maia to Kaimund. His mouth fell open, but he said nothing.

"Oh," said Princess Maia, twisting around. She glanced down and around at the icy ground, then tilted her head to the side. "Sorry! Sometimes a Frost has to expel ice when upset. I don't usually lose control like this. It's embarrassing!"

Will's mouth snapped shut, and he stared at Princess Maia with a bewildered expression. After all her talk of not trusting him, she was *covering* for Will!

What was happening?

"The grass *should* survive once the ice melts," Princess Maia continued, scampering over to lay a hand on Kaimund's arm. "Oh, you won't tell anyone I lost control like this, will you? Hans would never let me live it down."

Kaimund laughed lightly as he smiled down at her. "Don't worry. Your secret is safe with us. Isn't that right, Ginny?"

Ginny blinked. "I—"

"Of course, it's safe with her," said Will, his hand landing solidly on Ginny's shoulder. "This is to be our secret. Yes."

His voice was so *tight*. As though he dared everyone to argue.

"Yes," said Princess Maia.

Everyone was far too silent for far too long. Will's hand was too cold. Ginny leaned into him, calmed by the chill, but still confused.

Why was Princess Maia covering for him?

And *what* was she covering?

"We should get back to the others before they worry and investigate," said Will. He removed his hand from Ginny's shoulder to offer her his arm. She took it and let him pull her away from the ice patch.

He was *so* cold. Had he absorbed the brunt of Princess Maia's ice blast? How much had she expelled? Was she all right? Ginny was sure that Will would be fine – he handled cold as well as she did.

But Princess Maia…

Ginny glanced back over her shoulder at Kaimund and the princess. She *seemed* all right. As placid as ever, yes, but all right. Ginny frowned at the way that Kaimund stared down at the princess. Then she twisted away. Why did she have to torture herself like this?

No, better to focus on Will and what it meant that he was back in her life. Did she really need Kaimund now that she had her brother?

But she couldn't think about what her life might be without Kaimund. Will was still so much of a stranger.

And Princess Maia was so sure he was hiding something.

Ginny stayed silent as they rejoined the others. But, then, she had been silent before, as well. Eventually, everyone finished eating, and the party broke up, everyone drifting in their own directions. Will stayed seated, lost in thought, no matter how hard Robert tried to engage him. Ginny remained at Will's side.

She didn't know what the future held, but if trouble was coming, well … Will had been through so much alone. Since he was here, she had to stand by him.

If only she knew what he was hiding!

She knew she probably *should* know. But she didn't. She could remember so little from her childhood. And so little made sense.

~

"I've shaken Kaimund, finally."

Ginny snapped her book shut as Princess Maia sat down beside her in the library, her breath catching. "Wha—"

"I know, I know, but the poor fellow does not know how to give it up!" Princess Maia was shaking her head. "But I need to talk to you and your *brother*, and I'm going to give you the dignity of having the conversation alone."

"Why?"

"Because while I understand why Will is lying, you deserve to know the truth. I like you too much to see you taken in like this, as I said. Come."

"But I said that we didn't need to talk about him." Ginny shook her head and hugged the book to her chest.

Princess Maia shook her head. "You can't hide from something like this. Come. Do you know where Will is right now?"

"What do you think he's hiding?" Ginny sunk deeper into the couch, not wanting to go anywhere. Not wanting another crack in her world.

"I will give Will the opportunity to explain to you," Princess Maia answered. "I won't say what I know until we're in … his presence. But it's no longer just a guess. I'm sorry, Ginny. For your sake, I wanted to be wrong, but I can't deny the truth. Nor can you hide from it. Come along."

Ginny allowed Princess Maia to remove the book and pull her to her feet. She didn't help her. Nor did she fight. Why did this have to be happening? Why couldn't Will have just been *Will?* Why couldn't her life be orderly and simple?

But the pieces had been falling apart for so long.

He was in his bedroom, according to the servant they asked, so Ginny led the way there. There was no answer when she knocked, but Princess Maia insisted she knock again.

"Will, if you insist on hiding, then I'm just going to tell Ginny," Princess Maia spoke aloud when there was still no answer. "And if you don't care to explain yourself, I may just tell everyone else and see what they do about it. I have a feeling that that's the last thing you want."

Ginny's breath caught, and she wanted to run. She couldn't. Not with Princess Maia standing there beside her. Not with the burn of curiosity pricking at her heart.

What was Will hiding?

The door opened, and there Will stood, hair and clothes a mess, staring at Ginny with a dark frown. He said nothing as he turned and headed back to his bed, throwing himself down and pulling his knees up to his chest as he stared at the wall.

Ginny hugged herself as she watched him. She wanted to help him, but … *what was the matter?*

"That's not your brother, Ginny," said Princess Maia after a moment, and Ginny's breath caught.

Will swallowed visibly, still not looking at them.

"She's a Frost. She's a woman. Men aren't Frosts."

"Oh." Ginny took a step back, her arms falling to her sides as a frozen flurry of memories rushed through her, and that jagged piece fell into place. "*Oh.* She's my sister."

"No, Ginny—" Princess Maia tried to protest.

"She's my sister," Ginny repeated, sending the princess a glare. "I never had a brother. Everything makes sense now."

"You do remember," Will whispered. He – no, *she* – took a deep breath and released her legs to turn and face them, and when she spoke again, her voice was softer. Lighter. "Yes, I'm a Frost. I am a woman. I am Ginny's sister. Will is short for Willhilmina. Which is a terrible mouthful, but can be shortened nicely enough."

"I knew something wasn't right," said Ginny, taking a step towards Will. "But I wasn't *sure*. And I couldn't remember enough to make sense of it."

"You really thought you had a brother and not a sister?" Will tilted her head to the side. "*Gin!*"

Ginny lifted her hands, palms up. "I never told anyone one way or the other! I only ever said your name, everyone just assumed you were my brother, and I was too shy to protest! And they said it enough … I was seven when I last saw you, and that was twelve years ago. I wasn't sure one way or another until you walked in with Robert, and you were a man, and then when I asked, you *said* you were my brother. You could have told me, but you didn't!"

Will took a sharp breath and stood. "I'm sorry. I *should* have told you. I just … I've been living as a man for so long, when I found that that was what you believed, it felt easier to confirm that belief and continue on the way I always had." She bit her lip and leaned awkwardly against the bed. "I never meant to live this lie. But … there aren't many opportunities for girls. It isn't safe for girls on the street. I found that people made assumptions when I said my name, and it was easier to not argue. As I got older, I learned to hide my feminine features, and I thankfully have a boyish enough face and figure, and I *almost* managed to convince myself it was the truth. Almost, but not quite."

"And it also kept people from assuming that you were a Frost," said Princess Maia.

"Yes," said Will. "Things have been easier for our kind in recent years, but there's still a lot of prejudice to dispel in Howsill."

"A lot in the North Country, too," Princess Maia agreed.

Ginny shifted her weight awkwardly as she stared at Will, leaning against the wall with a forlorn stare. Swallowing, she rushed over to throw her arms around her sister.

Will's breath caught, and then she wrapped her arms tight around Ginny and held her close. "I've missed you, little sister. I'm so sorry that I didn't trust you."

"You've not had anyone *to* trust for a long time," said Princess Maia. "And Frosts tend to be suspicious." She took a deep breath. "But the prejudice against our kind is waning. And now you have found your family, so…"

"I'm a member of the guard now," said Will. "They don't allow women among the guards. No, this is the life I've carved out for myself, and I don't know how I would be able to take care of Ginny if I have to."

"Ginny has a home here," Princess Maia pointed out. "And if they turned her out, then she would have a home in the North Country, I promise you that. And you can have a home in the North Country, too. Or in the Forest. Aunt Elin said that your father must have come from the Forest, and if that's true, then you have a home there for sure."

"Maybe," said Will. She took a deep breath. "I don't want charity, though. Not for myself. If things come crumbling down around my ears, then that is definitely an option for me to consider. But, for now, well, I *am* a guard. That is the life that I've made for myself. Maybe it's a risk to stay with them, but I … I don't want to leave my friends."

"I understand," said Princess Maia. She gave a long sigh. "You have an ally in me. I want you to know that. You're a fellow Frost, and as such, I will protect your secrets. I was just concerned that you were taking advantage of Ginny. If you *are* her sister, then all is well."

"Thank you for watching out for her." Will gave a small laugh. "I knew if someone would see through me, it would be you, your highness. One recognizes their own kind."

"One does," said Princess Maia. "One looks out for their own kind, too. Just, I don't think you can live a lie forever."

There was the click of the door, and the princess had left the sisters alone.

"I know I can't," Will whispered in Ginny's ear as she gave her one last squeeze and released her. "I don't *want* to live this lie forever. But, for now, it's what I know. And it's what keeps you safe, Gin."

"I think I'll be fine," said Ginny. "Really, I will be. I'm just happy to have you back again, no matter how. And I want you to be happy."

"I'm happy enough," said Will. "I've never been trained how to act like a lady. Maybe, someday. But not until it's safe. Or I have to. It's not what I want, but it's what's comfortable."

Ginny nodded. "I understand that." She gave a nervous laugh as she sat down on the bed. "You really are my sister. Really."

"Really," said Will, with a laugh of her own. "But I'm still your Will."

"I know that." Ginny rubbed her temples. "I always knew that. I thought I had trapped you in this lie, but … if you've been pretending to be a boy for years…"

"You just helped me keep appearances," said Will. "Perhaps it was Mother and Father who trapped me, in the end. By giving me this name. Making it easy for everyone to make assumptions." She shrugged. "But we're clean now, and that's a load off my chest. I couldn't believe that you would have remembered wrong, but … I didn't know how to admit otherwise." She pushed away from the bed and pulled the curtain away from the mirror, frowning as she stared into it.

Ginny sucked in a sharp breath as she saw her sister's reflection, and she knew why Will fought so hard to keep it secret.

For it was no palace guard that took form in that frame. No, Will's reflection was that of a refined lady – the same facial features, sure, but dressed in icy blue dress that showed a feminine figure, and she had a braid as white as Princess's Maia's pulled over one shoulder. True to her claimed description, she was wearing jewels – a necklace, bracelets, and earings, so perhaps that had been less of a lie than Ginny had feared. She was charming, demure, and beautiful.

Will gave a long sigh. "That's who I should be. Who I *really* am. But I can't be that person. Not yet. Not until it's safe."

Ginny swallowed as Will covered the mirror again and turned to face her.

"Will it ever be safe?" Ginny asked, frowning.

"I don't know. I pray it will be. I also pray that it will be my own choice to leave, and it won't because I messed up as badly as I did today, and the *wrong* person saw me." Will shook her head. "I was so scared today, when Maia discovered my outburst. But then *she* took responsibility for it. I won't make another mistake like that, I promise. I can't risk you. I can't risk…" She trailed off with a long sigh. "My life is a huge tangle, and I don't know how to get out."

"You have me now, though," Ginny pointed out. "And I know the truth. So does the princess. You can trust us."

Will nodded. "Maybe, someday. I doubt Robert will ever see it that way. He wouldn't look my way if he knew the truth. I'm not his type. I know his type. The docile, pretty ones who titter and laugh and can't resist a uniform. No, it's better that I stay as I am, as his friend. His comrade. Watching his back and keeping him safe. He can't reject me if he doesn't know. And until he rejects me, my heart is safe."

"You're in love with Robert?" Ginny wrinkled her nose as she stared at her sister.

"And why wouldn't I be?" Will raised her chin and folded her arms over her chest. "He's my closest friend, charming, funny, handsome … I may dress as a man, but I still have the eyes of a woman. The heart … the heart of a Frost."

"I'm sorry," said Ginny.

"So am I," said Will. "I guarded my heart for so long, but Robert and his charming, *charming* grin just broke through all of my defenses, and he doesn't even know. He can't even guess that he holds my heart in his hands and can crush it in a moment as soon as he finds out the truth."

Ginny rushed forward to give Will another hug.

11 They didn't talk about it again. Not Will, not Princess Maia, and certainly not Ginny herself. There were only shared glances when they were in the same room as everyone continued to focus on the mirror. The night chosen to look into it was quickly coming, and everything was nearly ready.

Will continued to resist the request that they look at each other's reflections, yet with her own secret shared, she was less stalwart and quickly crumbled under the pressure and relented. She wasn't happy about it, and grumbled as much to Ginny, but also said that perhaps some secrets aren't worth keeping.

"Perhaps you should offer to let Robert see your reflection?" Ginny asked, biting her lip.

But Will just shook her head. "Never."

The day came, and everyone wore their very best. Ginny still refused to look in the mirror again, herself, but had agreed to stand at the entrance of the cave with a candle. She didn't like even this level of participation, but it was for Will, and since the mirror meant so much *to* Will, and Ginny now understood why, she was willing to do this for her sister.

She stayed quiet while everyone laughed and chatted happily, savoring the last few minutes of anticipation. What would everyone see? What were everyone's true selves? They had ideas – Rina was *sure* that Prince Hans was *just* as handsome inside as out, and Calla instantly made a counter-declaration that he had to be *handsomer*. Kaimund similarly tried to flatter Princess Maia, but while Prince Hans reveled in the attention, his sister just stood awkwardly and glanced towards Ginny as though she could save her.

Ginny didn't know what to do.

A cloaked figure swept into the room. Everyone pulled back in shock, but the figure threw back the hood to reveal Will's grinning face.

"So, all of you have gathered to see the most frightful thing in existence – your own true selves," she declared. "This is not a vision for the faint of heart, and I invite all who are scared to turn back now."

Ginny wished they all would turn back, but only an uneasy whisper rippled through the crowd.

"Very well then. Each of you will take your turn, according to my choice," Will continued. "As your name is called, present yourself at the entrance to the cave, and offer the guardian your token. She will give you your candle, and then you may enter. Look upon your true self with somber silence, and then you may retreat."

Ginny frowned down at the candle in her hands. Will had told her nothing about a *token* for entry. What was that supposed to mean? Why was it being handed to her? What was she supposed to do with them?

"Lady Nora, why don't you do the honors of being the first to look upon the Mirror of Thurt?" Will concluded with a bow. "So come forward, present your token, and look upon your inner self."

Lady Nora stepped forward with a proud lift to her chin, and she stared down her nose at Ginny. "Young man, we are allowing you to stay under our roof and eat our food. Yet you still have the audacity to *charge* us for the use of the mirror?"

Will held up her hands. "Must you be so mercenary in your thinking? The magic must be appeased, though your hospitality has been appreciated."

"Aunt, just go along with it," said Robert, with a roll of his eyes. "It's all in good fun, and you're getting to go first, so I don't know why you're complaining."

"This is all ridiculous," Lady Nora declared before storming out of the room.

"Ah, but the Mirror of Thurt is only for those who are true of heart!" Will declared, shaking her head. "If there any yet here who are unbelievers, let them turn back now!"

Everyone shifted. Ginny took a step back, gripping her candle tighter, but no one else left.

"Miss Rina, will *you* be the first to look upon your true self in the Mirror of Thurt?"

Rina scampered forward, thrusting a jeweled comb into Ginny's hand, and tilted her head to the side expectantly. Ginny gave her the candle, and then Rina plunged into the cave as Will lifted the curtain for her.

"Ah, nice," Will muttered as she took the comb from Ginny, and it disappeared into her cloak. "Very nice indeed. You're doing a wonderful job, little sister."

Ginny swallowed and nodded hesitantly. Rina appeared again and returned the candle. She gave a self-satisfied laugh and then disappeared into the group.

"Prince Hans, are you brave enough to look upon your own true self in the Mirror of Thurt?" Will asked.

Prince Hans sauntered forward, dropped a ring into Ginny's outstretched hand, and then gave her a roguish wink as he took the candle from her. Will opened the curtain for the prince and then took the ring from Ginny, giving her another proud nod.

Ginny's eye strayed to Rina, who stood beside Calla, chattering away with a proud lift to her chin.

Clearly, whatever *she'd* seen, it had pleased her. Why would *Rina* see something good in the mirror when Ginny had seen nothing at all?

Prince Hans came out of the cave with a loud laugh, declaring it to be good fun indeed. He nodded to Will and then sought Rina in the crowd to talk to her.

"Kaimund, my good friend, will you be the next to look upon the Mirror of Thurt, or shall you fail at the threshold?"

Kaimund cautiously approached and offered Ginny a small smile as he reached her. His "token" was also a ring, but a smaller silver band compared to the heavy, gaudy ring that Prince Hans had offered. Ginny closed her fist around it as she handed him the candle.

"I think I might let you keep that one for yourself," Will said, leaning over to whisper in Ginny's ear. "I have a feeling that it means far more to you than its actual monetary worth."

Ginny swallowed and slipped it into her pocket. It felt wrong to keep it for herself, and yet…

And yet.

It was a piece of him she could treasure forever, wasn't it?

Oh, that this whole affair was over, and she could look at it properly!

Kaimund stayed in the cave for a very long time. Or maybe he didn't, and it just *felt* like a long time. Ginny shifted her weight from one foot to another, wondering what he saw. It had to be something good – this was *Kaimund,* after all. Maybe he saw no change at all.

She was so focused on Kaimund that she didn't notice the commotion on the other side of the room. Didn't realize that the office door had opened again and *someone* was shouting.

"What's all this? What is going on in my office?"

Lord Bethim had come home.

~

No one was *quite* sure how it happened, afterward. Lord Bethim had meant to surprise everyone with his return home, as the political matter had been tied up quite suddenly, and no one had wanted to linger in the capital when there was no more need. He and Lord Graham had thought that no message could have reached home before them and had simply returned, as quickly as possible.

The journey had been long and hard, and Lord Bethim had looked forward to a relaxing evening alone in his own office. In his own order and space.

Lady Nora had met him at the door, and, upset as she was

by the "tokens," she had eagerly brought him to the office, priming him with warnings that the "children" were up to all sorts of trouble.

When he had walked into the room to find a crush of people, the space dimly lit and everyone dressed up, he had been *quite* annoyed. This was not the relaxation he had expected.

In the shift and panic as everyone tried to clear space away from the entry where Lord Bethim stood, someone knocked into the cave, and then another. It had been built well enough, certainly, but it hadn't been meant to take the brunt of several people pressing against it at once.

There was a crash from within and a cry from Kaimund. Will gave a sharp gasp of alarm and darted inside, while everyone shared worried glances and shifted uncertainly.

"Well, what's going on in here?" Lord Bethim demanded.

"The mirror has fallen on Kaimund!" Will announced, emerging from the cave again. "He's been injured!"

Ginny took a sharp breath. Kaimund hurt? Oh, how could everything go so wrong so quickly? She'd known that this was a disaster in the making, but this was far worse than even she had imagined.

Robert and Prince Hans darted into the cave after Will, and they hauled Kaimund out together and laid him out on a couch. Ginny's stomach sank. Was that blood? It was hard to tell in the dim lighting of the room.

What had happened to the candle? Eyes widening, Ginny darted into the cave. She snatched one of the candles from the wall and plunged further in, rounding the corners until she found the mirror's frame leaning against the wall, jagged pieces everywhere.

What happened when one broke an enchanted mirror? Oh, Kaimund! *Poor Kaimund.*

The candle he had carried into the cave was there, lying on the ground, thankfully extinguished, and as Ginny brought the candle she held closer to the broken glass, she saw that it was just that – glass. Clear as any glass she had ever seen, and no hint of the enchantment.

Shaking her head, she quickly extinguished every candle in the cave and emerged again.

The room had emptied while she was inside. Lord Bethim stood over his son, who still lay on the couch, and Will shifted uncomfortably from one foot to the other at the other end of the couch, Robert beside her, equally distressed. Her face lit as she saw Ginny emerge.

"Where did everyone else go?" Ginny asked in a whisper as she rushed to her sister's side.

"Lord Bethim asked everyone to clear the room, and Lady Nora is fetching a physician," Will quickly explained, pulling Ginny against herself. "He insisted that Robert and I stay because, well, he has it in his head that we're responsible."

"He's not wrong," said Robert. "That was your mirror, and the cave was my idea."

"I *told* you this was all a foolish idea from the start," Ginny said in a hiss.

"So you did, Gin, so you did." Will gave a long sigh. "In the future, I shall remember to listen to you."

"Uncle Bethim wasn't supposed to come home again for several weeks yet," said Robert, shaking his head. "The negotiations were going *terrible* still when we were there. I really thought we were safe and would have time to take down the cave, and he would never be the wiser."

"Is Kaimund going to be all right? He shouldn't be unconscious like this *just* because a mirror landed on him – but it was an enchanted mirror." Ginny slipped her hand into her pocket and squeezed a fist around the ring that Kaimund had given to her.

Will gave another long sigh just as Kaimund gave a low moan and the physician finally arrived, Lady Nora just a step behind him.

"I hope you're proud of yourself, young man," Lady Nora announced, staring at Will with a curled lip. "I knew you were trouble the moment you stepped through that door. I can't imagine the mischief you've gotten Robert into with your friendship.”

“Not nearly as much trouble as I've gotten him into, I promise,” Robert declared, stepping forward, between Will and Lady Nora. “Really, Aunt, Will's a good sort. He never meant for any of this to happen – we were the ones who made it so complicated.”

“I lost my mirror, and a good man is injured,” said Will, raising her chin, even as she hugged Ginny closer. “None of this is what I intended.”

Lady Nora sniffed and turned away. Will gave a sigh of relief, and her grip of Ginny loosened.

Kaimund groaned again, louder this time, and then suddenly sat up, holding his head. “Wha-what happened?”

“Sir, I don't think you should be straining yourself like this,” the physician protested. “You were just unconscious, and we still don't know if you'll be fine. The mirror that fell on you was magic, they said? Who knows what kind of trouble that might cause?”

Kaimund rubbed his temples, shaking his head, and slowly opened his eyes. He jerked back as his gaze focused on the physician. “Get away from me!”

“Sir!” the physician declared, pulling away as Kaimund lashed out. “I'm not here to hurt you, I promise. Just calm down and take a deep breath. How are you feeling? Your cuts seem fine enough, though that burn looks like it hurts. Your eyes, though – did you get glass in your eyes? Your eyes seem fine, but this whole business is trouble all around, I say.”

“That's clear enough!” Lord Bethim declared, shaking his head. “It's very bad business for a man to return home and find his space invaded for such frivolity as this! And now my own son is injured, and for what?”

Kaimund seemed to calm as he focused on his father, and a frown spread across his face as though he saw him for the first time. But he jolted again as the physician loomed closer. “I said get away from me, fiend!”

It was more than Ginny could bear, seeing Kaimund so distressed. She darted forward, calling his name as she caught his arm and pulled him back. He froze, blinking as he stared at her.

No.

Through her.

"Ginny?" he whispered. "Ginny, why can't I see you?"

Ginny fell back, her heart suddenly pounding in her throat. As her hand left his arm, he grabbed for her, but as she dodged away, he only swung helplessly at the air.

He couldn't see her.

"What has happened to my eyes?" Kaimund pulled back and covered his eyes with his hand, taking a long shaky breath. Then he lowered his hands and focused again on where Ginny *had* stood. "No one looks right, and I can't see Ginny at all."

"You did just have an enchanted mirror break on top of you," Robert said in an attempt at a glib remark. "Perhaps you might have absorbed the magic? Ginny, is your true self invisibility?"

Kaimund seemed to relax again as he focused on his cousin, but when Ginny gave a distressed squeak at Robert's question, his focus snapped right back to her as he frowned.

"*Nothing,*" Will suddenly hissed. "Oh, *Ginny.*" And she marched forward to catch Ginny into a tight hug.

"Will?" said Kaimund, his frown growing. "You're … you're a woman?"

Will went stiff, her arms growing tighter around Ginny. "I—" The word came out strangled. "I have to go."

And she was out of the room before any of them could even process another thought.

Ginny rocked back on her heels and squeezed her eyes shut. She could deny it. She could tell them all that Will *was* her brother, and they would believe her. Wouldn't they? Will was Will, and they'd known her as *him* since she'd first uttered his name.

But it was a lie. And while it'd been one thing to not protest the common belief, it was quite another to push it back into place now that it had been challenged. *That* would be a lie, no question about it.

"Will's a *woman?*"

She glanced toward Robert, who looked like he'd just been slapped. Then her gaze went to Kaimund, staring forlornly towards her, but not seeing her. There was no way that she could force any words from her throat, in support or denial. Oh, but today was a disaster.

She turned and ran after her sister.

12 Will's room was freezing as Ginny darted inside, shutting the door behind herself. Her things were strewn about, and Will stood in the middle of it all, packing frantically.

"Are … are you all right?

Will spun around and ran a hand through her hair as she focused on Ginny. She was breathing hard. "I'll be all right. I just have to get out of here before … before…" She shook her head. "Don't worry about me, Gin. I'll be all right. I always have been, and I always will be. This was a good run. Now it's time for the next thing."

Ginny swallowed. "I'm sorry."

"It's not your fault. Gin, you of all people have been blameless in this whole affair." Will's eyes hardened, and she stalked forward to lay her hands on Ginny's shoulders. "And you are *not* nothing. I don't know why the mirror shows you that, but its meaning isn't always clear. Maybe … maybe I was wrong about it showing a person's true self, though I don't know what else it might be. But you are my dear little sister, and you mean so much to not just me but plenty of people in this very house. A *princess* has decided to make you her constant companion. That doesn't happen to a nobody."

"Princess Maia doesn't exactly have other choices," Ginny

pointed out. "She doesn't like Rina and Calla, and I'm the only female here her age."

"Perhaps it began only as a matter of circumstance, but her loyalty to you is far more than necessity." Will pulled Ginny into a tight, desperate hug. "And she'll make sure you're taken care of. She promised me that much."

Ginny swallowed, not sure what to think of such a promise. "Are you sure you're all right? You're absolutely frozen."

"I'm a Frost," Will answered. "That's kind of our deal. Freezing."

"Will…"

"I'm going to be fine," Will promised. "I've known that this day would come. I didn't expect to lose the mirror the same day, but that just means one less thing weighing me down. It was a heavy mirror, you know."

Ginny sighed. "You're really just going to run? After we only just found each other again?"

Will pulled back and shook her head. "I can't stay. But, I promise, as soon as I have found something again, and I *will* find something, I will send for you. You won't have to stay here much longer. We can be together again. I just have to get back onto my feet."

Then she turned away again and focused again on her things. On the bag on the bed, into which she was folding everything.

"I'm not bringing my uniform with me," she declared. "Give that back to Robert, and he can … get it back where it belongs. It never should have been worn by a woman in the first place. Let him know that I never meant to hurt him. Let him know … no, don't tell him that I loved him. He doesn't need to know that."

"*Loved?*" Ginny repeated, her voice rising in pitch. "Will, what do you mean *loved?*"

Will just shrugged. "Tell him I'm sorry and that I'm going to be all right." She snatched a silver knife from her bedside table and slid it into a sheath on her belt. "Tell him it was a great time, and I'll never forget it. That's all he needs to know."

Ginny hugged her arms around herself, shaking her head, not sure what else to say. She could only stand there and watch Will throw all of her worldly possessions into that bag, muttering about the worth of jewels and how much she could sell them for. Her stomach sank like a frozen stone as she realized how little her sister actually had.

And now Will was going to start all over again. Doing what? Ginny couldn't believe that everything was breaking apart so quickly. How had Will supported herself before joining the guards? She didn't know. How was she going to support herself now? That seemed like an even more impossible question.

All too soon, the last thing was shoved into the bag. Will sinched it closed and turned back to Ginny with a half-grin. "I couldn't lie forever," she said. "I've always known that. I took the risk of having the truth come out when I accepted Robert's invitation to stay in this house, where I knew I'd left you. That everyone had assumed I was your brother was a providence I hadn't expected. It was a good run. Now it's time for the next one."

She stepped forward and pressed a kiss to Ginny's forehead. "I'll write you when I can, and when I can take care of you, I'll let you know. Don't be afraid. You aren't alone anymore." Then she turned away and slipped out the window.

Ginny's breath caught, and she rushed forward – they were on the third story, after all – but she looked down to find Will climbing expertly down, using icy handholds to prevent herself from falling. Will glanced up with one last grin and a wave before jumping down the last few feet and running off into the night.

"Will?"

Ginny spun around. Robert hovered in the doorway, looking pale and distressed. She swallowed. "She just left."

Robert winced, stumbling over to the bed and sitting down heavily. "It's true, then? She really was a woman all this time?"

Ginny shrugged. "I never had a brother, but no one would listen when I tried to say that Will was my sister. Eventually, I gave up trying and began to wonder if *I'd* been the one wrong the whole time. But it's true."

"She must think me the greatest fool, then. All this time, my greatest friend was a woman. I told Will all my secrets. He … she … Ginny, how could I not see it? He was always so private, never would talk about women – and I always was teasing him about the fact that he never shaved. How did I not guess the truth? How can I still *not* see it? Is Will even his name?"

"Will is short for Wilhelmina." Ginny offered Robert a weak smile.

"It would be, wouldn't it?" Robert shook his head. "The world's all wrong tonight. Kai now sees people wrong because it seems like he absorbed whatever enchantment the mirror had. Will's a woman, and now he's gone. And I didn't even have a chance to tell him goodbye or anything, like a good friend should. What's he going to do now? I bet he expects me to tell my superiors the truth, and that's why he ran. She."

"She left the uniform for you to return for her."

Robert blinked as he picked up the fabric he was practically sitting upon. "I should burn it," he growled.

"But…" Ginny took a step forward.

"I don't know what Will has in her head about me, but I don't do my mates wrong like that." Robert shook his head. "He was a woman this whole time? Fine! He's covered enough for me that it's time I did the same. If he's gone, then there's nothing I can do, but I can keep them from finding out *why*." He swallowed. "I'll tell them Will's dead. That we were camping on our way back, that he went out into the woods alone, and that all I found of him were bones and the tattered remains of his uniform."

Ginny froze, blinking. "That sounds … horrible."

"It'll keep them from looking for him. Her. Will. Wilhelmina."

"Are … are you drunk?" Ginny frowned as she noted the flush of Robert's skin.

"A man needs a bit of liquid courage before he confronts the friend who wasn't who he thought he was, the whole time he knew him." Robert ran a hand through his hair. "But it seems I just wasted time, and it meant I missed her entirely. Now I … I can't do anything for her. Except keep the secret. Poor Will. What's he going to do now?"

Ginny sighed and shrugged. "Survive, I guess. She's done it before, and she'll do it again. We … we just have to pray to Austere that she'll be fine."

"I'll be leaving, myself, in the morning," said Robert. "My leave is about up, and Uncle Bethim is upset. If I don't stick around, he'll calm down soon, I'm sure. If … if you find your sister again, before I do, let him – her – know that I get it. That we were friends, and it doesn't matter if she isn't the man I thought she was. She's still Will, isn't she."

"Oh, certainly," said Ginny.

"She's a Frost, isn't she?" Robert concluded. "That's why she hid. I know your father was a strong Zephyr, and it doesn't make sense that neither of you would have inherited his magic, and he's always been far better in cold situations than even you are." He gave a long sigh. "You don't have to answer that one. I think I know. And I'd better go prepare for my own journey, shouldn't I?"

He stood, snatching the uniform up and stormed out of the room, leaving Ginny alone. She stared after him, a lump forming in her throat. Then she sank into the bed and cried herself to sleep.

~

Princess Giana of Ember and her family arrived the next day.

Ginny had received surprisingly little condemnation for sleeping in Will's room. A servant had woken her, only to give her a sympathetic smile at her halting explanation and to escort her back to her room.

No one else had actually noticed. Nor did anyone else notice her exhaustion and still-puffy eyes. She took her place at the breakfast table and sat at Lady Bethim's side in the sitting room, but everyone else was far too concerned with their own business to give her any attention.

Lord Bethim was back in his place at the head of the table, and he wasn't pleased.

Princess Mayblossom seemed happier now that she had her husband again, so that, at least, was good.

Kaimund didn't join them for breakfast. He was sequestered in his room, and only certain servants were allowed to wait on him. That's what Ginny heard Lady Nora tell Lord Bethim. She didn't dare ask about him herself.

But, eventually, enough of the day dragged by, and their guests arrived. Ginny didn't hide when the household went outside to greet them and instead stood in the line next to Princess Mayblossom. Kaimund was still absent, and there were no marriageable members in Princess Giana's party for Ginny to distract from Calla.

She shrank back as the carriage door opened and their guests emerged. She'd never seen Dwarven or Cinders before. Princess Giana, Lord Yarro, and their children were human enough, but as dark as Will and Princess Maia were pale.

Princess Giana and Princess Mayblossom rushed forward to exchange hugs and for Princess Giana to express her congratulations. After greetings were properly exchanged, everyone turned to go back inside, the two princesses arm-in-arm as they chatted merrily.

"Giana's probably the best person for Blana right now," said Princess Maia, falling into step beside Ginny as the young Dwarven and Cinders raced around them. "Her mother *also* died when she was born, you see, and since she's survived five children of her own, she has enough authority on the subject to put Blana in her place when her nerves are acting up."

"Will you and your brother remain in Snowfield, then?" Ginny asked, frowning.

"Oh, surely." Princess Maia put a hand on Ginny's arm. "I noticed a few faces absent at breakfast, and, well, I did make a promise to Will. Terrible business, but I already talked with Lord Bethim and Lady Nora about the importance of keeping *his* secret. You don't have any worries there, but I am sorry that he's already gone."

"Last night was horrible."

"And barely any of us actually got to see the mirror for ourselves." Princess Maia sighed and shook her head. "I know, you don't like that thing, and I certainly didn't want anyone else to see my reflection, but I still wanted to know what mine was."

Ginny sighed.

"Yes, I know, apparently, Kaimund has absorbed the enchantment, and I do understand how horrible that is," said Princess Maia. "No man should have that power, and what will it even mean for him? Will he see people's true selves forever? Or will it eventually wear off and be lost forever? Will he be able to learn to control it, like others can control their magic?"

Ginny just shrugged, thinking that it sounded worse by the moment. Poor Kaimund!

They all settled in the sitting room, except for Princess Giana's younger children, who had been redirected into a nursery.

"So, Giana, what do you know about a Mirror of Thurt?" Princess Mayblossom asked at length. "I know, I know, it's a strange name, but I think it might be a Dwarven creation, and I know that Ember has records that many of the other countries have lost."

Lord Yarro, who had been standing on the edge of the room with their eldest son, raised his head at the question. "Thurt, you say? I've heard that name before."

"Was he a Dwarven?" Princess Maia asked as she leaned forward.

"One of the most powerful who ever lived," Lord Yarro answered. "But he was also a bit of a madman. There are a lot of legends and myths about him, and little is known for certain as the years have gone by. He left behind many artifacts, and a mirror might have been one of them. Why do you bring it up?"

"Because we had a friend bring a Mirror of Thurt into Snowfield Palace, and it had a mysterious enchantment that no one is quite sure what it is," Princess Mayblossom explained. She leaned back against the couch. "It broke last night, and my nephew seems to have absorbed the enchantment, so we would very much like to know what that enchantment *was*."

"Or is, since the enchantment still seems to exist, even if the mirror shattered," said Prince Hans. "Will said that he thinks that it showed a person's true self, and since I actually got a chance to see it, I'm inclined to agree."

"But Will didn't *know*," Ginny muttered.

Princess Giana frowned as she shared a glance with her husband. "I believe I once came across a book about Thurt and his creations in Ember's libraries. I don't *remember* a mirror, much less what such a mirror would have done. But I promised Darren that I would come see him *just* as soon as I found a hazel tree, and since you have one, Mayblossom, I shall avail myself of it." She tilted her head to the side. He was so *loathed* to let me marry a Forest Dwarven and leave him for three years, but he could hardly let Lizzy be his ambassador in these matters. She has to be queen."

"You're welcome to it," Princess Mayblossom assured her, grinning. "If you can find the book and bring it back with you, it would be wonderful."

"I've never heard of anyone absorbing the enchantment from a Dwarven's creation," said Lord Yarro, shaking his head. "I don't like it, but I suppose there's a first for everything. Have you asked the Gardener if she can remember anything?"

"The mirror only broke last night, so not yet," said Princess Mayblossom. "Perhaps I should accompany you as far as the Forest and ask my own questions. Poor Kaimund."

"Poor Kaimund, indeed," said Lord Yarro. "It sounds like terrible magic, made worse by the fact that no one knows what it is for certain."

Ginny shivered and shrunk back into the couch.

13 The Gardener could remember nothing about the Mirror of Thurt, and Princess Giana couldn't find the book. So, the mystery remained. Kaimund's vision remained distorted by the mirror's magic, even as his scars and burn healed.

He only stayed sequestered in his room for a few more days before he rejoined the family, albeit greatly subdued. He claimed that he had to learn how to live with his new vision, as it seemed to be his new reality, and he couldn't hide forever.

A few were brave enough to ask him how he saw them now. Calla practically demanded it. Kaimund would just frown and shake his head, saying that he didn't want to explain.

"It's not fair that you get to see everyone's true selves, and you're keeping it to yourself!" Calla declared. "Only Rina and Hans got to see the mirror for themselves, and now you won't tell anyone!"

"I think a lot of people are better off not knowing how they appear in that mirror," said Kaimund, shaking his head again. "I don't believe that it's anyone's true self; not anymore. I don't know what I'm seeing. You're not a shadow, Calla. Why do you look like a shadow? And Ginny..." He sighed and closed his eyes. "And now I've gone and said too much."

"A shadow!" Calla gave a huff and stood. "Well, that is

horrible." Then she turned and flounced away.

But the thoughtful look that twisted her face as she sat down on the couch next to her sister caused Ginny's heart to give an extra beat. As long as she had known Calla, she had been following behind Rina, trying to *be* Rina, and gain the praise and adoration that her sister enjoyed.

She had been Rina's shadow.

Maybe, just maybe, learning this would be good for her, giving her a chance to break free and be herself? Ginny didn't have high hopes, but this could be the *one* good thing that came from this whole terrible affair!

But how could Ginny herself break free of *nothingness*? She was a nobody. No matter that she lived here in Snowfield Palace as a trusted companion, she'd been born on the streets and had risen this far only out of charity.

And she was also very alone. Yes, Princess Maia still sought her companionship whenever possible. But it was worse now because now there was a level of desperation to it that Ginny found unsettling.

Kaimund was drawn towards Princess Maia even more strongly than before. *Apparently*, she was one who appeared less disturbing to look at with his new vision. He still wouldn't explain what he saw, but she at least seemed grounded.

Having his constant attention only made Princess Maia more uncomfortable, and now it was harder for her to deflect his attention to Ginny. He couldn't *see* Ginny, after all.

He could hear her, though, and the way his head would snap in her direction and his eyes would fill with such despair any time she so much as sighed was enough to silence Ginny completely. She hated the reminder that she was now invisible to him – her best friend in all the world.

Rina's wedding to Lord Reynard hastened on, even faster than originally planned, for after a private conversation with Lord Bethim, they decided to move it up by two months. It was unorthodox, yes, but Rina declared that she hated waiting and that after everything that had happened, it was time to focus on something *positive*.

Ginny wanted to think that it was a good thing, but something just didn't sit right with her. Rina had never been more than polite with her intended, and so declarations that she couldn't wait to marry him didn't seem *right*.

But Lord Bethim accepted it, and Ginny's opinion was the last that he would have sought. The wedding was happening, with all the pomp and festivity demanded by any event that had Rina as the center of attention. It was a distraction, certainly, and that's precisely what they all needed.

Meanwhile, Lord Yarro and the Dwarven who came with him focused on the mountain pass they were building. Princess Maia brought Ginny to go see it one day. Kaimund went with them, making it awkward.

"We need to do something about the fact that he can't see you," said Princess Maia, folding her arms over her chest as she stared after Kaimund, who was currently talking to a Dwarven about their progress. Which wasn't much, as they had only been at the task for a week, but it was still remarkable compared to what ordinary men would have been able to do.

"What is there we can do, though?" Ginny shook her head as she whispered. "He sees what the mirror showed, and if it didn't show me at all—"

"Will let you see yourself in the mirror, before anyone else, didn't she?" Princess Maia suddenly concluded. "That's why you disliked it so much. Because it showed you what you feared. Is that what the mirror showed people? Their worst fear?"

Ginny wrinkled her nose and shook her head. "I think that's a question that Kaimund is far more qualified to answer. I know it showed Will that she was, well, a she, and that's what she most feared anyone else finding out. But, then, it doesn't seem that everyone sees something horrible. Rina and your brother both liked what they saw, though, well, Kaimund does seem disturbed by them. But he doesn't seem to mind seeing you or his father at all."

Princess Maia nodded. "I wish they would find that book. Giana says that her brother is looking for it, and Lizzy will bring it as soon as they have it. I hope it does have answers. But, until then, I choose to believe that it has something to do with your perception of yourself, because I know that Rina and my brother each have a far-too-puffed-up image of themselves. Meanwhile, you seem to think you aren't anyone at all. However, *I* know that I'm just a normal girl, just caught in a huge mess of politics due to the circumstance of my birth. And thus it just goes to show that, no matter how she might disguise herself, Will never lost sight of who she was."

Ginny swallowed. That might be true, but still…

"I am a nobody," she said. "Maybe it's for the best that Kaimund can't see me anymore. I can't distract him from the life that he should live."

"Kaimund is absolutely lost without you." Princess Maia rolled her eyes. "Don't you see how he looks for you every time he thinks you might be in the room? I know, I know, he's deadset on wooing me – and I will admit for your sake that he is a good young man. But I have my reservations, and besides, he's Blana's nephew. Maybe she's ten years my elder, but that wouldn't make it one whit less awkward. He's just never seen that you *could* be an option."

But Ginny just retreated as she saw Kaimund headed their way again. "We promised to not talk about him. I think … I think I'll go ahead and walk back to the palace, now."

She didn't even wait to see Princess Maia sigh in frustration.

~

The wedding came. It was beautiful – if a little heartless. Prince Hans wasn't there – the week before, he announced that he needed to visit his father to discuss the state of their kingdom and that he would be gone for three weeks at least.

Rina stamped about for a whole day after the announcement, while Calla sighed in despair – until she realized that she would have Prince Hans *all* to herself once he returned. After all, if Rina was away, properly serving as the mistress of Sothers, all would be well and good. Indeed, it was a wonderful thing that he was away.

Ginny raced here and there on Lady Nora's orders, making sure that every little thing was completely perfect. It meant that Princess Maia could demand her presence less often. It meant that she had to risk interaction with Kaimund far less frequently.

When the wedding itself came, Kaimund sat with his family while Princess Maia had Ginny at her side. Ginny knew without a doubt that, without Princess Maia, she would have been left to stand with the servants, hiding in the back, where no one could see her. But, no, she was properly in attendance and Princess Maia had given her one of her own dresses to wear.

But, then, she had always worn Rina's and Calla's cast-offs. This dress was just a little bit nicer and a little bit newer. It fit her better, too, as Princess Maia was closer to Ginny in size, and she had asked a seamstress to take it in for her instead of making Ginny do it herself.

And it really, really was a beautiful ceremony, and Rina preened and postured like she was the most important princess in the land while Lord Reynard stood at her side, as handsome and as bland as could be.

Ginny, honestly, truly wished them all the best, though her quiet fears kept her from being hopeful. Rina was not one for contentment and was always reaching for what she thought she deserved. How long before she wanted more than Lord Reynard could give her? And how far would she go to get that *more*?

But that wasn't hers to worry about, and there was nothing she could do about it. She could only do everything in her power to make Rina's day as perfect as possible, because Rina demanded perfection.

Calla suddenly threw herself into a seat next to Ginny's, a gloating grin spread across her face. "Rina *lost*," she declared. "All those years of preening and declaring herself better than me, and she's *lost*. She's stuck forever with Lord Reynard, who is the *stupidest* man she could have chosen, and now it really is my turn."

Ginny bit her lip and nodded, unsure what to say to either encourage or discourage Calla. She felt sorry for the younger Bethim sister, especially if Calla only saw herself as Rina's shadow. But when would she ever decide for *herself* what she wanted instead of chasing after what Rina had? Or for better than what Rina had.

Who was Calla, if not defined by her sister?

Calla dropped her voice. "When Prince Hans returns, I shall have him all to myself, won't I? Rina hates that. She wanted him to propose to her before she had to marry Reynard. And now it really is my chance."

But, alas, Calla's ambitions weren't to be, for as Rina was finishing her preparations for her honeymoon to the capital, she suddenly declared that she couldn't do without her sister and that Calla *had* to accompany her. Everyone proclaimed that a wonderful opportunity for Calla – surely her sister would help her find a suitable husband in the capital – and so there was nothing that Calla could do. The servants prepared her things, and the two sisters rode off with Lord Reynard the following day.

 Ginny received a summons from Lord Bethim just two days later, insisting she come to his office. There was nothing she could do to argue, so, despite her pounding heart, she climbed the stairs back up to the room where the fateful accident had occurred.

Nothing remained of the constructed cave or the mirror it had concealed. The servants had carefully removed all offending evidence of that horrible night.

Ginny's heart pounded faster as she approached her benefactor. Lord Bethim stood at the window overlooking his grounds, hands tucked behind his back. He was a tall, imposing man, and she'd always been frightened of him, but he seemed somewhat ... *smaller* today.

"Is that you, Miss Ginny?" he said, twisting around to stare at her. "My, but you're as silent as a mouse!"

Ginny froze, tucking her hands behind her back as she glanced down. "You needed me, sir?"

Lord Bethim awkwardly cleared his throat. "Need you. Well. That's not really the word for it, now, is it?" She glanced up to see him sit down at his desk and motion to a chair in front of it. She quickly hastened forward to do as she was bid. "Miss Ginny, it has been brought to my attention that, during that whole affair with the mirror, you were the only one with a head on your shoulders, declaring how bad an idea it was."

She swallowed and glanced down again. "And ... and who

told you that, sir?"

"It hardly matters – but, if you must know, it was Robert, Kaimund, and Princess Maia, all three," Lord Bethim answered. "If it had just been Robert, I would have just considered it him trying to keep you out of trouble, given your vulnerable position. And Kaimund has always been your advocate."

Ginny's heart gave an extra beat at the thought of Kaimund advocating for her, and she fought down an ill-advised smile.

"But Princess Maia, it seems, has taken an interest in you and praises your judgment," he continued. "So, naturally, I should take notice of that, shouldn't I?"

"Princess Maia is a good young woman," said Ginny. "If I had any sense at all in the matter, it was only because Will let me see the mirror early, and I feared what I saw in my own reflection."

"But it was still caution that everyone should have heeded," said Lord Bethim. "How old are you these days, dear?"

"Nineteen, sir." Ginny bit her lip.

"The same age as Calla, yes? Why weren't you included when she came out last year?"

Ginny shrugged. "There was no need for me to take any attention away from her," she explained. "Since Rina was not yet married, she was still competing with her for attention."

"And yet you can hardly expect to stay under this roof your whole life – surely you plan to find your own home someday?"

Ginny's heart gave an extra beat before sinking like a lead weight. "Sir, I'm a nobody. I'm forever grateful for your charity, yes, but what lord would ever want, as his wife, one such as me? My mother rejected her inheritance, and my father was a footman." She shook her head. "No, I couldn't compete against Calla."

"But Calla isn't here anymore, now is she?" said Lord Bethim. "And there are plenty of lower-ranking nobles who would be desperate enough for a connection-by-proxy to Snowfield Palace. You're a pretty enough young thing, too, if in a childish way. I'm sure there's a husband out there for you, even if they don't have the grounds to rival Sothers. You can do well enough for yourself, I promise. No, dear, we will hold a ball for you because you deserve it just as much as either of my own daughters did. You're a good young girl, and you'll make some man an excellent wife."

Ginny nodded, all protests dying on her tongue as she looked up at him. His eyes were too hard for her to argue. He would have his way, because he was a powerful lord, and this was his household, and that was how the world worked.

But one protest finally did work its way loose.

"What about Lady Nora? She won't like it."

"I shall tell Lady Nora myself, and if she *doesn't* like it, then she always has the option to return to her nephew's lands. I'm sure he would love to have the responsibility of her. My dear late brother aside, she's here on my charity just as much as you are."

"Very well," said Ginny, the warmth of self-satisfaction welling in her chest at the thought that Lady Nora's position in the house could be so vulnerable. However, she didn't think *she* might be the more valuable member. After all, Lady Bethim didn't know the first thing about running the household, and who would ask that of Princess Mayblossom? For all her cruelty, Lady Nora at least kept things running smoothly.

"You're a good girl," Lord Bethim declared. "Don't forget that. Now be off with you and be about your business. I'll talk to Nora about the preparations and see what she can do for you."

Ginny mumbled her thanks and hastened away before he could see the redness of her cheeks.

A ball, in her honor! She would never have imagined such a thing, but it was happening, it seemed. She wanted to crawl under a rock and hide, but she also wanted to shout from the rooftop.

Both were silly ideas, and so she wound up in her bedroom instead, legs pulled up to her chest as she considered what this strange future might hold for her.

Perhaps, perhaps she *would* meet someone else, someone

who could take away the pain in her heart whenever she saw Kaimund with Princess Maia. She didn't think it possible – Kaimund was the best person she knew – but, then, did that really mean anything when she knew so few people? He was better than Robert, he was certainly better than Prince Hans, and he was better than Lord Reynard – but that was the extent of young men in Ginny's acquaintance.

Maybe there was another out there. A man who *would* see her. Who would want her. Who wasn't …

Wasn't Kaimund.

~

She didn't know how long she sat there, alone, only that Princess Maia came bustling in, all smiles and laughter. "I just heard the news!" she declared. "A *ball!* In your honor! Can you believe it, Ginny? Why, I told you you weren't nothing, dear, and doesn't this just prove it? Lord Bethim is throwing a ball just for you!"

Ginny sat up straight, blinking. "This is your doing, isn't it?" she asked, staring at the princess. "You put him up to it."

"I did nothing of the sort." Princess Maia shook her head. "I merely pointed out your virtues and how it's a shame that you think of yourself as a nobody. It's awkward, the way you float, not a servant, but not really a member of the family, either. No wonder you don't feel like you have a place!"

Ginny took a long breath and sighed. "It's better than someone like I deserve. I could have died on the streets."

"But you didn't – Austere made sure of that," Princess Maia insisted, sitting down beside Ginny. "Not every girl had the promise of a rich lady to protect her, and then Austere made sure to soften Lord Bethim's heart to make sure that you weren't turned away, despite the promise. Now, if just for my sake, please stop with the self-deprecating and lift your chin. You're going to be the belle of the ball, and I plan to make sure of it. That means your *own* dress this time – no borrowing one of mine, though I insist you keep the one I gave you. We shall go to the seamstress at once because you can't imagine how long it takes a dress to get made, especially if it's a proper dress like you're going to have. No, don't worry about the expense; I'm paying for it myself. I have a good allowance for my dresses and far too many of them. And my mother does like it when I share."

"But nothing too fancy, yes?"

Princess Maia laughed. "Oh, you *are* funny, dear! No, nothing *too fancy*. I agree. That would never do for you. The word I have in mind is *exquisite*. There won't be a single eye there capable of looking away from you, because you are a beautiful young woman, and it's time everyone noticed."

Ginny sighed. "But what if I don't want everyone looking at me?"

"Oh, come now, silly! It's not so bad as all that, I promise. Why, I've had the eyes of a nation upon me since the hour of my birth, and I've not suffered for it, now have I?" Princess Maia stood and tugged Ginny to her feet. "When I'm done with you, none shall *recognize* you for that shy ghost you've always been. And *you* will see that you aren't a nobody, no matter the circumstance of your birth and no matter what the mirror showed you. We will get you a dress, and who knows what heart you might win!"

"Does my heart not factor into it?"

"Certainly!" Princess Maia declared. "And you, my dear, shall have your very *pick* of suitors." She rocked back and tilted her head to the side as she sized Ginny up. "We'll need to do something about those braids of yours, too, now that I think of them."

Ginny pulled back, taking a braid in both fists as her eyes narrowed on the princess. "What's wrong with my braids?"

"Nothing at all," placated Princess Maia, patting Ginny's arm. "It's just that they … are better suited to a schoolgirl than a debutant at a ball. They're charming, certainly, but they make you seem more like a child than a grown woman, and what *good* young man seeks a child as his partner? Oh, Ginny! You are a dear young thing – just imagine how beautiful you'll be if you just wore your hair *up*, like a lady should!"

Ginny *wasn't* a lady, though. She didn't deserve a whole room of attention. And she didn't like the thought of Princess Maia dressing her up and doing her hair like a doll.

But would it be worth it if it might find her a suitable husband who would give her her own place and cure her of her unreasonable obsession with Kaimund? She would prefer a husband who loved her for herself, but who would love a nothing like her?

She closed her eyes, brushing aside memories of Will braiding her hair, as she would do each morning until she had to leave her on Snowfield Palace's doorstep. For so many years, her braids had been the only part of Will she could cling to, and so she had resisted all pressure to change her hair, no matter how she might be ridiculed for it.

However, Will was no longer a faded memory. She might have run again, disappearing into the night a second time, but Ginny now had a letter tucked into her dress pocket that promised that Will was all right, just as she always would be. She survived. That's what she did.

And, maybe, if Ginny found a noble husband, she would be able to help Will, too. Give her a home. Perhaps even find her a husband of her own, if she wanted one. Perhaps Robert would look her way if she was the lady she was supposed to be.

"If you think it's best," she finally whispered. "But, please. Nothing too elaborate. I don't want to lose who *I* am, under it all."

"Never," said Princess Maia. "Those who use dresses and hairstyles to hide a girl's real beauty are never in the right. Now, come along. And don't you worry one thing about the ball — I've already promised Nora I will handle the whole thing for her. She won't be allowed to sabotage it, not on my watch, and neither will you be overwhelmed by it."

"Thank you," said Ginny, with a surrendering smile. "This is all more than I could ever ask for."

"But everything you deserve. Remember that, my very dear friend. Who is *not* a nobody! In fact, the people who'll attend the ball won't deserve to stand in *your* presence! Not if they think such silliness!"

15 The ball happened, despite any feelings Ginny had about it. Maia was a whirl of excitement, and it was thrilling to watch. Ginny just wished that it wasn't to make herself the center of attention.

But now she stood in the milling room, wearing a ballgown far finer than anything she had ever dreamed of wearing, her hair wrapped around her head instead of down in its familiar braids.

She barely knew even a tenth of the people in the room. She'd seen enough of them, as she'd observed balls in the past, but who had ever noticed the quiet ward who lurked in corners and never interacted? And in a milling crowd of nobles, who was worthy of *her* notice?

Well, they all were, since they were all far above her in station. But there were just so many!

"Well, well, well," said a voice at her side, and she twisted around to stare up at Prince Hans. "It seems I have returned from my errand only to find that Snowfield Palace has lost half its young ladies. The fairer half, I had thought, but I wonder if I was wrong in such an opinion."

Ginny narrowed her eyes as she stared up at him. "I didn't realize that you had arrived at Snowfield again. I … trust that your journey went well?"

"It was an excellent journey," said Prince Hans, laughing. "So considerate of you to ask! Now, I promise that I'm not just here to steal your time. I promised Maia that I would lead you on your first dance, as would be proper. And who can resist you after you've had the attention of a prince? Come now, what do you say?"

Ginny took a step backward, her mouth dropping open. "I…" She glanced about, looking for Princess Maia, but she was nowhere to be seen. "Are you sure? You don't have to. Even if you promised your sister, I would hardly expect you to devote your time to me when there are so many other, more lovely ladies here."

"But you're the maiden of honor; nothing is more proper." Prince Hans shook his head. "I imagine it might be better for Kaimund to stand up with you, but since circumstances have conspired against the two of you, I shall valiantly try to act as an adequate substitute for him."

Ginny took another step back and fixed her glare on him again. She didn't answer. She had no answer. How did Prince Hans *possibly* think he might be a substitute for Kaimund, even jokingly! Kaimund was everything Prince Hans wasn't, even without the shiny title.

"So, what do you say?"

He didn't even seem to notice her glare. If anything, he just grinned brighter.

She sighed. Prince Hans was the last person she wanted to dance with, especially not her first dance, but, then … she knew exactly two young men here tonight, and one of them couldn't see her. Prince Hans was her last choice, but her first choice wasn't an option.

She nodded, but only barely. She didn't like Prince Hans one bit, and she was sure he was only doing this to remain the center of attention. But any eyes on him were eyes not on her. That, she could appreciate.

"Excellent! Dear Ginny, don't fret at all. I know how intimidating it is to be forced into the limelight like this, especially when you've hidden in the shadows for so long."

Prince Hans gave her one of his smirking grins that had always made both Rina and Calla practically faint with silliness.

Ginny just sighed and looked away from him to the rest of the guests. Would any of the other young men ask her to dance? Would she accept? Would anything come of any of it?

Or would she run from the room?

"Come now," Prince Hans said after a moment. "They seem to be arranging themselves for the first dance, and we need to go take our place."

She glanced back to him to see that he offered her his arm, and she took it reluctantly. Appearances, after all, though she didn't like it at all. He guided her carefully through the room, and she could ignore most of the people around her.

Everyone except Prince Hans. It was impossible to ignore him. He just took up way too much space, even if he was short and *not* a large man.

Ginny swallowed as they took their place and his hand rested on her waist. No, she shouldn't have agreed to this. She was too close to this too-charming man, and it was too late. The music started, and the prince whirled her across the floor.

She knew how to dance, having learned alongside Rina and Calla, but this was the first time that Ginny had ever danced with a man. While Kaimund and Robert had frequently been recruited as partners for the girls, there were only two of them, so Rina and Calla had been the priority. Ginny had had to practice on her own, or, if Robert was away, she would dance as Calla's partner – much to Calla's distress.

And to have Prince Hans as her first partner was...

Not as bad as she feared it might be. He complimented her when she did something right and ignored any mistakes she made. He led her confidently across the floor but with a gentleness that was easy to follow. The smile never left his face, and it was dazzling.

If she hadn't watched him flirt with Calla and Rina for three months, Ginny might have fallen for that smile. He was like the sun. She had observed it from the side for so long, and suddenly his light was turned upon her.

But having seen it from afar, she recognized it for what it was. Charm. Nothing more and nothing less. When the dance finished, and they left the dance floor, she quietly thanked him as she took a step back.

"Ah, but that was an excellent dance! I should be thanking you, my dear – after all, this is your night, and you have shared it with me. Now, I shall not bother you for any more dances tonight – it wouldn't be proper, and I want your night to be a whirlwind of dancing as gentlemen fight for your hand. Ah, but you're a dear, pretty thing. It's good that people can finally see it."

He gave a dramatic bow and disappeared into the crowd, leaving Ginny breathless.

She shook herself and forced her eyes away from his retreat, sternly reminding herself that he was just flash and show. Perhaps he had done this as a favor for his sister, but that only proved how disgenuine he was.

There was Kaimund, standing next to Princess Maia. They had just stepped off the floor together and were laughing. Ginny's heart gave an extra beat, but she couldn't look away from them, for Princess Maia then twisted around and met her eye. With one more sentence exchanged between them, she broke away and rushed to Ginny's side.

"Oh, but you *do* look lovely tonight, dear," she declared. "Was that my brother I saw you dancing with?"

Ginny swallowed and folded her hands together at her waist. "He told me you told him to ask me for my first dance."

Princess Maia laughed. "Did he now? Ah, but you know Hans – always such a tease. You know he never listens to me about anything, so clearly, that was all his own idea, and he just refuses to admit as much."

"Oh." Ginny frowned. "Well, he does love attention."

"He does." Princess Maia took Ginny's hand and squeezed it. "And he can't resist the prettiest girl in a room. Now, what other dances do you have lined up, or do we need to go find you your next partner?"

Ginny bit her lip, her gaze returning to Kaimund, who was

staring after them with a lost expression. She shook her head. "No one has asked me yet, no."

Honestly, if this ball wasn't in her honor, she would have slipped out already. But she couldn't slip out unnoticed, and Lord Bethim would be upset if she committed such an act of ingratitude.

"Ah, I'm probably scaring them off, aren't I? Well, let me scurry off and let the gentlemen approach. Why, I think I see a young man staring already."

Then she was gone.

~

Ginny wasn't sure how she made it through the night, especially since it was early morning before it ended. As she collapsed into her bed, she finally understood why Rina and Calla always slept past noon after balls.

She didn't have a partner for every dance. In fact, she was only asked by five other gentlemen the whole night, and then Prince Hans took pity on her again and asked her a second time. None of the gentlemen were particularly notable, all of them bland, nervous young men or notorious flirts cut from the same cloth as the prince.

She woke with a pounding headache, but a glance at the clock told her that it could still be called morning. At least the day could be salvaged. But for what? What did Ginny do with her time?

Sighing, she pulled her wits together, put on one of her own dresses, and bound her hair into its familiar braids. Then she slipped out of the room and down the halls to seek the rest of the family.

She found Prince Hans, before anyone else.

"Ah, Miss Ginny!" he cried, holding out an arm to her. "I had feared that the vision I'd seen last night was just a dream, and yet here you are, as beautiful as ever!"

Ginny frowned and did not accept the offered arm. "I'm back to ordinary Ginny again, I promise."

"I stand corrected. You are twice as lovely now as you were

last night."

"You, sir, are bored because Rina and Calla are gone, and you can no longer play them against each other." Ginny's headache sharpened her words. "Please don't use me for your entertainment in their absence."

"Ah, such a horrible image you have of me!" Prince Hans threw his hands into the air. "I am injured, fair maiden. How may I ever make amends?"

"I'm not the one you injured with your antics," said Ginny. "So I don't know what you expect to do."

"Ah, a feisty mouse you are today, aren't you!" Oh, why wouldn't he go away and leave her alone? "Your charms only increase each moment. Here I had always thought you a ghost in the corners. I've never been more wrong in my life – you're a beautiful young woman and an absolute gem."

Ginny's frown only grew. "Do you know where the others are? Or … perhaps some breakfast?"

"Ah, poor dear – that was your first late night, wasn't it, and you couldn't go until it was actually over!" Prince Hans shook his head. "Let me take you to the kitchens and find you a good breakfast. You didn't quite dance the night away last night, the way you should have, but it was still far more excitement than I sense you're used to, and you need some sustenance to restore you."

He offered his arm again, but Ginny continued to ignore it. He wasn't wrong, but why did it have to be *him* here, all attentive? This was the final shard of her world turned upside down and thrust into her heart.

Kaimund couldn't see her, and Prince Hans *only* saw her. Last night, she had hoped to find some alternative to Kaimund, but all she'd done was become Prince Hans' latest conquest.

But he did escort her to the kitchen and procured her a bowl of stew that was being prepared for lunch. It was good stew, and she thanked Cook profusely for it. Then he brought her to the sitting room, where everyone was gathered.

It was so good to slip away to her own sofa and resume one of her knitting projects. Prince Hans didn't follow her, and no one else seemed to notice her, all talking about the night before with far more enthusiasm than she felt.

"She did look well enough last night," Lady Nora was saying. "She's not Rina or even Calla, but she did turn enough heads. Perhaps your husband's charity will pay off, and one of those young men will take her off our hands."

So mercenary, that woman!

"Oh, but does she have to go?" asked Lady Bethim. "We've already lost both of my girls. I don't think my nerves could take the loss of Ginny, too. Oh, but this whole idea was silly."

"You, of all women, know the value of a good marriage," said Lady Nora. "Come now, Else. This would be good for Ginny. She needs her own home one day; you can't keep her forever. And even if a gentleman proposes to her today, propriety will keep her with us for a good several months at least, still. Perhaps we'll have Calla again by then. Or, perhaps, Kaimund will have the good sense to marry and give you a permanent companion in his wife."

Ginny sighed and knit faster. At least Kaimund himself wasn't here right now. She hated being grateful for his absence. It was just one more sign that everything was wrong.

Princess Maia stumbled into the room and then hastened immediately to Ginny's side to chatter merrily about the night before. Ginny barely listened but let her ramble.

Everyone else considered the ball a success. Ginny hated that she thought it anything but.

Everything only worsened after lunch when Lord Bethim summoned her to his office again. She went with twice the trepidation she'd had before. Now she had a thousand ideas, none of which appealed to her. Chastisement because she'd behaved badly last night? Or had someone already expressed interest in her already? She certainly didn't have an interest in any young man, yet!

She stepped into the office and closed the door behind her as quietly as possible, her eyes wide as she turned to the desk. "Yes, sir?"

"Ah, Ginny! Good girl."

He was grinning broadly, which made her think that a suitor was far more likely. Her stomach sank.

"You know, I really didn't think it of you, but in hindsight, I shouldn't be surprised," he continued. "You're a beautiful young woman, after all. My dear Ginny, you have won a most prestigious suitor – so far above you in station and prestige."

"Really, sir?" Ginny tucked her hands behind her back. "I'm afraid I didn't notice that anyone gave me any marked attention last night. Who is it?"

"Prince Hans, my dear!"

Ginny took a step back, shaking her head. "You must be mistaken, sir. Prince Hans ... he wouldn't ... yes, he danced with me twice last night, but it was only to help my reputation because his sister asked him to." Princess Maia might deny it, but the only other option was to tell Lord Bethim how Prince Hans had behaved with his daughters ... and she couldn't do that. "I promise you, he has no further interest in me than that."

Lord Bethim gave a stern "harumph" and stepped around his desk and towards her. "I'm afraid that *you* must be the one mistaken – but it only goes to show your humility, doesn't it! No, he was just in this very room this morning to ask if he had my permission to court you, and I have given it with my blessing. You are a lucky young lady, and I couldn't be prouder of you!"

"No..." Ginny shook her head harder. "No, he couldn't ... I ... I'm not a good wife for him. He's a prince! He'll one day be a king! I could never .... I..."

"I understand that it is surely a shock to you, but do at least consider him," Lord Bethim instructed. "Whatever you might think of yourself, it is a very advantageous match, and for not just yourself, but for the whole family as well. Now, go ahead and be off with you. I know you'll do the right thing – you're a good young girl, after all."

Ginny nodded sharply and then fled the room.

Prince Hans, courting her! He really must be bored to go this far. She wanted nothing of it, but Lord Bethim had asked, and, well, Lord Bethim was her benefactor. She couldn't disappoint him, now could she?

129

16

The following week was absolute misery. Prince Hans seemed to lurk around every corner – she didn't know how he managed it – and Princess Maia only laughed when Ginny brought up her concerns.

"My brother *will* do what he wants, you know that, dear!" she declared. "And he's always drawn to the most beautiful woman in a room."

"I'm the only young lady in the house, except yourself, and you're his sister," Ginny countered. "Can't you make him leave me alone?"

"Except that I really think he is taken with you," said Princess Maia, tilting her head to the side as she stared across the room where her brother sat, talking with Kaimund. "I've never seen him so aggressive in a chase! But, then, most young women he's chased have been thoughtless fools who have been too flattered by the attention to run. You have a good head on your shoulders, Ginny, as I've always said."

Ginny pressed her lips together, frowning harder. "And yet you still think that I should be flattered by his attention?"

"Of *course* you should be!" Princess Maia shook her head. "Because whatever you think of yourself, you are entirely worthy of being loved by a prince. I agree you could do far better than my brother, but he's here, so take a compliment."

Ginny frowned and sank into the couch. She didn't consider it a compliment at all, and she hated that Princess Maia was pushing her like this.

No matter how she dressed or did her hair, no matter how determinedly an overly-flirtatious prince might flirt with her, it didn't change who she was. Princess Maia needed to stop trying to make her into something she wasn't.

Ginny sighed as she focused again on Kaimund. He sought her less and less as the days went by and reacted with less desperation each time she spoke. On one hand, it meant that he was moving on and focusing on what mattered most, but on the other...

Well, it meant he was slipping that much farther away from her.

He'd never been hers to begin with. She needed to stop obsessing over him. Ginny shut her eyes and took a deep breath. She needed to escape. If only she'd had a more serious suitor than Prince Hans!

And then an escape came, in the form of a letter from Will, that very afternoon. Will had found stability already and was begging that Ginny come stay with her.

Ginny tucked the letter into her pocket as she considered. Will didn't say what her new life would be, but it had to be better than lurking around Snowfield Palace, watching Kaimund with Princess Maia. It was only a matter of time before the princess gave in – Ginny saw how he could draw a smile from her. And they both deserved happiness!

Drawing in a deep breath, she went to the garden to pace and think. The summer was still strong, and she soon found herself walking down the familiar paths toward Kaimund's garden.

She hadn't been down these paths in several weeks. It'd been too painful to see Kaimund with Princess Maia, or to think of them together. And it was already impossible for her to stand in this clearing and not think of them.

But it was still a piece of Kaimund that he had given her, and if she was going to leave, she needed to give it a proper good-bye. She tucked herself into the alcove and threw herself onto a bench, pulling her knees up to her chest.

Could she really leave Snowfield Palace? She couldn't stay, she knew that, but this had been her home for twelve years. The only home she knew.

Her breath caught in her throat as she heard heavy footsteps, and Kaimund came storming into the alcove and started pacing.

Ginny's eyes widened, and she pulled herself further back. This had been a mistake. *Oh,* how this had been a mistake!

Kaimund suddenly stopped pacing and swung his gaze wildly about. "At least my plants still look right," he muttered. "Roses are roses, and they don't have any opinions about themselves to distort their appearance."

Ginny swallowed, squeezing her eyes shut.

"My life has fallen apart, ever since that mirror fell on me," he continued. "And I don't know what to do. I can't go back. Everything is wrong."

Would she be able to escape without him hearing her? She opened her eyes to see that he had pulled out pruning shears to tend to his roses. He stood so close to her that she would brush against him if he leaned any closer. She leaned away.

"Ginny..." he muttered, sending her heart pounding right into her throat. "Ginny, where are you? Where do you hide? Walking into a room and not seeing you makes me feel like my very heart is gone from my chest."

He pruned another branch with a harsh snip. Ginny pulled her knees closer to her chest, forcing down a sob that tried to rip itself from her throat. She shouldn't be here, oh no, she shouldn't – but how was she to get away?

She stared up into Kaimund's face. His eyes, once so clear and blue, were now swirling gray with lines of silver, ever since he absorbed the mirror's enchantment.

"Is she scared of me? I'm the same man I've always been. And she's the same Ginny, I'm sure of it!" His shoulders slumped, and he gave a heavy sigh. "At least Maia is still around, the pass is going well, and Aunt Mayblossom is doing better now that she has Princess Giana to talk with." He shook his head. "But everything is now so empty. I never even thought that I would miss listening to Rina and Calla fight."

Ginny bit her lip. She'd never thought that she would miss watching Rina and Calla fight over Prince Hans, but here she was.

"I. Wish. I. Had. Never. Looked. At. That. Mirror."

Ginny gasped as he began attacking the rosebush with each word, not caring where his shears snipped, and branches fell recklessly. His beloved rosebush that he had cared for with such love for so long!

"Kai!"

His name slipped from between her lips before she could stop herself, and she sprung to her feet before she could think.

He froze, and his hand shot out and caught her shoulder before she could escape. "Ginny," he whispered. The shears fell to the ground, and his second hand cupped her face as his eyes slid closed. He leaned forward, pressing his forehead against hers. "Ginny, were you here this whole time? Oh, you shouldn't have had to see that." He swallowed. "It's good to find you. Tell me, my dear friend, what have I done wrong?"

Words couldn't make it past her heart, still pounding in her throat. She couldn't tell him that he had done nothing wrong at all. He could never do wrong.

But without a need to stay silent to escape his notice, her tears broke free in ugly sobs. And once they started, they couldn't stop.

"Oh, Ginny," Kaimund muttered. "I'm so sorry, whatever happened to make you hide. I … I don't know what to do to make it better, but … I'm so sorry."

His thumb wiped clumsily at one of her tears, because even though he opened his eyes again, he still couldn't see her. He pulled her into a tight hug, burying her face against his chest.

This was exactly where she wanted to be. This was exactly what she could never have. But as long as the tears came, she couldn't fight, and just stood there, letting him hold her world together. For a moment, she could pretend. She could imagine that Kaimund was hers, the way she wished he was.

He held her tight enough, it was so easy to pretend.

Slowly but surely, her tears subsided, but still he held her. Reluctantly, she took a deep breath and pulled back, frowning up at his closed eyes. "Kai, Will has sent me a letter. She's able to take care of me now, and she wants me to go live with her."

His hand found hers, and he held it tight. "You're part of the family here, Ginny. You don't have to go. You never have to go."

She swallowed, dropping her gaze from his face. "It's where I belong. I'm grateful for the home here – I'll always be grateful. And I don't *want* to go. But she is my sister, and I didn't get to grow up with her. Our time together was cut short so unexpectedly, and I want to make the most of every moment."

He sighed. "I understand. Will's the good sort, even if her mirror has caused me a world of trouble. And she is your sister. I—" He wrapped his second hand around hers too, squeezing it tight. "Just promise to stop hiding. Until you leave, at least. I can't bear the thought that you're in a room even right beside me, and I don't even know."

Ginny bit her lip and nodded – and then realized that he couldn't see that. "I'll try," she whispered.

"I don't know what I'll do without you, though," he continued. "You've always been there, my quiet voice of reason. Who will be there to help me see the world clearly, now?"

"I will miss you, Kai," she confessed, not knowing what else to say. "You've always been the best friend a scared little girl could ask for. You're a good man, and you deserve all the happiness in the world. Please remember that for me. And remember that I will be fine. Will is going to take care of me.

"If you ever need a home, please come back here." Kaimund suddenly leaned forward and pressed a kiss to her forehead. "I don't care what Aunt Nora or my father might say. You'll always have a place here. This is where you belong."

Her breath caught, and one last tear squeezed out of her eye as she pulled back. "I'll remember that."

Then she pulled free of his hold and fled the alcove, only briefly glancing back over her shoulder as he slumped onto the bench where she had sat, staring into space as he ran a hand through his hair.

~

Ginny still had to convince Lord Bethim to let her leave without seeming ungrateful for the home he had given her. Because she was infinitely grateful – just not enough to put up with Prince Hans' nonsense. And it *was* all nonsense, whatever anyone might say. No prince in their right mind would ever consider her.

Prince Hans certainly wasn't in his right mind, but that was all the more reason for her to ignore his advances.

She requested an audience with her benefactor and went into his office affecting more confidence than she felt. She held out the letter, her chin raised, and explained the situation with as few words as possible. Lord Bethim listened silently, his frown growing with each word.

"Please don't think that we're trying to scare you away," he said. "You've been a wonderful companion for my wife, all these years, and I don't think she can do without you."

Ginny swallowed and gave a light shrug. "I know, and I hate to leave Lady Bethim, but Will and I have been parted for so long. If she wants me to stay with her, then I can't say no."

Lord Bethim gave a sharp nod. "I suppose not. But, would you really leave now, when you have the attention of a prince? Wouldn't you prefer to see yourself settled and then invite her to stay with you?"

"Sir, I don't understand why a young lady should be expected to automatically return a gentleman's affection just because he turns his attention upon her," she answered. "Perhaps I'm too much like my mother, but it seems unfair to me."

"I see." Lord Bethim stared at her sharply, and she squirmed under his gaze. "But you can't argue that you'll never have another opportunity like this."

"It takes more than just a title, money, and a pretty face to make happiness," she argued. "I honestly believe that both he and I will be happier if we don't pursue this relationship. Please, just let me go, and let him forget me."

Lord Bethim sighed. "I don't suppose that I can keep you here if your mind is made up, and Will is your family. But, Ginny, you don't know your sister's situation – and she is a young woman alone in the world, even if she can disguise herself as a gentleman. Don't you think…" He trailed off and tilted his head to the side. "Perhaps this will help you learn to appreciate what you have and what you've been offered. I'll arrange your journey to this address your sister gave you. Just send a letter when you're ready to return – and don't wait too long. You never know how quickly the prince's attention might drift."

"If it does drift, then that will just prove how wise I was in rejecting his suit," Ginny countered. "Thank you, sir. For everything. My whole life. You've been far kinder than I ever deserved."

"I've only ever done what Austere could ask of me," he answered. "And you're a dear young woman, so it was no trouble at all."

She nodded and slipped out of the room, pausing to breathe hard in the hallway. Now to only face everyone else begging her to stay once they found out that she was leaving. And beg they did.

Kaimund had already had the news of her departure, so he just sat silently staring. Lady Bethim fainted on a couch and complained about everyone leaving, causing Lady Nora to chastise her and tell her to be reasonable.

"Oh, do you really think that you have to go?" cried Princess Maia, taking Ginny's hands and pulling her onto the couch next to her. "I mean, I know what Will means to you, but we are getting along so well, and it seems a shame to break everything up. At least wait until Calla returns, perhaps?"

Ginny glanced across the room to Kaimund and then to

Prince Hans. "I know. But I've never left home. Never left Snowfield, that is, not really, not since I came, and I need to know where I belong. I need to see what the world is."

"You're choosing a difficult life." Princess Maia shook her head. "But, then, Will did, too, even though I told her to go to the Forest if she was found out. She's not in the Forest, is she?"

Ginny bit her lip and shook her head.

"Well, I'll be praying for you, and we're all going to miss you – don't you dare imagine otherwise." Princess Maia sighed. "And I don't know who will miss you more – myself, Kaimund, or my brother. Ah, who am I fooling? It's going to be Lady Bethim. She's going to be in a sorry state – maybe I should go play the harp for her to help her nerves?"

She squeezed Ginny's hand and then went to take up the instrument.

But it was when Prince Hans cornered her in the hall afterward that was the worst of all.

"Am I really such an ogre that you must run away like this? Dear Ginny! Don't you know that I only have the noblest of intentions?"

Ginny narrowed her gaze. "No, sir, I don't know that. Your intentions certainly weren't noble with Rina and Calla."

"I had no intentions at all, with them – distracting though they were." Prince Hans laughed and then snatched Ginny's hand, giving it a desperate squeeze. "Tell me where you're going and that I'm allowed to visit you! I'm afraid you have stolen my heart, and if I don't follow it, I shall die of grief. I know you have your reservations – and such a wise, sweet thing you are to have them – so give me a chance to prove myself to you."

His face was so unguarded and earnest that the air nearly snatched from Ginny's lungs. "I—"

"You're not heartless; I know you're not. Say yes."

Ginny glanced down, collecting her thoughts. She hated the thought of him following her, but, perhaps, this was for the best. She knew that life with Will was going to be hard. Perhaps if he saw her degraded in the world where she really belonged, he would come to his senses and forget her.

She looked up and gave a sharp nod. "You may visit."

17

It was a three-day journey by carriage. Lord Bethim didn't send her in his own carriage – of course he wouldn't do such a thing! – instead, Ginny's journey was with the post, alongside strangers, staying at a strange inn where she kept to herself and tried to avoid notice. On the second night, there was no inn for them to stay at, and they made camp alongside the road.

She quickly understood why Princess Maia despised travel so thoroughly. This was a special brand of torture.

But come mid-afternoon of the third day, it was over, and she and her trunk were let off in front of a once-grand house on a street of houses that had all seen better years. As she watched the carriage rumble away, she sat down on the lid, drew her knees up to her chest, and fought to catch her breath.

It was done. She was here.

What was this place, and did Will really live here?

Ginny knew that she should go up to the door and knock. Let Will know that she was here, but the whole of the journey and what she'd done crushed down upon her. She had left Snowfield. Possibly forever. Would she ever see Kaimund, or any of the others, ever again? Prince Hans had begged to come visit her, but would he really make this journey just to continue a flirtation? It was ludicrous!

"Hey! You there! Are you Ginny? Will said that I'm

supposed to be watching for Ginny. You're here now, so are you her?"

Ginny blinked as a dirty child of indeterminate age or gender appeared over the wall, staring at her boldly. With trembling lip, she nodded. "I'm Ginny, yes. Who are you?"

"Suzy," the kid answered. "I'm one of Will's girls. She said that you're going to come teach us how to be ladies. You don't look much like a lady, though."

"I'm not one," said Ginny. "But I grew up with some. Where is Will? I know she wasn't sure when I was arriving, but we sent a letter in advance…"

"And that was why I was sitting here, watching," Suzy answered. "I got distracted, I'm sorry, but it was taking a long time, so I took a nap. Will's on a run. She'll be back soon, but you and I need to get that thing inside before anyone else sees it and decides it's worth your life."

"Worth my…" Ginny's heart sped up. "What sort of place is this?"

"Not anything like those fancy places you're used to," Suzy answered, skipping over to lift one of the handles of the chest. "But it's a roof over one's head, and I'm thankful to not be out on the streets, and I know Will is, too. But I think she wants to explain everything to you, herself, so I won't say no more. Come on."

Suzy tugged at her handle, so Ginny had to climb down from the trunk and take the other one. They passed through old, rusted gates, which protested as Suzy closed them behind her, and then hefted the thing up the grand, but crumbling steps up into the house. However, the girl stopped as soon as they were inside the house and had shut the door behind them.

"That's far enough, as far as I'm concerned. When the rest are here, they can help you take it the rest of the way, but this is heavy, and I don't want to take it any further.

Ginny nodded and sat back down on the trunk.

"What's in it, anyway?" Suzy continued. "Pretty dresses, maybe? I've always liked pretty dresses, though I know one like me has no business ever wearing one myself."

"Maybe … maybe if you take a bath, I'll let you try some of them on," said Ginny. After all, she had once been a little girl admiring pretty dresses, and she knew how much it meant to taste that world.

Suzy's eyes widened. "Really? Oh, joy! But are you sure about that bath?"

"Very sure," said Ginny. "It's much easier to scrub the dirt off of your skin than from these dresses."

Suzy tilted her head to the side as she thought and then shrugged. "I should go start dinner before the rest arrive. You can come with me if you would like. Or you can guard this trunk until the others arrive. You probably want to do that – they'll have it open and your dresses strewn about as soon as they see it."

"It's locked, and I have the key," Ginny pointed out.

"Doesn't matter." Suzy shook her head. "Button can pick locks faster than you can blink. Wish I could do that. She gets to go on *all* the runs, while they always leave me behind to cook."

And then Suzy dashed away, leaving Ginny alone in the crumbling corridor.

What was this place? Why was Will here? What was Will doing, and who was this Button, picking locks, and why was Will with her? What did any of this mean?

And, to think, she could have still been in Snowfield Palace, in her own place on the couch, living her life the way she always had. It had been her choice to leave.

It had been a choice she'd had to make. She couldn't stay there, caught between Kaimund and Prince Hans, with Princess Maia a confusing tangle of encouragement. Ginny belonged with Will, her flesh and blood, whatever Will was caught up in.

If Will was caught up in something bad, she would just have to encourage her sister to turn back onto the right path. Maybe that was why Austere had led her down this path?

Had Austere led her down this path?

She realized that she'd not consulted Him in the decision,

as she should have. She'd just run as soon as she'd seen a way out.

~

Ginny heard her sister and her girls before they were in through the door. The whoops of delight and cries of success split the air, and then the doors swung open again, the dying light of evening spilling into the hallway.

"Ginny!" a grin spread across Will's face as she saw her, and she rushed forward to catch Ginny into a hug. "You've made it – ah, it's good to have you again. My family really is complete now."

Though she had a thousand questions, Ginny relished the chill of Will's hug, relaxing as she centered herself again. Then she took a deep breath and pulled back to examine her sister.

Will was more feminine now than she had been before. She still wore pants, with a knife hanging from her belt, but there were curves to her figure that she'd previously concealed, and her hair had grown out, now hanging in uneven waves nearly to her shoulders.

"I've missed you, Will. I'm glad to see that you're well." Ginny forced a smile as her gaze swung towards the group of girls behind Will – though at least one seemed to be a boy. Each was as dirty as Suzy, of varying sizes, colors, and ages. "What is this place?"

Will's smile faltered, and she glanced over Ginny's shoulder to her trunk. "You know what? We should get that thing up to my room – you're going to share with me, I insist. You're soft, sister, much as I hate to say it, and this is a hard town. So you're going to stay where I can protect you."

Ginny took a sharp breath and nodded. A thousand questions swirled, but she pinched her mouth shut as she watched Will and three of the other girls take up the trunk and haul it away. She followed, arms hugged around herself, up a rickety staircase and down a hallway to what might have once been a grand bedroom. The frame of a bed stood in the corner, but it was the only furniture, and it was covered in random valuables and weapons. A few blankets spread across the floor. The trunk was set at the end of the bed, and then Will shoed the girls away, shutting the door behind them.

"You have questions, don't you," she stated. "Of course you have questions. Because I know how bad all of this looks, especially to someone like you."

Ginny's breath caught, and she chewed her lip. "What is this place? What are you doing here? Who are all of those girls?"

Will tilted her head to the side, folding her own arms over her chest as she leaned against the door. "This is a house that our grandfather owned," she explained. "It was abandoned when mother was a child, when a plague went through this town, and then thieves and gangs took over this neighborhood when everyone else was dead or away. He couldn't sell it, and not even the creditors wanted it, so when I showed up, claiming to be his heir, willing to pay off the last of his debt and then fight off the ruffians that had made a nest in this place, I was welcome to it. So, it's mine now. A home. I always wanted one of those, you know."

Ginny swallowed. "And those girls?"

"They needed someone to protect them, so I invited them to stay with me." Will shrugged, a small smile tugging at one corner of her mouth. "They're a good lot, and I want to give them a better life. That's why I asked you to come – you've been taught manners and booksmarts. You can help them."

"Oh." Ginny slowly nodded as she processed the request. "That's why you asked me to bring books?"

"Did you?"

"A few." Ginny gave a small shrug. "Books are expensive, after all, but Kai made sure that I had some."

"I can get you more if you need them," said Will, with a nod of her own. "Can't promise any specific books, though, because it's all luck and chance."

"Will…" Ginny took a deep breath, raising her chin. "What are you doing here? Suzy said that you were on some sort of 'run', and one of the girls picks locks?"

"Several of the girls pick locks," Will answered. "They come from rough backgrounds. Don't worry about it, dear."

"How are you supporting yourself? What *work* are you doing?"

Will's breath caught, and she pushed herself away from the door, shaking her head. "Don't look at me like that, Gin, all self-righteous. *Our father* was a thief. Oh, he gave a good go at an honest life, but when he had a family to support, and no one wanted to hire him, he reverted right back to his old ways. Then he left us." She drew the knife from her belt and glared at it. "He left us with money, which lasted a few years, but he still left us, and then mother died."

"Oh."

"Oh. Exactly." Will sighed and jammed the knife back into her belt. "He was good at what he did, at least. And so am I. So don't think about it. *Please* don't think about it. We do what we must to survive, and you can help those girls someday achieve a better life."

"But Austere…"

"I know Austere doesn't like this," Will answered. "But Austere isn't exactly looking out for us right now. We have to look out for ourselves. It's the way of the real world." Then she sighed and pulled Ginny into a hug. Ginny relaxed into it, despite her tangled feelings. "I know I shouldn't have brought you into this, but … I've missed you, Gin. I need you."

"Promise me that if we find a way out, you take it."

"If we can take the girls, then yes. I can't leave them here to grow up the way I did. Someone has to look out for them." Will held Ginny tighter. "Now, why don't we go see what Suzy has scared up for dinner? Poor girl isn't meant for this life at all – she reminds me so much of you. A terrific cook, too. Can make meals out of the meanest of supplies. I think she might be a Sensitive, because she keeps a garden in the backyard that's remarkable."

Ginny nodded as Will released her, only to tuck an arm around her shoulders and guide her out of the room and back down the steps to a long dining hall where the others were already gathered, Suzy presiding at the head as she guarded a pot of stew with a ladle. "Good!" she announced as they entered. "I was fearing mutiny if you didn't get here soon, Will."

"I'd promised them that they wouldn't have to wait for me to arrive before eating," said Will, shaking her head as she took her seat, giving Ginny the place beside her. "I should have given you the instructions, too, but…"

"You got distracted, that's fine," said Suzy, nodding for the children to bring her their bowls. "I would have been distracted, too, if I saw my sister again after not seeing her for so long. If I had a sister. 'Course, I don't know anything about my family, but who does in these parts?"

"It's what you make of yourself, not what your family makes of you, that's important," said Will. "You're a good sort, Suzy, and you're going to go far. Now, I'm sure everyone here has seen my sister, Ginny – and you know that I've told all of you to watch out for her. She's not used to places like this, and she doesn't know her way about. But she's here to teach all of you to be ladies, so you can get honest work as servants when you're older and can get out of this town."

One of the boys raised his hand. "She's not gonna teach Tom and me how to be *ladies*, now is she?"

Will tilted back her head and laughed heartily. "She'll teach you manners and how to read, but it's always easier for boys to get work than girls. Now, all of you, sit still for a second while I introduce you lot – there's my girls – so she can tell one of you from the next. Gin, you've met Suzy already, I know, who's my second hand and takes care of the house for us while the rest of us are away – she'll probably be your best student – and I'm already sure she'll make an excellent cook for some grand lady, just as soon as she's old enough. Then we have Jan, Airy, Tina, Faye, Button, Caro, and the boys, Rick and Tom. Rick and Tom are Faye's younger brothers, and she's all they had, so we took them in, too. But, generally, we're here to watch out for the girls lost in this town. Maybe, someday, we'll all make it out again."

And then the room exploded in chatter and shouts as

everyone talked among themselves while wolfing down their food. Ginny sat silently through it all, quietly spooning her own stew into her mouth as she listened. This was her new life. This was the price of her escape. No matter how little she liked all of this, she had to make do.

Will's intentions were noble. Even if Ginny didn't like the methods, she could still appreciate the goal. After all, where would she be herself it not for the charity of the Bethims? These kids might be rough, but they all just needed a bit of charity, themselves.

She just prayed to Austere that she would be strong enough for the task ahead of her.

18

"Do you know, our mother used to be terrified to let me even touch you, when you were born, scared that my ice was going to hurt you?" Will said as they prepared themselves for bed. "But then you were always so fussy, she thought she was never going to get any sleep, and the only time you stopped fussing was if I was holding you. So she gave it up and let you sleep in my cradle with me, and we were inseparable ever after." She concluded with a sigh, sitting on the edge of the bedframe. "Until I had to leave you on the doorstep of Snowfield Palace. Almost didn't have the heart to do it, you were crying so hard, but I couldn't take care of you on my own."

"It's okay," said Ginny, fidgeting with her silk nightdress. It was an ugly thing, worn out by Rina before it became Ginny's, but it was far finer than anything those girls had ever even seen. She tilted her head to the side. "You know, Robert isn't mad at you for lying to him. He's confused, but he's told his commanding officers that you're dead and never plans to betray that you were a girl."

Will shrugged, her eyes fixed somewhere on the wall. "He's a good sort. Of course he would do that. I wish I hadn't put him in that position, though. My lies were only ever supposed to be that. My lies."

"And yet you constantly covered for him."

"Nothing he did was ever worse than my pretending to be a man."

Ginny sighed. "Well, I think you still could have told him the truth long ago. You decided for him how he was going to respond, and you never actually gave him a chance."

"And either he was going to reject me, or I would still be at his side, trying to hide my feelings," Will answered, shaking her head. "Neither outcome was worth it."

"You never gave him a chance to *return* your affection," said Ginny.

"And what good would that have done? I was still his fellow soldier! Whether or not he knew I was a woman, I still had to act like I was a man. Him not knowing made it easier."

"But now he does know, and you're no longer his fellow soldier!"

Will froze for a long moment, and then she shook her head. "Gin, I know you want me to be happy, and I love you for it, but it's too late. I don't … can't … it's too late. One look in his eyes, staring at me as though I was a foreign creature and not at all the friend who had been at his side for a year, and it was too much. It broke me, and I couldn't afford to be broken." She gave a long sigh and rubbed at her heart. "Once broken, a Frost's heart heals with ice. That's the way of things."

"Oh, but Will—"

"He's going to forget me, make new friends, and move on to the next pretty face," said Will. "That's the way of it. And I don't care."

"You loved him!" Tears sprang to Ginny's eyes as she watched her sister, so quiet and subdued. Tears she feared that Will had never indulged in for herself. Tears because how could her sister sit there and act so careless about a man she'd professed to love. When Ginny herself broke a little bit more each time she even thought of Kaimund and Princess Maia…

"I loved him, yes," said Will. "And that's why I had to set him free. I don't want him to have *this* on his conscience."

Will suddenly unfolded, marched over to Ginny, and wrapped her in a chilly hug. "Oh, Gin. You're just so soft."

Ginny didn't think that her sister meant it as an insult, but there was an edge to the word, just the same, that made her tears flow faster. Something *had* broken within her sister, and now all the world was wrong.

"Gin, answer me truthfully – are those tears just for me, or has your heart been broken, too?" Will suddenly asked.

Ginny's breath caught, silencing her for a heartbeat, but the tears came again before she answered.

"It's – it's not his fault," she managed to force out between the sobs. "I'm just a little sister to him. I was the fool, falling in love where I shouldn't."

"Aren't we all, Gin, but a broken heart is a broken heart." Will's arms tightened, and then she pushed Ginny back to stare into her eyes. "And I think I watched you break, piece by piece, while I was at Snowfield. As you faded more and more. I should have seen it. What kind of sister am I to not notice a thing like that?"

Ginny wiped at her tears. Several answers sprung to mind, but too many were accusatory, and accusations were the last thing she wanted to give Will. "You hadn't had your own heart broken yet," she finally said.

Will just pressed her lips into a harder line. "And now you're a mere shadow of yourself, even compared to then. Oh, no, I'm not going to accuse him of it, because I know you'll defend him the same way I defend Robert. He didn't *know*. But how could he not know? You were right there, the whole time, and I could see the way he gravitated to you, so it must be mutual somewhere? Of course you loved him." She shook her head. "And I was too focused on all of my secrets and the mirror to *notice*."

Ginny shook her head. "What could you have done about it? Kaimund is Lord Bethim's heir. They might have taken me in as their ward, but I would never be fit for his wife."

Will swiped at one of Ginny's tears, frowned at it, and then laid a hand against Ginny's heart. "There might not have been anything I could do about his ignoring you, but there's something I can do about the pain you're in now."

Shards of cold shot from Will's hand, so intense that Ginny cried out in actual pain as it spread to her extremities. Then the chill settled into a numbness that quieted the ache in her heart of just moments before. Ginny's breath caught as she realized what her sister had done.

"You're Frost enough for your heart to break, but not enough to heal yourself," Will said, pulling Ginny back into the hug. "I'm sorry."

"You … you didn't even ask if I wanted…"

"It's not a choice that Frosts get. That broken heart would have killed you, if you left it long enough, and I think we were even past it being healed by Kaimund returning your affection, after all. There was blood in your tears."

Ginny tried to keep crying, but the tears were gone, swallowed up by that overwhelming numbness.

"You can still have hope, though," Will continued, pressing a kiss to the top of Ginny's head. "You're not fully Frost, and that ice isn't yours. If you should find yourself the focus of an ardent enough affection – Kaimund's or otherwise – the ice can melt, and you can love him in return. At least, this way, you'll know that the love is genuine. Now, let me undo your braids, and we can sleep. It's been a long day for you, especially with a broken heart."

~

Thoughts of Kaimund soon faded into her new routine. Princess Maia would come to her senses, and all would be well. There was no reason for Ginny to worry herself about it. It was good that two people so dear to her would be happy.

It did alarm her, especially in the first few days, how easily and painlessly she could think about Kaimund and the princess together, but soon even those worries faded. In the absence of heartache, she threw herself into the new task of teaching the children, as Will had asked. An early order of business was baths for everyone, but when it proved too much of a hassle and both boys disappeared before their turn, she surrendered to the fact that baths just weren't a priority in a town ruled by thieves.

So she would save that battle for another day.

Once clean, Suzy actually appreciated the effort, squealing as Ginny let her borrow one of her dresses. So it was a battle won on at least one front.

She spent most of her time with Suzy. The rest would disappear each morning with Will, not to return until the evening, and so it was with the oldest girl that she spent most of her time. Suzy was glad for the company and eagerly soaked up all of the information Ginny had to teach her – though she would often complain if a task was too hard, before disappearing into the garden. She'd never had to apply herself before, so it was only natural. In exchange, she taught Ginny the ways of the kitchen.

It wasn't a perfect life, by any means, but it was a new life and a way to move forward. She didn't approve of what Will did, but Will claimed that they only stole from those who deserved it – whatever that meant – and, well, there weren't many honest folks in this town.

She still wished that Will had found any other means to support herself, noble as it was for her to try to form a better life for the girls.

A week passed quietly. She almost didn't realize that it was gone, so easy was it for her to live from moment to moment. So necessary. It was better to put Snowfield Palace out of her mind entirely, so that is what she did.

"All right! Who took my knife?" Will came down the stairs shouting, startling both Suzy and Ginny as they cooked. "I left it on our bedroll this morning as I didn't want it for this run, and now it's gone."

Ginny took a step back, shaking her head. "I—"

"I know you didn't take it, Gin," said Will, waving her away. "Though you have the best access to the room, you would never do such a thing, innocent thing that you are. And if it was you who took it, I would not be upset because it just means that you were being proactive about defending yourself, and he was your father, too." Will folded her arms over her chest.

"No, it's one of the others who has taken it, and I have a fair idea of who."

She stormed back out of the kitchen, leaving Suzy and Ginny to share a nervous glance.

"Button," said Suzy after a moment. "She always has her eye on Will's knife – the little thief." She shook her head. "I know we're not supposed to judge each other, but I tell you, Ginny, if there's any one of us who's a hopeless cause, it's her. She's just here for a free roof over her head, and Will finds her too useful and is too sympathetic to throw her back out onto the streets."

"You don't think that this is where Will is going to draw the line?" asked Ginny, fidgeting with the soup ladle.

Suzy shrugged. "If there's going to be a line, this is it. Button is only six, though, practically a baby, and so Will just *keeps* forgiving her. Button knows that sentimental things are off-limits, but she doesn't have any of those of her own, so she doesn't care. She sees a shiny knife, she wants the shiny knife, and so she takes the knife. Doesn't hurt that the knife can turn people invisible."

Ginny blinked. "What?"

"Oh, it's a remarkable enchantment – it's how Will is such a good thief. Apparently, your father was even better, because his Zephyr magic also meant that he could fly," Suzy explained. "Has Will not told you? Well, it's terribly good for getting into places one shouldn't be in, and if Button has it now, things are going to get rather frosty until she comes back out of hiding."

"What if she doesn't come out of hiding? What if she leaves us completely?"

"Then that's between Button and your sister," said Suzy. "Meanwhile, you and I shall do our part and ensure that no one gets any of this stew until Will has her knife back. A code is a code, after all."

The commotion lasted the whole rest of the day until Will finally found Button and secured her knife again. Button was not thrown back onto the streets, remarkably, but she was threatened within an inch of her life if she ever even thought of stealing it again.

"This will teach me to not leave my things around, even in locked rooms," Will then confided to Ginny, laughing. "After all, this is hardly Snowfield Palace, and I shouldn't be expecting honor among thieves. Indeed, if you hadn't still been in the room when I left this morning, and the run such a dull one, I never would have done it. Gin, next time I leave my knife behind, make sure you put it on your own person. It's because I want you to have some protection."

Ginny swallowed, trying to make sense of it all, and slowly nodded. While she hated the thought of using the knife in self-defense, knowing that the knife also granted invisibility made her feel better. Will was just trying to take care of her in her way.

"Oh, and in all of that fuss, I completely forgot that there was a letter for you." Will pulled an envelope from her pocket and shoved it into Ginny's hands. "I haven't read it, I promise. But I think it's from Snowfield, even if I don't recognize the address."

Ginny frowned down at the envelope, not recognizing the handwriting either, and then she tore it open and shook her head. "It's Prince Hans."

"*Prince Hans?*" Will repeated and gave a low whistle. "How'd you score that correspondence? I never saw the two of you together unless you were glaring at him."

"He's gotten it into his head to court me now that Rina's married and Calla's gone to the capitol with her." Ginny glanced over the letter, barely comprehending the words before she jammed it into her pocket. She would read it later, if only in hopes that it contained news of home.

Home wasn't Snowfield Palace.

She shook her head.

"Ah, but your heart was too fixed upon Kaimund to give him a second thought." Will tugged on one of Ginny's braids. "Perhaps Prince Hans will be the one to melt the ice?"

Ginny took a long breath and shook her head. "I gave him permission to visit – but I'm sure he'll run as soon as he sees this place. You said that it has to be a true, *ardent* affection, and Prince Hans might make a good show of the latter, but I don't think he's capable of the first."

"And does he know he suffers such sharp censure from you?" asked Will.

"I've told him as much to his face," Ginny answered. "Not that he's capable of comprehending that a female wouldn't appreciate his attention."

"A shame. He's fine to look at – you can't deny that!"

19 Another week passed. Ginny received a second letter from Prince Hans. Neither one was long – mere notes, really. Both were filled with inane praise of her beauty and laments over her absence. Each sent love from his sisters. The second did say that Princess Mayblossom and the baby were doing well. The impending birth was twisting her nerves to a feverish level, but Princess Giana could still talk sense into her. Just a few more months...

Both letters were put out of Ginny's mind as soon as she had read them. The latter only served as a reminder to redouble her prayers for Princess Mayblossom's health and peace of mind. Will said nothing when she saw Ginny praying. Suzy just wrinkled her nose and asked if it helped.

"Austere watches out for us," Ginny explained. "He made this world, and so He has the power to make things better for us, if we ask Him. He doesn't always do it – He's not a wish granter, after all, but it's good to ask, especially on behalf of others."

"It's hard to think anyone's watching out for us in this town."

Ginny chewed her lip, fidgeting with the dress that she was mending. "Well, He had to have been watching out for you, to lead you to Will," she pointed out. "And I know He watched out for me, softening Lord Bethim's heart so he would let me stay with them, growing up." Though she had often wished that Lady Nora's heart had been softer! "But He doesn't stop bad people from making bad choices, and bad choices can hurt innocent people. And even good people can make bad choices, and hurt themselves and others."

Suzy swallowed, staring at the pair of trousers that was her task. "I suppose that I understand that. Still doesn't seem fair."

Ginny shrugged. "Well, that's why we must always make the best choices we can. Even if it isn't easy."

Not many people made good choices in this town, and she wasn't sure that Will was an exception. She hated thinking ill of her sister. So she shook her head.

"Well, I suppose that meeting your sister, and you, too, are good things, and maybe that's proof enough that there's an Austere looking out for us." Suzy frowned. "But there are so many girls out there who don't get help. And not just girls. And it's hard to make good choices when all the choices are bad."

Ginny nodded. It was easy for her to condemn those who made choices when she was safe in Snowfield Palace. But now she was here. And where would she and Will be if they hadn't had a Snowfield Palace to send her to?

But wasn't it still best to make the best choices that one could, even if it was hard? How could one tell what the best choice was?

"I think I hear the girls again," Suzy announced, tilting her head to the side. "Home already. They're early."

Ginny pulled the last stitch tight and tied off the thread. "Well, I just finished this, so I'll go see how today went, if you would like to stay here and continue sewing."

"Go ahead," said Suzy. "My hand is cramping something awful, but I'll keep at the task. Oh, but boys can put holes in their pants faster than anything!"

"I'll be back as soon as I can," said Ginny, giving Suzy an encouraging smile. "Maybe I should come back with at least one of the other girls and make them help. I'm supposed to be teaching them to be ladies, after all."

Suzy's nose wrinkled. "None of the other girls have even

halfway decent stitches."

"How can they get better if they don't practice?" Ginny shook her head and slipped out and down through the halls of the house.

Will stood in the foyer, her hands on her hips as she surveyed the girls already scattering around her. She broke into a grin as she saw Ginny. "Ah, good. You're already here, and I don't have to go look for you."

"You needed me?" Ginny frowned.

"I always need you, Gin-dear." Will laughed. "You've been stuck in this house the whole time, and that's just not right. So come with me for a bit of an adventure."

"But…" Ginny's protest hovered with uncertainty. "But you told me that you didn't want me out on the streets. And I never really went out when I was at Snowfield, either. I'm fine. Really."

"You shouldn't have been kept cooped up at Snowfield; we are going out," Will declared. "I don't want you on the streets alone, but I'll be with you, so you'll be safe. And we'll be going to some of the better parts of the town."

"Suzy and I are in the middle of mending – I can't just abandon her!"

"Jan, Faye, go help Suzy with the mending – with as poorly as you both did this morning, you might as well go do something useful," Will ordered. "There, now Suzy won't be without help, and you can come with me."

Ginny's frown grew as the two girls hurried past her in obedience. Why was Will being so insistant about this? Everything she had said until now was about how Ginny was too soft for the town, and she needed to stay inside, unseen, as much as possible.

Was this another evidence of her sister's sharp edges? She saw them more and more as the days went by. They had been there at Snowfield – formed by years spent alone and fighting for survival – but with her frozen, broken heart, they were worse.

Ginny hoped that she might never be that way, even with

her own heart broken. She prayed every night that her heart would remain soft, though the numbness made it hard to care.

"Ginny?" Will sighed and skipped up the stairs to take Ginny's hand. "Come along – I know the world is frightening, but you have to be brave and step out into it. You can't go your whole life hiding. You have to live, and this is the first step." She tugged Ginny down the stairs.

Sighing, Ginny complied. She didn't have the strength to fight her sister, and if Will was determined to take her out into the world, then Will would take her out.

She blinked against the sun – maybe she really had been inside too long. She shook her head.

"Will, do you really think you're helping the girls if all they ever do is go out with you on these 'runs'? You say that you had me come here so I could teach them, but Suzy is the only one learning."

Will's step faltered, and she glanced nervously about. "Look, Gin, I know I have a long way to go. But I can't just look at the long term – they need to eat. But Suzy is doing so good! The others will see, and they will follow. Just give it time. They have to want this."

Ginny chewed her lip and sighed. "And why do you always make your runs during the day? Isn't … what you do … better to be done in the dark?"

"Well, if I was robbing honest folk, maybe," said Will. "But I'm stealing from thieves, so we go when their guard is down. It's a dangerous game, I know, but we never take enough from any one gang to make them suspicious."

"Dangerous?" Ginny's voice rose a pitch.

"Nothing we'll let come your way, I promise, Gin. You're perfectly safe in that house." Will took Ginny's hand and squeezed it. "And you're perfectly safe when you're with me."

But Ginny didn't feel reassured. Her sister was involved in such bad business, no matter how she tried to justify it.

"Why don't you take the girls to the Forest?" Ginny asked. "We're near it, and I'm sure the Gardener will do something for them. Especially if Suzy's a Sensitive herself."

Will's step faltered, and she shook her head. "I know you only know good things about the Gardener and her Forest, but there are other stories about her, and I have never liked charity."

"You don't like asking people for things, so you just take what you need from them." Ginny frowned harder.

"Ouch." Will inclined her head. "You certainly have strong opinions, despite your quietness."

"And what have you heard about The Gardener that makes you think she won't help you and the girls?" Ginny asked. "Because I've *met* her. And you know Princess Mayblossom, her niece. She *would* help us."

Will shrugged. "But Father made Mother promise that you and I would stay away from the Forest. Nothing good comes from that place, and especially not for the likes of us."

"The Gardener said that our father was probably from the Forest," said Ginny. "But that would have been back when the Mistress ruled it. The Gardener's grandmother. And the Gardener isn't a bit like the Mistress."

"It's still the Forest." Will shook her head. "And … here we are."

She pushed open a door and pulled Ginny off the streets and into what seemed to be some sort of inn or tavern. The room was quiet right now – no doubt because it was the middle of the day. Ginny's eyes widened as she saw a young man sitting alone at a table.

Prince Hans.

She barely had a chance to gasp before Will shoved her down at the table next to him.

~

"Here she is," Will announced. "It's good to have you here, sir. I'm afraid that Ginny has desperately missed everyone at Snowfield Palace."

Prince Hans laughed. "And we have all missed her. She's a dear thing, after all, and now Snowfield feels positively empty!"

Ginny swallowed and folded her hands in her lap, refusing

to acknowledge Prince Hans' too-charming grin.

"And I barely know what to do without her, so I can well imagine," said Will, with a laugh of her own.

"You know, I must say that you're looking a little different than you did when you were at Snowfield, Will," Prince Hans observed, leaning back to cross his arms over his chest.

Will chewed her lip for a moment before she shrugged. "Must be my new hairstyle."

Prince Hans' eyebrow arched as he noted the frost that spread across Will's hand for the briefest moment. "Must be."

"What brings you to a place like this?" Ginny asked, lifting her chin. "Because I'm pretty sure this isn't a good place for the crown prince of a foreign country."

Prince Hans shrugged. "I know how to handle myself; don't you worry. And I had to come see you, Miss Ginny. You told me that I could, and here I am."

Ginny frowned and took a deep breath. "Well, I didn't think you would."

"I hope I shall always have the ability to delightfully prove you wrong," He gave another laugh.

"You don't belong in a place like this," Ginny insisted.

"No less than you do," he countered. "And your sister has given me leave to visit with you. Come now, won't you let me rescue you from this dreadful place?"

"I only agreed for you to *visit* me," said Ginny, her gaze narrowing. "This is where my sister is, and she will take care of me."

As much as she disagreed with Will's lifestyle, she trusted Prince Hans even less. At least she knew Will's motivation. Prince Hans might forget her in a moment.

"Our father abandoned our mother, my dear prince," said Will. "You must bear that in mind – we don't trust easily."

"And my mother's heart was broken," said Prince Hans. "I know how delicate a Frost's heart can be." He leaned his head to the side as he focused on Will. "You should go see my Aunt Elinrose. She has a lot of experience thawing the broken hearts of Frosts, and she would be more than happy to help you."

Will opened her mouth and then rocked back in her seat, blinking as she folded her arms over her chest. "I'll bear that in mind," she said.

Ginny chewed her lip. If Will could just get to the Forest and meet the Gardener for herself, everything would be so much better – but to have it be because of *Prince Hans*...

He would hold this over her, wouldn't he? She didn't know his motivation in courting her – other than passing the time – and she didn't want him to have any leverage.

But Will needed her heart thawed. If not because she deserved a real chance at happiness with Robert – because even Ginny could admit that it would take a true miracle for their paths to cross again – then at least to remind her of her morals.

"How are your sisters?" Ginny asked instead, sitting straighter. "Princess Mayblossom, especially."

"Maia and Blana are both excellent," said Prince Hans. "Both send their love. I think Maia would have come with me, if she could, but I had to ensure that your new living situation was safe for her. No offense, Will – is your name actually Will?"

"It's short for Wilhelmina," Will answered.

Prince Hans nodded. "Well, even though I never would accuse you of willfully trying to endanger your sister, I couldn't know for sure what your new situation might be, so I had to be careful."

"Little sisters must be protected, I understand," said Will.

Ginny took another deep breath and then stood, folding her arms over her chest. "Is there anything else you need to say, or should my sister and I be returning home again? I'm sure Suzy doesn't want to be left alone with all of the girls for too long."

"She'll be fine – she has *such* a way with them," said Will, waving Ginny off. "There's no reason for us to rush away."

"And there's no reason for me to keep the two of you," Prince Hans countered. "Perhaps I can take Ginny out into the countryside in a day or two? She looks like she could use some fresh air, and this town doesn't seem like it has much of that."

Ginny's frown grew.

"I think that can be arranged," said Will. She sighed as she stared at Ginny and then also stood. "And don't worry – I shall talk to her."

"I do understand what competition I have," said Prince Hans, also standing. "I only ask for a chance to prove myself. And perhaps to take her back home with me."

Ginny blinked and took a step back.

"To Snowfield Palace," he quickly amended. "Because I'm not the only one who misses you."

"I left for a reason," said Ginny, and she turned away.

"Call on us tomorrow – you know the address," said Will. "Hopefully, she'll be in a better mood tomorrow – I thought this would be a pleasant surprise for her, and it seems I was wrong."

Ginny's frown only grew as Will took her hand and guided her out of the tavern. Will had *known* that she didn't welcome Prince Hans' attention and had still thought that this would be pleasant?

Did her sister really know her so badly?

"I'm really sorry if that was disagreeable," Will said once they were on the streets again. "But you can't stay obsessed with the loss of Kaimund. Even if Kaimund were to finally wake up and see you for what you are, he's not the one who's here. Prince Hans is – and can you really spurn the affection of a prince?"

Ginny just shook her head. "I don't believe for a moment that he's genuine. I don't trust him, and his being here only makes it all worse."

"Gin, you deserve to be a princess." Will sighed. "I shouldn't have sent you that letter. I should have left you at Snowfield Palace. Even with your broken heart ... I'm sure Maia would have seen it and helped you, eventually."

"Will, no prince in their right mind would want me – especially after seeing me here." Ginny shook her head. "Please, let's just take the girls and go to the Forest. We'll all be much happier there."

But Will just sighed and shook her head.

20 Ginny managed to convince Will that going alone with Prince Hans was a terrible idea. So, when Prince Hans *did* appear the next morning to take her out into the countryside, Suzy came with them as an escort, and Ginny had Will's knife strapped to her own waist. She didn't like wearing a knife, but it did lend a sense of security.

Prince Hans laughed when they insisted that Suzy come with her for the outing, but he put the two of them on his horse good-naturedly and led them through the twisting roads out of the town.

Ginny breathed a deep sigh as she took in the bright sky and the rolling countryside. Even if it was with Prince Hans, it was good to get away from that house.

"Oh, this is *nice*," Suzy declared, spinning around as she stepped down from the horse. "There's not much of use out of the town, so I don't get out much. Thank you so much, sir, for bringing us."

"It's an honor to be of service to such lovely young ladies," Prince Hans declared, grinning. "And I made arrangements for a picnic, so we can have that now, or we can do some exploring first."

"It's a bit early for lunch," said Ginny. "I suppose we can explore a bit, first." She chewed her lip.

"A marvelous idea," said Prince Hans, holding out an arm

to Ginny. "Will you come with me?"

Ginny had already come this far with him, so she nodded slightly. She didn't take his arm, however, instead gesturing for him to lead the way. He hesitated for a moment, then shrugged and walked down the hill. She followed.

"I know you don't believe me that my affection for you can be anything but shallow," he said, shoving his hands into his pockets. "But there really is something special about you, Miss Ginny.

Ginny shook her head. "You've seen where I come from now. You know that I could never be a fit wife for a prince. You need to focus on finding a wife who will be a good *queen*. And stop toying with the heart of every maiden you meet. I don't know why you are this way, and I know it's not my place to tell you to stop, but I can tell you to stop pursuing me."

"My mother wasn't a princess. She was a Frost with a broken heart," he countered. "And I know you underestimate your own value. You'll make an excellent queen. I'm sure of it."

"Your surety won't change what I am," she countered. "What *are* you doing here?"

"If you must know the truth, my sister did ask me to court you," he explained. "She wants you to know your own value. But when I saw you at the ball, all dressed up and beautiful, I'm afraid you quite stole my heart. And I know you're Frost enough, and you've fallen in love already, but will you please just give me a chance to show you how valuable you really are?"

Ginny sighed as she stared up at him and then glanced over her shoulder at the town behind her. This was the world where she belonged, but would she ever be content here? Or had her years at Snowfield Palace spoiled her forever?

"Are you sure you don't want me to take you back home with me?" Prince Hans asked. "Your sister might be here, but you don't belong. You don't want to live here in a place like this, and if you just said the word, I would take you back to your old life again."

"But I never fit in that old life, either." Ginny sighed again.

"I'm caught between worlds, I know that. And, right now, I'm needed more in this one than the other."

"I don't know if I agree with that," said Prince Hans. "You're very needed in Snowfield Palace, even if they don't know it. It's been so quiet without you – everyone says so."

"It's quiet without Rina and Calla," Ginny countered.

"Insist that, if you must, but it doesn't make you correct," said Prince Hans. "You were an intrinsic part of life at Snowfield Palace." He shook his head. "And Maia, especially misses you. She's never made friends well, and the two of you just clicked together. Now she's left alone with Kaimund. Poor fellow – has no idea at all how to charm a girl."

Ginny balled her hands into fists and then uncurled them, shaking her head. "Kaimund is…"

"Yes, you would defend him, the blind fellow – couldn't see well even before the mirror fell on him." Prince Hans laughed. "Ah, if he had only ever realized the treasure that could have been his if he'd just opened his eyes!"

Ginny swallowed. "I don't want to talk about Kaimund."

"Of course you don't," said Prince Hans. "What would you like to discuss instead, then? That tree over there? It's a lovely tree, you know? Or perhaps I shall regale you with poetry about the blueness of your eyes. They're such a lovely shade – such a rich blue compared to the iciness of a true Frost like our sisters."

Ginny sighed. "Please, no flattery."

"I know, you're a humble little thing, but you *do* deserve to know how special you are. Because you are a bright light in this world, and it would be a darker place without you."

"Do you think we should head back and eat now?" Ginny asked. "I think it might be lunchtime."

"A marvelous idea," said Prince Hans, spinning around to face her. "I'm beginning to feel hungry myself, so let's go find that escort of ours and pull out the basket I brought with us."

He offered her his arm again. She continued to ignore it. Together they made their way back up the hill. Suzy was found, and lunch laid out. Ginny kept her lips pressed together, her frown growing darker the more Prince Hans talked.

"Have you ever thought about the magic that people have?" asked Prince Hans, as he distributed sandwiches. "I often have. I'm surrounded by Frosts, Sensitives, and Cinders, not to mention their male counterparts. And it makes a body think – fire and ice. Opposite magics. Might Sensitives, with their magic of life, have some form of counterpart as well? Not a male Sensitive – Beasts, I think their proper name is, if they're strong enough, like my cousin Hansel – but a proper *opposite*."

Ginny pulled back, even as she took the sandwich he offered her. "I've never thought about that at all."

"Neither have I," said Suzy. "I don't think about magic much in general, though. It's a thing, I know, but it's never been anything much to me. Until Will came, but even she never uses hers much."

"The opposite of life is death," said Ginny. "What sort of magic would that be?" She shuddered. "What sort of person would *have* that sort of magic?"

"An interesting thought experiment, yes?" said Prince Hans.

Why in the world had he thought that *this* might be an acceptable turn for the conversation? Ginny didn't understand this man at all.

"I'm glad that no magic like that exists," she stated. "What we have is strange enough."

~

After the picnic, Prince Hans frequently visited, confusing Ginny more each time he came. But, no matter how she tried to distrust him, his presence chipped away at her heart more each time.

She missed Snowfield Palace. That was the long and short of it. She missed the place that had been her home for so long, and her heart had latched onto the piece of home that had found its way here – no matter that it was the most distasteful piece. If only Kaimund had been the one lovelorn enough to follow her!

But, no, it was Prince Hans. Far-too-charming Prince Hans. He came every day – if only for a few minutes to bestow some trinket upon her. Her collection of treasures on the bedframe was growing steadily – and she had given Will permission to sell them when she could.

He didn't take her out again, instead talking with her in the sitting room of the house. He offered, but Ginny firmly insisted that they not waste Suzy's time again. They'd barely had time to finish dinner for the rest of the girls, when arriving home from the picnic, and they'd not been able to do any of the housework.

"Ah, Miss Ginny – are you sure you want to stay in this house today?" Prince Hans asked as he walked into the sitting room one morning. "It's a lovely day out, and I won't have many more chances to take you out again."

She frowned as she glanced up from the skirt hem she was letting out – Button was growing like a weed and would need a completely new dress soon if she kept up like this. "What do you mean?"

"I can't stay in this place much longer," Prince Hans explained, and he shrugged as he sat down on the floor across for her – oh, but their lack of any real furniture could be embarrassing! "I'm actually supposed to be in the capitol with Maia right now, but I sent her on ahead and detoured here. Now I have to catch up and pray they'll forgive my distraction."

"I see." Ginny sighed, though she didn't quite know what that sigh was for. Frustration that he had been here when he should have been somewhere else? Sorrow at the loss of this connection to home?

She could no longer lie to herself that she considered Snowfield Palace home.

Prince Hans nodded. "I'll leave tomorrow – though, if you just said the word and asked to come with me, I would delay so you can prepare."

Ginny pinched her lips tighter and ultimately shook her head. "You should have gone to the capitol in the first place," she said. "I apologize for being a distraction."

"Oh, no, Miss Ginny – you need never apologize for that," said Prince Hans. "I am the weak one, and the task I had in the capital was nothing but drudgery, and Maia could handle it well enough on her own." He shook his head. "She and I both agreed that this was as good an excuse as any for me to slip away and visit you. I know that our time has been short, but have I not stolen away any bit of your affection? Come now, Ginny. Tell me that I have hope."

He leaned forward, his expression so earnest, Ginny's breath caught in her throat.

"I … appreciate that you came to visit," she finally said, ducking her gaze and fidgeting with the needle. "I can admit that. Thank you for taking time from your journey to make sure that I'm doing okay."

Prince Hans took a deep breath and nodded. "I shall accept that. I would do it a thousand times over, just so you know."

Ginny sighed. "Please focus on the life you lead. Don't make impulsive sacrifices on my account."

"I make no promises on that account – not unless you agree to come with me to the capitol, for Maia desperately misses you." Prince Hans shook his head.

"Go without me," Ginny insisted. She stabbed the fabric with her needle. "This is where I belong, as I've told you, and you need to go where you belong. Don't worry about me. Learn how to love someone in your own world, and stop toying with the hearts of women. I think your sister would have so many more friends if she didn't lose respect for every young woman who loses their heart to you."

Prince Hans frowned. "I'm pretty sure she has no friends because she's a regular ice princess and scares other girls away."

Ginny sighed and shook her head. "Go do your business. Forget about me. Learn to be a better prince."

They sat in silence for a few more minutes, and then Prince Hans sighed and stood, muttering a "good day to you" before he left the room. Ginny's heart lodged in her throat as the door shut behind him. Had she *really* just told off a prince like that?

A real, actual prince?

He would never listen to her. She knew that. Yet...

Yet, as he'd sat on the floor next to her, with that open smile, he had seemed like just a normal man. For a moment ... for one strange moment, she had felt that it was Kaimund sitting next to her, the way it used to be, before Princess Maia had come between them. Before the mirror's magic had made her invisible to him.

He used to value every word she said. Even when everyone else would dismiss her, he would seek her out.

But there was too much distance between them. He should never have catered to her the way he did. She should have never fixed her heart on him the way she had.

Ginny frowned and pressed her hands to her still-frozen heart. She didn't know what direction her life would take, but she knew what would never be. Kaimund. Prince Hans. She needed to put them both out of her mind.

21 Yet, even though she knew what she needed to do, it was much harder to make her heart comply. It was hard to quiet the threads of warmth that had crept back into her heart with Prince Hans' visit.

Ginny tried to not cry. Not in front of Suzy or Will. Suzy would never understand, and Will would understand all too well. It was tempting to let Will ice her heart again, to let herself fade back into the uncaring haze she'd been in before Prince Hans had warmed her heart.

But she didn't want to lose the ability to feel. She didn't want to stop caring. It was hard enough watching Will.

More days passed. More weeks. Princess Mayblossom's baby would be born soon. Ginny wondered if it would be a boy or a girl. Would she ever get to meet the child?

Would she ever be part of that life again?

No, no, don't think about the old life.

Will was away with most of the girls, and Ginny was alone in the house with Suzy when they had a knock at the door. They shared a glance before rushing to a window to peek out at the young man who stood on the threshold.

"That's not your Prince Hans," Suzy muttered, her head tilted to the side. "That's who I thought would be here."

"It's Robert," said Ginny, pulling back with a frown.

"Robert?"

"He was also a ward at Snowfield Palace," Ginny explained. "Lady Nora's nephew. He's a guard and was best friends with Will when she was a guard, too."

"And now he's come and found Will!"

Ginny shrugged. "He knew her as a man, but learned the truth right before she ran. We should go let him in and see what he's doing here."

Quickly, she went through the house and down the stairs, Suzy at her heels, and she threw open the door just as Robert was knocking again.

"You best get inside quick, sir," said Suzy, lifting her chin. "They don't much like the likes of you around here, so you should get out of sight."

Robert nodded, stepped inside, and let Ginny close the door behind him. The frown he wore made Ginny's stomach twist. She wasn't used to Robert frowning. It made the world feel wrong.

"I'm glad I found the right house, Gin," he said after staring at her for a long moment. "I was beginning to wonder, standing out there." He swallowed. "Where's your … sister."

"Will's out with the girls," said Ginny. "They … they have things they do in town during the day. Suzy and I stay behind to take care of the house and do the cooking."

Robert nodded. "Right. Ginny … it's good to see you again. You're … looking as well as ever. I don't like the looks of this town, but you have a roof over your head, and that's what matters, right? So many can't even say that much."

Ginny nodded. "That is … true enough. And Will spent a lot of her life on the streets."

Robert sighed. "I'm glad she has a roof over her head now. And you with her. No one deserves to be alone in the elements like that."

"What are you doing here, Robert?" Ginny asked, raising her chin. "I didn't think you would have leave again for a while. And to come here?"

"Why wouldn't I come here?" Robert shoved his hands into

his pockets and leaned against the wall. "Will was my best mate, *saved my life multiple times*, and so naturally, I'm going to make sure she's doing all right for herself. Still so strange to think that he was a woman this whole time. Why didn't you ever say anything, Ginny? That was your sister!"

Ginny opened her mouth, then realized she really didn't have an excuse, and so shrugged.

"Then again, it would have required arguing, and we all know how much you hate to argue." Robert gave a wry laugh. "Ah, dear Ginny, Snowfield Palace isn't the same without you. So quiet, so empty."

"I'm not the only one who left," Ginny reminded him.

His eyebrow arched, and he suddenly straightened, the wistfulness leaving his expression as his posture turned serious. "No, you're not, and that's why I'm here. I think."

Ginny frowned and shook her head. "What do you mean?"

"What I mean is, Prince Hans has run off with both Rina and Calla, his sister with them, and no one knows where they've gone," Robert explained. "I got leave to take the news to Uncle Bethim, and Kaimund had disappeared the day before I arrived. None of this makes sense. Reynard is furious. The princesses went to ask the Gardener about it, and they couldn't use the hazel tree."

Ginny swallowed. "Something couldn't have happened to the Gardener?"

"We don't know. It could just be the tree itself. I said I would go investigate, but I'm here instead. Truth is, I'm scared of what this all means, and I don't want to venture into the Forest alone."

"So you came *here*."

"I know, I know, I'm a fool. But something in my brain insisted that if I just had Will with me, everything would be all right." He sighed and leaned back against the wall, running a hand through his hair. "I'm an idiot, aren't I?"

Ginny took a deep breath, a bloom of hope rising within her. "No, I don't think you are at all. It's dangerous to go into the unknown, and you know that as a guard. Will and the girls will be back home again soon enough. Go ahead and rest. Dinner isn't quite done, but we might have some bread for you."

"Bread would be good enough," said Robert, nodding. "And I am an idiot, whatever you might say. What kind of man can't see it when his best friend is hiding something like that?"

Ginny just laughed. "If you're an idiot, then I'm twice that, because she's my sister – and I *knew* that – but I still believed her to be my brother when she walked through that door at your side, dressed as a man. Princess Maia was the first to figure it out."

"One recognizes their own kind, I suppose," said Robert, shaking his head.

~

They left Robert in one of the empty sitting rooms, where he took it upon himself to repair a broken chair that someone had left behind. Suzy and Ginny didn't say much between themselves as they retreated to the kitchen again to work on dinner, which had fortunately not burned during their distraction.

Time passed, and as soon as Ginny heard shouts in the hall, she quickly rushed to warn her sister of their guest.

It was apparently a good run, because Will was all grins, her hands on her hips as she ordered the girls about. But the grin fell when Ginny told her they'd had a visitor while she was gone.

"You know I've told you to not open the door to strangers," Will stated, shaking her head.

"He's not a stranger," Ginny countered, with a shake of her own head as she took her sister's hand. "And he's still here, waiting to see you. So come along."

"Oh a *he*," said Will, reluctantly following. "It's even worse knowing that a strange man was in the house with you all this time."

"He's *hardly* strange," said Ginny. She couldn't quite bear to tell her sister outright that it was Robert. No, it was best for

Will to see for herself. "And you didn't think a thing of it when you let Prince Hans come court me!"

And now, to hear what Robert had said had happened between Prince Hans and the Bethim girls…

"Well, we knew him, so that hardly—" Will broke off as Ginny pulled her into the sitting room, and she saw Robert sitting there in the middle of the broken wood. "Robert…" The whisper was breathless.

Robert quickly stood, running a hand through his hair as he approached them. "Will. It's you. You…" His gaze traveled down her figure and then settled again on her face as he went still, as though his very brain had stopped working. "You really are a woman."

Will drew in a deep breath, pulling herself to her full height and folding her arms over her chest. "Yes, I am. Did you come all this way just to gawk at me and see if I really had been lying to you this whole time?"

Robert took a step back, shaking his head. "I – no—"

"And just what is your commanding officer going to say? We can't desert our posts!"

"He's on emergency leave!" Ginny quickly inserted, pulling her sister back. "Prince Hans and Princess Maia have disappeared with Kaimund, Calla, *and* Rina, and the hazel tree they use to reach the Forest isn't working. He's come to ask for your help. Because he trusts you. And even if you weren't the man he thought you were, you're still the companion he wants at his side in the face of danger."

Will went slack, tilting her head to the side. "Is that so?"

Robert took a deep breath and advanced again. "Essentially, yes. I don't care that you're a woman. I'm hurt that you never trusted me with it, but you've had my back too many times for me to assume it was malicious. You earned my trust a thousand times over. I just wish I'd had your trust."

"It wasn't that I didn't trust you," said Will. Ginny could feel her trembling, oh so slightly. "I – it doesn't matter. Not anymore. You need my help?"

A frown flickered across Robert's face, but he nodded. "If

you'll give it. Something is wrong with the Forest, and so I've got to go see what's happened. I would like a strong Frost at my side. Just in case. I don't know what I'm going to find."

Will's chin lifted. "Someone told you I was a Frost?"

Robert laughed and took another step closer. "*That* I figured out on my own. I'm not completely blind. Of course, it's just a guess that you're strong, but regardless, you're who I want at my side."

The temperature in the room dropped by several degrees, and frost spread along the walls with audible crackling. "I'm strong enough," she said. "But I also have people here who rely on me. I can't … I can't leave my girls."

"Right," said Robert. His shoulders sagged. "I should have known you would say something like that."

Will suddenly pulled her hand from Ginny's and stalked out of the room without even a glance behind her.

"I'll talk to her," said Ginny, giving Robert what she hoped was an encouraging smile before she rushed out of the room after her sister.

Will hadn't gone far. Ginny found her leaning against another doorframe, breathing hard, her eyes fixed on some unknown target.

Ginny swallowed. "I want you to know, people I care deeply about are probably in danger right now, and if you don't go, *I* will. I don't know what good I can do, but I can't sit idly by."

Will's gaze snapped towards her, and her frown darkened. "Did you see the way he looked at me?"

Ginny sighed. "All I saw is that he's trying to figure out what your friendship is now that he knows this about you. Will, he has *covered* for your absence from the guards. He's come here because he wants you at his side in the face of unknown danger. Stop panicking over your broken heart and do what you can for your friend. Or is your heart too frozen to care about the people you used to love? Because lately, I've begun to wonder if *I'm* safe staying here with you."

Will sucked in a breath and dropped her gaze. "Oh, Gin. You don't understand, I—"

"I think I understand perfectly well," said Ginny. "My heart was also broken, and you froze it for me. But if Kaimund were the one in that room, begging me to save the people he loves, I would follow him in a moment. Robert doesn't have to know why you left – though I do think he deserves to know – but you should help him. The girls can take care of themselves. They have a roof over their heads, and Suzy will keep them in line."

"But if I'm not here, who will keep them from falling back into old habits?" asked Will. "We don't take the easy route. What will I have to return to?"

"Leave that to Austere or bring them all with us," Ginny countered. "We aren't too far from the Forest here, and it would be a much better place for them unless something has gone horribly wrong there. The Gardener isn't the Mistress. Maybe our father distrusted the place, but it's a different Forest than the one he left."

Will tilted her head to the side, considering. "I'll give them the choice," she said. Then she straightened and marched past Ginny back into the room where Robert waited.

"I'll help you," she said. "My sister would never forgive me if I tossed you back out onto the streets and made you fix your own problems." She thrust a hand out towards him. "I'll save your skin for you once again."

A grin lifted the corner of Robert's mouth, and he stepped forward to take her hand in both of his. "Thank you. From the bottom of my heart. I've missed you—" He tilted his head to the side, his grin growing. "Mina."

"Mina!" Will tried to pull back, but couldn't, since Robert had her hand.

"It's short for Wilhelmina, the same as Will is," said Robert. He lifted her hand and pressed a kiss to her knuckles. "I think you deserve to be treated as a woman, even dressed like that, and your name is a good place to start."

Will's mouth fell open, and she did yank her hand away this time. "Bold of you to assume that I would want that."

"When have you known me to be otherwise?" said Robert,

holding up his hands. "Maybe I don't know you as well as I thought, but you know me, and I look forward to getting to know who Mina is."

"Right," said Will. "I should go talk with the girls. There's no time to waste, and we need to prepare. You can sleep with Rick and Tom tonight, and we'll try to leave in the morning. Some of the girls might come with us, because I'm giving them the option, but I don't know who will agree."

And she hastened out of the room, leaving Robert grinning after her.

22 Ginny made the announcement over dinner that night since Will was too out of sorts for it. Suzy was going to stay in the house and keep it for them, and the others were told that if they were going to stay in the house, they would have to remain honest, and Suzy would have full rights to kick anyone out who didn't comply.

Faye quickly agreed to stay behind, with her brothers, and help Suzy uphold those standards. The boys cried out in disappointment, but Faye insisted they were too young for such a mission – which was correct – and they could wait until Will came home and reported on the state of the Forest. The others would decide in the morning.

Will scowled as she ate, and the room's temperature was noticeably frosty, though no one said anything about it. As soon as she'd had her fill, she left the room without a word.

"I think Will isn't sure what to make of her old life finding her," said Suzy, wrinkling her nose.

"I'm hardly her 'old life,'" said Robert, frowning after her. "'Friend under false pretenses,' perhaps, but I've told her I don't hold that against her. But I'm just glad to have her back, under any condition. Even as horrible as this. Kaimund and the girls disappearing being the horrible part, that is. Not anything about current company."

Ginny excused herself soon after that and went up to find

Will in their room. The girls could entertain Robert well enough.

Will was already in her nightshirt, lying on her back on their bedroll, staring up at the ceiling, hands in her hair. The room was completely iced over, but Ginny didn't care. She made her way over to her sister and sat down beside her.

"Are you all right? Did seeing him again hurt?"

"I don't feel anything," Will whispered. "He stands there, the exact man I loved – ready to accept me as I am, and I think he was even *flirting*. But I'm just so cold."

Ginny sighed and laid down, wrapping her arms around Will. "I'm sorry."

"I had to freeze my heart – I *had* to. But now I can't even cry. It doesn't hurt, and that's what's so terrible." She rolled over and wrapped her arms around Ginny, hugging her tight. "But he's here. And I'll relearn how to be friends with him – *actual* friends. Oh, but why did he have to get it into his head to call me *Mina*?"

"You don't like the name?" asked Ginny. "You could tell him to stop. If you have a good reason, I'm sure he would listen. He doesn't *want* to hurt you, and he is your friend."

Will sighed. "I don't know. I can't feel anything, Gin. The name … part of me is asking if he expects anything from me if he uses it, and part of me wonders why I never thought to use it before."

"Let me get into my nightdress, and let's just go to sleep," said Ginny, giving Will an extra squeeze. "We need to get an early start tomorrow morning, I'm sure."

"You don't have to come with us," said Will, releasing Ginny and rolling onto her back again. "Except, I guess you probably do. Kaimund is missing, and I just can't seem to freeze him out of your heart."

"I'm soft," said Ginny, quickly changing into her nightdress.

"You are, aren't you?" Will gave another sigh. "It's not a bad thing, Gin. The world frankly needs more soft people. Just as long as you have people around to protect you."

"And, thankfully, I have you." With that, Ginny laid back beside her sister and curled up close.

Ginny didn't sleep well, if she was to tell the truth. As soon as her mind cleared from worrying over Will, Kaimund's situation crashed upon her. And, not just Kaimund, but Rina and Calla, too!

But morning came, and she rose when Will did, quickly changing into her sturdiest dress and following Will down the stairs where Robert and Suzy had their packs and breakfast prepared.

"None of the other girls are going," Suzy declared. "Though I wish you were taking Button – I know she's going to be trouble, if any of them will be, and she's too young to throw back onto the streets." She shook her head. "But I wish you well, all of you. I'll … be praying."

"Who knows, this might all turn out to be nothing," said Robert with a hopeful grin.

Ginny just shrugged. "I never trusted Prince Hans. There was always something that wasn't quite right about him, and both Rina and Calla were too taken with him – and Rina was engaged! Princess Maia, though … that's what makes this all so strange. I trusted her. She seemed to want nothing to do with her brother. *So what happened?*"

The other three shared a glance before giving her a sympathetic smile.

"Let's not work ourselves up over the possibilities," said Will. "Maybe this Gardener will have answers. Maybe not. We won't know until we meet her. Let's just eat and get on with this."

Ginny could barely choke down the porridge that Suzy set in front of them, and she gave her new friend a lingering hug, wondering when they would meet again. Then they hastened out the door together and out into the streets.

Robert only had one horse, but he declared that they would take turns riding. But the only one who ever seemed to ride was Ginny, as Will and Robert walked, one on each side of the horse. She didn't ask for it – but neither ever seemed to want a break, and Will stated at one point that Ginny had no experience with long marches, and it was best that she save her strength. Besides, she was the smallest and easiest on the horse, especially carrying their supplies.

She hated that she could be a liability and often wondered if she should have stayed behind, but she didn't voice such concerns. Instead, she listened to Will and Robert slowly ease back into old conversations, soon laughing as though they had never been parted, though the topics always seemed shallow, largely concerning old escapades.

But, perhaps, given a need to redefine their friendship, they needed to start at the shallow end.

Ginny slept with Will at night, as always, and they entered the Forest some two days later. Ginny's eyes widened as she glanced around herself, marveling at the trees surrounding her and the eerie light that filtered through the leaves. She'd never seen so much greenery in her life, and after spending weeks in that town, it was positively shocking.

"Nothing seems wrong so far," Robert remarked after a few minutes. "The place is strange, to be sure, but it's just the amount of magic here. We need to find the Gardener."

"How do we do that?" asked Will. "This place looks like a headache to navigate – but where is she? I'm sure she has some seat of government…"

Robert laughed. "Oh, she does, and she takes it with her wherever she goes. I've stated a desire to find her, and now we just need to walk. As long as she doesn't find us a threat, she'll have the Forest take us right to her."

"And if she finds us a threat?" asked Ginny, her voice small.

"I don't think we need to worry about that." Robert patted his horse's flank. "She likes you, after all."

Ginny blinked but made no further protest as they plunged deeper.

~

She wasn't sure how long they walked through the Forest. Time was strange in this place, and the shifting light hard to track. All Ginny knew was that, somehow, the weight of this place sent the conversation between Will and Robert to more serious topics.

"You know, I can't help but replay every conversation we've ever had, trying to determine what ... *this* meant."

"And, by *this*, you mean the fact that I'm a woman," said Will, her voice turning frosty.

"More or less, yes," said Robert, shrugging. "I ... I try to tell myself that it means nothing. That you were my friend regardless, and it doesn't matter what secrets you kept. But then I'll think about things you said that didn't quite make sense at the time, strange looks in your eye, the way you didn't like it when I would flirt with other women..."

"Well, no woman likes to see her best friend toy with the hearts of fellow women," said Will. "I don't think you noticed how Maia and Ginny would glare at Hans for his escapades."

Ginny swallowed.

"Ah, true enough," said Robert, and he gave a long sigh. "But are you sure that's all it was?"

"If you think for a moment that *I* was susceptible to your charms, then *please* think again," said Will. "I was privy to all of your flaws, and I know just what sort of man you are. Besides, I – I'm a Frost. My heart is a block of ice, and that's that."

Robert tilted his head to the side. "To my knowledge – and bear in mind that I know a few Frosts since Uncle Graham married into North's royal family – a Frost's heart is only *frozen* after it's been broken. So who broke your heart? I trust you gave the scoundrel a black eye, because he would deserve nothing less."

Ginny bit her lip, wondering if she should say something. But it was Will's secret to tell, not hers. She would hate it if anyone told Kaimund about her own affection and broken heart.

"Well, he never knew, and I was the fool," said Will. "Let's not talk about this. My past is ... messy. A lot happened that I don't like to remember. But I'm standing here now, with my best friend and my little sister. That's all I need in life, you know."

"He was a fool if he never saw it," said Robert. "But, you know, if everything's fine with the Gardener, she's good at fixing frozen hearts. If she thaws yours, then you can have a second chance."

"Love isn't all there is in this world," said Will. "Do you really think that I have *time* for romance and all of that? And what fellow would want a wife who knows how to be a man better than him?"

Robert tilted his head to the side thoughtfully. "Maybe a fellow with a pair of eyes in his head. I don't know. Look, Mina, I'm not going to tell you how to live. I just … don't want your future to be the same as your past. All alone. I'm glad you have Ginny now, though. That's a good step."

"Exactly," said Ginny. "You're not alone anymore. I know you've spent your life fighting, but … you don't have to do it alone anymore. And *please* let the Gardener fix your heart. For my sake if not your own."

Will sighed. "Fine. If you ask her for it, I'll do it. I—"

The path ahead of them suddenly opened up into a clearing. In the middle of this clearing stood a throne of twisted branches, and in this throne sat a woman – but not the Gardener. This woman had the same green eyes and ruddy complexion mixed with patches of green, but her features were sharper, her hair a golden blonde falling in a long braid pulled over her shoulder, and azalea flowers grew in her hair.

"Ah, Emmazel," said Robert, stepping forward with a bow. "We're here to talk to your niece."

Ginny frowned. She'd never seen the Gardener's aunt up close before, and now she couldn't dismiss a strange sense of familiarity. She looked like … she looked like Will, just with different coloring.

Emmazel rolled her eyes. "Oh, everyone is here for Elin, but it's her day off, and I told her that I would deal with complaints and problems today. She's better at it, I know, but I can't make her do it every day because she deserves time with her husband and family, the same as I do. So out with it, and

I'll see what I can do for you."

"It's about Hans and Maia," Ginny blurted, leaning forward. "I'm pretty sure she'll want to deal with this herself."

Emmazel's lips pressed into a line as she regarded Ginny. "I see. You make a good point. Yes, I think she should deal with this one. Follow me." She stood, and the throne receded into the ground as a black cat jumped off of it and wound around her ankles. "Oh, silly cat." She muttered before scooping him up.

"That's her husband," said Robert. "He's really a man but likes to be a cat most of the time."

"Don't be giving away all of my secrets, young man," said the cat, folding his ears back.

"And, yes, he does talk," Robert added. "Sensitive magic, you know."

"Ah," said Will. "I guess that makes sense."

"You're fortunate that Elin didn't leave the Forest today," said Emmazel. "She could have been visiting Mari or James, but no, she's at her cabin. What is wrong with Hans and Maia, by the way? And why didn't Mayblossom come to see us?"

"We should probably wait and tell the Gardener," said Robert. "It's rather serious, or, at least, we fear it is. Though if you could tell us if *you* sense either of them – and perhaps my cousins, too – in the Forest, that would be an excellent help."

Emmazel took a deep breath and closed her eyes. Two steps later, she stopped walking and stood still, gripping her cat-husband tighter. Ginny tightened her grip of the saddle horn.

"I don't sense them," Emmazel said after a moment. "Now, granted, my connection to the Forest is not as strong as Elin's, but my magic is stronger, so it balances out most of the time." She swallowed. "But there is a section I can't sense near the border to North." And then walked again with redoubled steps. "This is a serious matter. You were right to demand Elin's attention."

Robert urged the horse to go faster to keep up with Emmazel, and the world bent around them strangely as they moved through the Forest. Within minutes, they had arrived at a rose-covered cabin in another clearing. Emmazel tossed the cat to the ground as she rushed to the door, which flew open as she reached it. The Gardener now stood in the doorway, staring at Emmazel for a long moment, her expression worried, before her attention flickered to Ginny, Will, and Robert.

"Come on inside," she said. "The three of you look like you've had quite a journey and need some rest. And if you have bad news about my niece and nephew, don't hold back."

Ginny gratefully let Robert lift her down from the horse and followed them into the house.

23

It was a small, quaint room. There was just enough room for everyone at the table – Ginny, Will, Robert, Emmazel, the Gardener, and the Gardener's husband, Earnest, and their two children, Hansel and Ela. Night, Emmazel's husband, stayed as a cat, curled up in Emmazel's lap, though his gaze seemed fixed on Hansel. A handful of fairies buzzed about, piling the table with food. Ginny picked at hers, though Will and Robert fell to gratefully.

The Gardener didn't eat but listened with a silent frown as Robert told his story of the disappearances in the capital and Snowfield Palace and that the hazel tree wasn't working. At the end of it, she shook her head. "I wondered why Mayblossom and Giana didn't make their weekly visits the last two weeks, and I had to send a message to Darren about it – he doesn't worry about his sister *quite* as much as he used to, but he does like to keep track of her and her family. I should have sent Earnest to check on them but figured that there had to be a logical explanation."

"And it's another week before Mayblossom needs a new supply of potions," said Emmazel. "And it wasn't until she entered her last month that you planned to start making daily visits again, and that's not until next week either." She sighed. "So don't heap blame upon yourself the way you like to do."

Ginny pressed her lips into a line. "But what happened?"

"I don't know, but that dead zone that Emma sensed probably has something to do with it," said the Gardener. "I've already tried to send Earnest to Snowfield Palace, but I've lost connection to that tree. I should … see if the others work."

"We have been able to visit our other friends in the last two weeks," said Earnest. "It should be fine."

"Still best to check, and you should probably let your worrisome cousin know about the development with his sister," said the Gardener, waving a hand towards him. "So, off you go."

Earnest faded from sight.

"Do you think they're in that area you can't sense?" asked Robert. "This whole affair is so strange."

"It is," said the Gardener. "And the fact that this has happened right under our noses is even more worrisome. I don't know that they're in that section, but there's too much involved to be a coincidence. Something has happened, and we completely failed to notice."

"And there's nothing we can do to change the past, and you aren't responsible for everything, Elin," said Emmazel, reaching over to pat her niece on the shoulder. "Even if you are the Gardener of this whole Forest, that's why you gave half your power to me – so all of this responsibility isn't on your shoulders."

The Gardener gave a heavy sigh. "Of course. I know that. Still…"

"That's your niece and nephew and Mayblossom's new family, I know," said Emmazel. "But let's just focus on what we *can* do."

"Will and I are both trained soldiers," said Robert. "And we're here to help solve the problem – I went and recruited Will deliberately for the purpose. Whatever is going to happen, we don't want to be left out."

"Not going to lie, I thought you might have been the perpetrator," said Will, her eyes narrowed on the Gardener. "I'm still not convinced otherwise."

The Gardener gave another long sigh before turning to

focus on Will, then she frowned. "You would think, after twenty-four years, I would have escaped my grandmother's reputation, but every time I *least* expect it it comes back and bites me again."

Will snorted.

"Whatever has happened, we will get to the bottom of it," said Emmazel. "Both Elin and I are determined to keep each other from going down my mother's path. And it's not fair to make assumptions until you have all the details. Even if I think your nephew might be the one at the bottom of this, I'm not going to say that, Elin. I never liked the look of that boy."

The Gardener gave yet another long sigh. "We'll take all the help we can get, if you promise to get all of the information before attacking. Nothing good comes from acting on hasty assumptions." She focused again on Will. "Who are you, by the way? I don't think we've met before."

"She's my sister," said Ginny. "She's a Frost but lived as a man for a long time, to keep it a secret. And her heart's broken, and I've been trying to convince her to come and ask you for help. I know this isn't a good time, but she's finally here, so would you please…"

The Gardener's shoulders straightened, and a grin tugged at the corner of her mouth. "I can do that, yes. That's an easy problem to solve." She quickly stood and circled around the table to where Will sat, holding up her hand. "It won't hurt – not physically, at least, though you may be suddenly struck by any emotional issues you weren't able to process yet."

Will took a sharp breath, glancing quickly at Robert. "Sure. Do it. If we wait, who knows if we'll get another chance, and who knows if I'll keep my nerve."

The Gardener nodded and laid her hand against Will's heart. Will closed her eyes, bracing a hand against the table and slowly balling it into a fist as they sat. A minute passed, and then another, and the Gardener finally pulled back with a heavy sigh. "That was some deep damage," she said. "You've lived a hard life."

"That would be an understatement," said Will. "Lost my

father before Gin was born; lost my mother when I was ten. Spent the next eight years on the streets, eventually just gave into the inevitable, disguised myself as a boy, and enlisted in the guards. Even that fell apart a few months ago when…" Her voice caught.

Ginny jumped up from her seat, raced around the table, and threw her arms around her sister. "It's okay," she whispered. "You're not alone anymore."

"No, no, I'm not," said Will, sighing. "And yet I still can't help but wonder how long this really can last."

"As long as Austere wills it," said the Gardener. "There is no guarantee of happiness or prosperity. Life can change in a moment, but He is good, and I know he watches out for you the same as any of us."

Will nodded, relaxing into Ginny's hug. "Even after everything I've done?"

"It's not our own actions that make us valuable in His eyes," said the Gardener. "He loves us for His own sake."

"Well, it's a new start," said Will after a long minute. "Let's hope that I do better with this one than all the others. I mean, the last wasn't too bad, but I think, I think…"

"Your heart was frozen," said Ginny. "I think that kind of got in the way of making the best decisions."

"Yeah, basically," said Will.

"After watching my sister nearly freeze herself to death because her own heart was broken and she didn't want to freeze it, don't feel guilty for your body doing what it was made to do," said the Gardener. "You came here to me, and that's what matters."

"Right," said Will, taking a long, shuddering breath.

"Now, I am a little curious about your missing father, I must confess," the Gardener continued, tilting her head to the side. "Because I surmised that he was from this Forest when your sister was able to call me using a hazel tree – despite having Frost magic, not Sensitive. But now that the two of you are here and looking at your face, I have questions."

Ginny sucked in a breath, straightening.

"Yes," said Emmazel, her voice sharpening. "And why are you wearing my father's knife?"

~

Every eye was fixed on Will. They all knew that Ginny had no answers about her past.

Will's expression hardened, and her hand went to her belt. "Because it was *my* father's knife," she said. "It was the only thing he left me. I mean, there was money for us to live off of, but the knife was the only thing of real value."

Silence followed. Emmazel suddenly stood and stalked away from the table, trembling. The Gardener stood to chase after her, putting a hand on Emmazel's shoulder and giving some silent communication.

"Ginny is nineteen or so – the Bethims don't know her birthday, but she was seven when she came to them, and that was over twelve years ago," the Gardener said, turning back to them. "How old are you?"

"Twenty-two, near as I can figure," Will answered. "It's not exactly easy to keep track of that sort of thing on the streets."

"I can imagine," said the Gardener. "But that does mean that it's possible."

"What's possible?" asked Ginny, pulling away from Will.

"That your father wasn't just any escaped resident of the Forest – no, the amount of Forest magic in both of you is too much for that, and that knife seals it," said the Gardener. "The two of you are Emmazel's half-sisters."

"What?" Will flew to her feet, her hand on her knife hilt. "That – this knife means nothing. Our father was a *thief,* and I'm sure he would have happily stolen it from yours."

Emmazel gave a frustrated sigh. "What was his name? Do you know that much?"

"Jack," said Will, her stance shifting.

"Well, that was his name," said Emmazel. "I named my son after him."

"And he was a Zephyr," said the Gardener. "Will, you are the strongest Frost I've ever met apart from my own sister."

Emmazel turned away again, pacing up and down the length of the room twice before she turned to face them again. "My father … went and married again and didn't tell any of us about it. You didn't know anything, did you, Night?"

"I know that he was increasingly away towards the end," said Night, suddenly in the form of a man to wrap his arms around her. "*And* he was increasingly paranoid and distracted. But I never guessed something like this."

Emmazel sighed before focusing on Ginny and Will with a forced smile. "I'm not upset that the two of you exist. I just … how could he not tell anyone? Ginny was lucky enough for the Bethims to take her in, but you grew up on the streets, Will. And I could have kept you from that! How could he do that? If you had but stepped into the Forest, or come to Hightower…"

"I think he said something about Hightower," Will confessed. "But we were strictly warned to stay away from the Forest."

"Your mother left him a broken man," said Night, pressing a kiss into Emmazel's hair. "And he faded so fast, there at the end. Perhaps he meant to tell you, but his memory failed him."

"So he is dead then? He didn't just abandon our mother?" asked Will.

"Dead and buried some nineteen years ago," said Emmazel. "He … he was far from a perfect man, I know. He kept me in my tower five years longer than he needed to, and it's taken me years to unlearn the fears that he gave me. But … I always thought he tried to do his best."

"I'm sure he did," said Night. "But I know from experience that sometimes even the best-meaning fathers can make terrible mistakes."

"The two of them are here now, and we can move forward and make things better now that we know," said the Gardener. "I know I'm personally excited to welcome two such amazing young women to the family."

"Family," Will repeated, and she sat down hard. "This … this is a lot to take in."

"I'm sure it is, dear," said the Gardener, reaching over to squeeze her shoulder. "Don't believe for a second more that you're alone in the world. You have a large family now and a well-connected one, too. Let's see what my niece and nephew have been caught up in, and then we'll see what we can do for both of you."

Emmazel broke away from her husband to rush over, catch Will in a hug, and then turn to envelop Ginny. "The day I learned that *I* had an older sister was quite a shock – and I remember it well. If either of you is a thing like me, then I know that there may well be an upward journey ahead of us, but I can stand here and say that we can't let the mistakes of the dead define us."

"No," said Will. "No, we can't. And I'd like to think I'm smart enough to know when to not fight."

Emmazel sighed and shook her head. "It's just ... very strange. You're the same age as Hansel and Ela – and scarcely older than my own twins…"

"Don't forget that your twins grew up alongside their own nieces and nephews," said the Gardener. "Our family tree is very complicated. A lot of long lives and second marriages."

"That is true enough," said Night.

24

With that mystery discussed, the more pressing mystery gained priority. Earnest had not yet returned, so the Gardener decided that it was better to let him stay in Ember, and she also sent Hansel and Ela to go stay with their Aunt Mari and Uncle Barend in Farra, much to their protests.

"We don't know what has happened," the Gardener told them, shaking her head. "Hans and Maia have already been targeted, and I can't let the two of you be used against me, either. And, don't worry, Jack and Jana would also be sent away if they weren't already with their sister for the day."

She kissed them both, and then they faded from sight.

"I would send you away as well, Ginny, but your connection to the Forest – while very strong for having stepped foot here for the first time only hours ago – isn't quite enough for me to send you anywhere. So, I'm going to have to ask you to stay here in this cabin, where you should be safe."

"But…" Ginny protested.

"Gin, I know you want to help Kaimund, but how much can you really do?" Will asked, standing to wrap Ginny in a hug. "We knew that the Gardener liked you, so we brought you this far, but if she and Emmazel are scared, then…" She shook her head. "Please stay safe, and Robert and I will save Kaimund for you."

Ginny sighed and squeezed her sister tight.

"Everything is going to be fine, I'm sure," said Robert, giving Ginny one of his best smirks. "We'll all just have a laugh about it later."

"Unless something is very wrong," said Ginny.

The things that Prince Hans had told her while trying to court her that week pricked at her heart. About magic and what might be the opposite of Sensitive magic. She hadn't been able to guess what he'd meant then, and she didn't know now. But if it was connected … should she say something?

But thoughts of that magic completely flew from her head as Will suddenly twisted away, grabbed Robert by the collar, and pressed her lips against his. He tensed, but as she started to pull away, he wrapped his arms around her waist and kissed her back.

"Well," said the Gardener. "She acts fast."

Robert finally let Will pull back and stared down at her with a smirk. "So, that was you resisting my charms?" he asked, reaching up to play with one of her curls.

"That was me trusting you with my heart, the way I should have done years ago," Will whispered, her eyes still closed. "We're a pair of fools, but we work well together, and … I think you look exceptionally handsome in a guard's uniform."

"You know, I've heard that before, about the uniform, that is," Robert answered. "But I've never cared so much about it until now. I would say the same about you, but I think I prefer your current outfit."

Will gave a nervous laugh, steadying herself by resting a hand against his shoulder. "I should have said something sooner … but … I didn't know how … I didn't think that you would ever look my way if you knew. And I still don't…"

Robert stole another kiss. "My dear Mina, I don't think I'll be able to look at another woman the same way again. From the moment I saw you like this, knowing the truth about you, you've quite eclipsed every other woman in my mind."

"That's your sister, all right," Night told Emmazel, wrapping his arm around her waist.

"I have no idea what you're talking about," said Emmazel before she grabbed him by the collar and kissed him. "Just in case you need to be a cat again. I can't leave you without a proper share of magic," she explained, pulling back.

"Good call," said Night before hugging her close.

Will and Robert eventually finished their conversation, and Will turned back to Ginny, beaming. "And that's that. Remember to stay safe, little sister. I'll be back soon, and you'll have a chance to claim your own happily ever after."

Ginny opened her mouth to protest and then just shook her head. Things weren't that simple for her. She knew the way that Kaimund looked at Princess Maia. And she was a nobody…

She was Emmazel's younger sister. Yes, by her father's second marriage, when he was acting as a thief and not … whatever position he'd held in the Forest as the Mistress's consort, but … the connection still stood. And the look in Emmazel's eyes as she'd declared their relationship had been fierce.

"We *will* be back, I'm sure," said Emmazel, moving in to give Ginny her own hug. "Whether or not this is Hans causing trouble, Elin and I are *quite* a team, and he doesn't stand a chance, especially if we have a Frost as good as Will on our side. So, sit tight, maybe send up some prayers if you get scared, and let us handle this, okay?"

Ginny bit her lip and nodded. She knew it was silly to worry. She wouldn't gain a family just to lose it all in one day, right? Even she wasn't that unfortunate.

"I'm sure you would have been an amazing older sister if you'd known," she assured her. "I … I'm glad we finally have answers, even if they're a lot to process."

"You're a stronger young woman than I think you realize," said the Gardener as she moved to take Emmazel's place to hug Ginny. "I'm glad to have you in the family, and you've already done so much for us already."

"I … your nephew was trying to court me a few weeks ago," Ginny said with a sudden thought. "I don't know how serious he was, but he did follow me into the horrid town where Will was living and stayed there for over a week. That might have meant *something*. And if it did, and if he's the one behind this, then maybe I could be helpful. If only as a distraction."

The Gardener tilted her head to the side thoughtfully, then shared a glance with Emmazel. Finally, she shook her head. "I appreciate the offer, really I do, but I do think that this is too dangerous for you. There is already the possibility of hostages involved, and we don't need to have you to protect, too. So just hold tight until all of us return. You're going to be fine, and so will everyone you care about."

"You can't make that promise," said Ginny, shaking her head. "You don't know what has happened, so you can't promise everything will turn out okay. But if you think everything will go better if I stay out of the way, I'll do that. I just … I just think you should know that Prince Hans was talking about the possibility of a fourth type of magic – an opposite to Sensitive magic. I couldn't guess what he meant at the time, but maybe this has something to do with it? I don't know. It feels relevant."

The Gardener gave a solemn nod. "He's mentioned that theory before. I hadn't considered it relevant to the current situation, but if you think it might be, I shall bear it in mind. New magic could well explain the strangeness of this whole situation."

"It's got to be an awful sort of magic," said Ginny, shuddering.

"No magic is evil, in and of itself; it's just the user," said the Gardener. "The Mistress made Sensitive magic into a horror, and both Cinders and Frosts have been feared for good reason. We'll get to the bottom of this. This isn't the first time I've had to fight family, if that's what it comes down to."

She moved on, and then there was Robert, his grin more serious than Ginny had ever seen it. "Hey, kid. Just wanted to make sure you know that I have your sister's back, no matter what. I've always seen you as something of a little sister, and now I guess it's just more official. You know, if you're all right with it."

"I want her to be happy, and I think you make her happy." Ginny gave him an encouraging smile as she glanced toward Will. "She's loved you for a while, and I've known for a while. I told her to tell you much sooner, but she was … scared, and I don't blame her. I'm just glad that it seems to have worked out, despite everything."

"Yeah, despite everything." Robert shook his head. "Your sister is … quite a woman, and I'm a lucky man to have her at my back."

"She's lucky to have you."

"I'm going to leave you my horse, just in case," Robert added. "Everyone else will be walking, so I don't need it. And if you need to make a quick escape … well, I think he'll do you more good than myself; that's the end of it. He'll keep you company, at the very least."

~

And not long after that, Ginny was alone in the clearing as she stood in front of the cabin, with only the horse for company. She swallowed hard, then turned back and headed back into the house.

The fairies were still buzzing about. She'd forgotten about them.

"Bad business, bad business," one was saying. "All of this is bad business."

"The Gardener and Emmazel will take care of all of this," declared another, a male fairy. "Don't be all worrisome. There's nothing they can't do – and it's really just strange that it got this far before they found out about it."

Ginny bit her lip and sat down at the table again.

"Oh! Oh!" cried the first fairy. "You're still here! I didn't think they would leave anyone behind."

Ginny shrugged. "I'm not really a fighter, and they thought I would be a liability. They're … not wrong. They want me to stay behind in this house instead."

"Ah, poor thing," declared a third fairy. "Would you like

some more cake?" She didn't even wait for Ginny to answer, and cut a huge slice from the cake on the counter and flew it over to where Ginny sat. "There you go, dear. The world isn't that bad with cake, now is it?"

Ginny stared at the slice of cake and didn't pick up the fork.

"Oh, come now, they're going to be fine, you know they will be," said the male fairy. "This is the Gardener, after all. And Emmazel."

"I know," said Ginny. "But it's hard to not know what's going on. Especially when we have no idea what they're up against. Will I see any of them again?"

Where would she be if she lost everyone she cared about in one blow. She *could* return to that house and try to make the best of things with Suzy, but the thought of making a life in that city without Will was frightening.

"We should introduce ourselves," said one of the female fairies. "She'll feel better if she knows our names, right?"

"I'm Twig," said the male fairy, zooming around Ginny's head. "This is my wife Poppy and our daughter Lavender. Our family has taken care of this cabin for generations, and my own great-grandparents – Sir and Jenna – helped the Gardener fight the horrid Mistress."

Ginny frowned and nodded slowly. "Okay." Knowing their names didn't help that much, truth told, but it was something.

She should pray. She knew that. Emmazel had practically asked her to do that. She knew that it was far more helpful than sitting there worrying.

"Now the Mistress, she was scary, or so they say," said Poppy. "The whole Forest feared her. Except the Gardener. Nothing scared the Gardener – and when she discovered that the Mistress was torturing the people, she marched right up to the woman and demanded she stop. When the Mistress wouldn't stop, she took the Mistress's power from her, and that was that."

Ginny frowned harder. "I … I lived with the Gardener's niece, Princess Mayblossom. That's not quite the story she told me."

"Well, Princess Mayblossom was a mere child at the time," Twig pointed out. "She can hardly be expected to remember all the details perfectly."

Ginny raised her eyebrows and then – she couldn't help herself – gave a small laugh. The faith of these fairies in their leader was so absolute, it was adorable. The faith she ought to have in Austere. He would see them through to the other side.

But, then, Austere didn't unmake people's bad decisions for them. What if the bad choices that had led to this situation were too much for good decisions to counter, and they all had to live with the consequences?

That thought did compel her to pray. There had to be a way out. Things couldn't be as bad as they seemed. Everything would be all right.

"You've still not even *touched* your cake!" Poppy observed.

Ginny blinked as she opened her eyes and focused on the slice of cake still sitting in front of her. "I'm not hungry," she whispered.

"We know, dear," said Lavender, landing momentarily on Ginny's shoulder to pat her cheek before she was zooming around again. "But it will make you feel better, we promise. No one *wants* to eat when they're upset, but food makes one less upset. So do eat the cake. Or we can get you something else, if you'd like something else. But I don't know why anyone would want something more than cake. Especially this type of cake. Poppy makes the best cinnamon cake there is, and that's that. So do at least try it."

Ginny sighed and took a bite of the cake. It *was* good. Really it was. She took a second bite, and then put down her fork. "I feel a little bit better now," she told the fairies before she stood and began pacing the room. She needed something to do – knitting, sewing, it didn't matter – but any of her projects were miles away, and she didn't know how to begin a new one in this place. Maybe the fairies could give her supplies if she asked, but did she dare ask?

"You're going to be fine. We're all going to be fine," Poppy declared, landing on Ginny's shoulder. "You really need to have faith in the Gardener. She knows what she's doing."

"No, she doesn't, though," said Ginny, shaking her head. "She doesn't know what has happened, so there's no way that she can prepare for all the variables. And if she can't prepare…"

"She'll figure it out," said Poppy. "Her and Emmazel both. They're really smart and very strong."

Ginny sighed, and at that moment, another fairy flew in through the window.

"Rosebud!" cried Twig, flying to meet her. "What brings you away from the village? What happened?"

"There's a man and woman headed this way," cried the new fairy. "And the Gardener sent me to tell the girl in the cabin to go meet them. They can't go very fast, and she has a horse that can help them go faster."

Ginny stood for a moment, blinking, and then she rushed out of the house, jumped onto the back of Robert's horse, and plunged into the Forest, trusting the Gardener to guide her path.

25 It seemed to take forever, and Ginny's heart hammered in her throat the whole way as she urged the horse to go as fast as it would.

Robert had led the horse for her on their way to the Forest, and she'd only ever ridden ponies before, not any creatures as large as this, so directing this horse herself was a bit intimidating. But if the Gardener had requested this from her, she would figure it out.

A man and a woman. Robert and Will? Perhaps Kaimund and … Ginny didn't know who she wished would accompany Kaimund. It was a strange affair all around, and she needed to focus.

Who was she being sent to meet? Was there a problem that necessitated her presence? What problem could *she* possibly help – unless it was the horse that was needed?

Focus, Ginny.

On and on she went, her heart beating faster each moment until she finally saw two figures headed towards her along the path. As she neared them, she recognized them – Kaimund and Princess Maia.

"Oh!" Princess Maia's face lit with relief as she saw Ginny. "Aunt Elin said she would try to have you meet us, and here you are! Kai…" She glanced up at Kaimund and then gave a defeated sigh. "I didn't mean for any of this to happen, really I didn't – but I had no choice. I had to freeze him!"

Ginny swallowed hard as she dismounted. "You … you froze him?"

"I had to!" Princess Maia pulled away from Kaimund, shaking her head. "Because otherwise Hans … Hans…"

Ginny opened her mouth, unsure whether to ask questions, try to reassure the princess, or make accusations. Finally, she shook her head and focused on Kaimund instead. His eyes stared lifelessly, his movements were stiff and jerky, and his skin was a pale shade of blue, covered in a layer of frost.

"I think he's fine; he *needs* to be fine," said Princess Maia, shaking her head. "Oh, if I've killed him, I – I don't know – but I couldn't let Hans hurt him. Not after what he did to Rina and Calla!"

"What happened to Rina and Calla?" Ginny finally asked.

"I don't know; nothing about this makes sense. But … but I think Rina *is* dead." Princess Maia shook her head harder. "Let's get him on that horse and get out of here. I've been able to get him to walk, but it's been like trying to move a glacier. None of this is right…"

Ginny chewed her lip, decided that it wasn't worth it to ask any more questions – not when the princess was so visibly upset – and so she focused instead on trying to get Kaimund to mount the horse.

It wasn't easy. Kaimund was so stiff, and he seemed to have little control over his own body. He was heavier than both Ginny and Princess Maia, and they couldn't lift him. Ultimately, Princess Maia grew a block of ice under his feet to push him up high enough to mount easily. As soon as he was in the saddle, the princess turned to Ginny with a more focused expression.

"Climb onto the horse behind him," she instructed before searching through the saddlebags and finding some rope.

"What?"

"You're a Frost, but you don't create your own ice," Princess Maia explained, almost too quickly. "You just absorb it. If you're in contact with him, you can help pull the ice out of him. We need to get him to a Sensitive or a Cinder – and I don't know which would be better – but it's better to do what we can now. I'll lead the horse after I tie Kaimund to the saddle. You can focus on pulling the ice out of him."

Ginny didn't protest but quickly climbed onto the horse, behind Kaimund, and awkwardly wrapped her arms around him, laying her head between his shoulder blades to achieve as much contact between them as possible.

He was *so* cold. It was frightening. His back, under her cheek, didn't feel like skin, but a block of ice. Even sleeping next to Will when she was at her frostiest wasn't like this.

"And you're not even a strong Frost," said Ginny, shaking her head.

"A little each day builds up," Princess Maia answered, tugging the horse forward at a determined pace. "I met with Aunt Elin and the rest. I escaped on my own – I don't know how, but Hans never was interested in Kaimund or me, just his *sick* experiments. How could that monster be my brother? He's always had his flaws, but *this?*"

"I'm sorry," Ginny whispered.

"Aunt Elin will take care of him. I know she will," Princess Maia continued. "She always takes care of everything. But he's already ruined so much – and he *can't* be king of the North Country after this. He just can't. This is going to change everything. How could my own brother be a monster?"

"Well, my brother turned out to be my sister, and I didn't know that, when I should have," Ginny said, trying to be helpful. "And then I arrived in her new home and discovered that she had resorted to thievery, and I hadn't thought her capable of that."

"Will grew up on the streets," Princess Maia countered.

"And your brother grew up as a spoiled prince," said Ginny. "I think … I think any way a person grows up, none of it is a promise that they'll turn out right. It depends on what sort of person *they* are, too. And if your brother was hiding some strange, unknown magic … he said something about an unknown magic to me, an opposite to Sensitive magic, and so I can only assume it's relevant now…" She trailed off with a shaky sigh.

"None of this feels real," said the Princess. "I feel like I'm in the middle of a nightmare that I just can't seem to wake out of. How could this happen?"

Ginny sighed. Was Kaimund feeling less cold? Ginny was feeling very cold now, herself. But she was *meant* to be cold, and he wasn't. She could hear his heartbeat from where her ear rested against his back, and it was so painfully slow.

"The Forest is so uneasy," said Princess Maia, after a short while. "I've known it to be upset before, but this? Oh, Hans, what have you *done?*"

Ginny didn't know what else to say. The princess had been traumatized by her brother's actions, clearly, and what could be done?

"Aunt Elin will take care of him," Princess Maia assured herself. "She'll stop this madness, and then she'll break the terrible news to father – she's always been so good with bad news – and Mayblossom will be the heir instead. This really won't change much of anything for me, will it? Except Hans will be gone. Mayblossom has often joked that she resents Hans for taking the crown, by the mere virtue of being a son – and I know she'll make a good queen. If she has to be. But that will take her away from Snowfield Palace, after all…"

"We'll figure out what will happen next as it comes," said Ginny. "We don't have to have all of the answers just now. We need to focus on getting Kaimund to safety, right?"

Why hadn't they reached the cabin, yet? Surely that was where they were headed?

"Right, of course, naturally," said Princess Maia, swallowing hard. "But I just don't know how my brother could do … what he did."

"I don't know either," said Ginny. "But … he made his choices. You made yours. That's all we can do."

"I don't like the choices I made, the choices he made me make." Princess Maia gave a shudder.

~

On they walked, and Ginny slowly came to the conclusion that they weren't headed to the cabin at all – though she hadn't a clue where else they might be going. The princess kept repeating herself, rarely giving new information, but seeming to need to process everything that had happened. Kaimund remained silent and frozen. Would he ever recover?

How could Princess Maia have used her ice magic like this? It was everything that Frosts were trying to prove they weren't! Hans had threatened her into it, and she'd seen it as the only way to spare Kaimund's life.

Hans had the strange magic that he had theorized about. It seemed that it was less theory than he had claimed. Ginny couldn't make sense of it all.

Run. Escape. Out.

The words echoed through the Forest with sudden force, a booming whisper that sounded like the Gardener and Emmazel and yet neither of them, all at once. The world suddenly bent, and glancing behind her, Ginny saw the trees closing in.

Princess Maia glanced behind them, too, and gave a strangled scream before breaking into a run, urging the horse to go faster. It complied, ears laid back, quickly going faster than Princess Maia could go on foot. It broke away from her hold and sped on, faster and faster.

"It's – it's fine!" Princess Maia shouted after them, "I'll keep on as best I can. Just get him to safety! He'll follow the path, and you'll be fine as long as you're on the path!"

Ginny couldn't move. She was stuck on the back of the horse, her arms around Kaimund. She could only stare back at the Princess until the Forest suddenly closed between them.

Run.

What had happened? Oh, *what* had happened? None of this was right. Were the Gardener and Emmazel all right? Were Will and Robert? Why were they running? Something must have gone wrong – but what?

She had Kaimund, at least, even if he was frozen solid. Ginny squeezed her eyes shut and held tighter to him. There was no way for her to direct the horse, so she had to trust the Forest and Austere. If she'd been forced to choose one person to save in this horrible situation…

She had to be honest with herself. That was a choice that she could have never made. But Kaimund had been the one constant in her life. If she was to lose everyone else, at least she…

She couldn't even finish that thought. Losing even one person that she loved was terrible. How could the world be so broken and twisted? Why did they have to flee the Forest? Did it mean that the Gardener and Emmazel had failed? That they had been hurt? Ginny caught glimpses of Forest Spirits in the trees staring at her mournfully, but none said a word, only closing the tree branches around her, preventing the horse from straying.

Her own heart raced while Kaimund's remained a steady far-too-slow rhythm. At least it was a constant. At least she could hear it. At least it was something.

She was grateful that Princess Maia had had the foresight to tie Kaimund to the horse. She was pretty sure that it was the only reason that they hadn't fallen off already.

Ginny closed her eyes again. On and on they went. There was nothing she could do but pray. So pray she did.

She prayed for Emmazel and the Gardener. She prayed for Will and Robert, that they would actually get the life together they deserved and that their story wouldn't end in tragedy. She prayed for Rina and Calla, though hadn't Princess Maia said that Rina was dead? She still prayed for them both, because she didn't know, and maybe there was hope. She prayed that she and Kaimund would escape, as the Forest wanted them to, and Princess Maia would *somehow* escape, too, despite having fallen behind.

But, most of all, she prayed that Kaimund would be able to survive the ice that had overtaken him because she didn't know how she would live without him. Even if she had to leave him again, even if she gave him up to Princess Maia, she just needed to know that the world still had him in it.

How much ice had she absorbed from his body, and he *still* was unresponsive?

And then the world shifted, and she opened her eyes to see the bright sun above, for they had emerged from the Forest. But her breath of relief couldn't come yet, for she was still on the back of a speeding horse, clinging to a frozen Kaimund.

But at least they had both made it out alive.

What had happened?

26 "Woah! Woah! Woah there! Sir? Miss? Is everything all right?"

Ginny pried her eyes open as she realized the world had stopped moving, and she stared, blinking down at the golden-haired young woman who now held the horse's reins. She blinked harder as a young man stepped up behind the young woman, looking entirely too much like—

"Will?"

The young man blinked and tilted his head to the side. "I think you might be a bit disoriented after your ordeal – but no worries, you're quite safe now, so catch your breath, take your time. People are pouring out of the Forest all along its border. No one quite knows what happened, but … it's clearly something terrible. I'm Jack, this is my sister Jana, and just know that you're safe. Your young man here doesn't seem to be in good shape. Did he run afoul of a Frost?"

Ginny hugged Kaimund tighter and focused on breathing, and she tried to relax herself. "Princess Maia had to, she said. She didn't want to."

"Maia did this to him?" Jack gave a low whistle. "Didn't know she had that in her. She's not the strongest Frost, after all."

"I've been trying to pull it out of him, but I don't … I don't think I've made much of a difference."

"Let's get him down from that horse, and I'll see what I can do for him," said Jana, smiling. "I'm not quite Cousin Elin, but I'll try."

Jack helped a still unresponsive Kaimund down from the horse with a strong gust of wind – he was a Zephyr, *of course* – and laid him out on the ground, and Jana laid her hands against his heart, closing her eyes in concentration. Ginny slid off of the horse, stood for a moment on wobbly legs, and then sat down heavily.

"Jack and Jana – you're Emmazel's twins, aren't you?" she realized.

Jana glanced up with a weak smile, while Jack answered.

"We are, and you're observant. Who might you and your young friend be?"

"That's Kaimund. Princess Mayblossom's nephew." Jack and Jana should know who he was with that explanation. "I'm Ginny. I … I think I'm your aunt."

"*What?*"

Ginny bit her lip, wondering if she should have admitted the relationship, but in light of everything … she needed to be connected to someone, and they might need the same.

"I just found out myself." She gave a slight shrug. "You don't have to believe me – I know it's a lot to accept, and I have no business claiming such a relation. But it's apparently true? I'm your mother's half-sister, and she didn't even know that her father had remarried until today."

Jack opened and shut his mouth before shaking his head. "Well, I don't have any protests, so I'm not going to say anything about it. I think there are more pressing issues. Like what happened. Jana and I were staying with Heather today so our mother could focus on governing the Forest – which is normal enough. But we needed to ask her a question a few hours ago, and when we tried to contact her via the hazel tree, there was no response. Which is less normal, but we still didn't panic until there was no response from her after several more tries over the next hour. So we started towards the Forest to see what had happened for ourselves, and were met by a mass exodus halfway."

Ginny took a shaky breath and pulled her knees up to her chest. "I think Princess Maia knows better than anyone what happened, but she fell behind, and I don't know if she'll be able to escape, herself. I know what she told me. And I know what your parents and the Gardener knew when they left to confront Prince Hans. I don't know what happened after that, though. None of this makes sense, and it's all wrong."

"Hans is behind this, then?" asked Jack, his frown growing.

"I never liked Hans," said Jana. "He always made me feel a bit sick. Physically sick, like my magic was dying when around him. I never said anything about it because he's Elin's nephew, and Elin loves her brother's children like her own. But I never thought he would cause anything like this…"

"I think … I think when one tries their very best to always make good choices, it makes it hard for them to accept when someone else tries the very opposite," said Ginny. She pressed her cheek against her knees.

"True enough," said Jana, and she removed her hand from his heart with a shake of her head. "That's as much as I dare give him. He's stable, and he'll survive the thaw. And I don't know what else will be asked of me. Even if this man is *nearly* family, I can't use all of myself up on him. Heather might have some potions that will help. Oh, but nothing is going right today, and if Kai here just survives, then that will be *one* good thing out of everything, you know."

"Thank you," Ginny whispered – and she couldn't help herself. She uncurled and hurried to Kaimund's side to take his hand now that Jana had stepped away. He was warmer now – but she could only tell it because she herself was so cold.

"So, you're our aunt, you said?" Jack prompted.

Ginny shrugged. "I think … I think it would be easier to explain if Will were here – you look so much like my sister. My sister being Will, the one I always knew was my sister. Except when I thought she was my brother." She frowned and rubbed her temple. "I don't mean for it to sound complicated, but …

it is. I know I look like my mother – which is why Lady Bethim took me in when I was seven, so I'm not sorry for that."

"I'm not disbelieving you," said Jack, a grin lifting the corner of his mouth. "I'm glad to count you as a part of the family if it comes down to that, and we aren't strangers to foundlings and secrets and stuff like that. I do find *that* particular relationship strange – but you look like the honest sort, and your shock at recognizing me was too pure for you to be making it up.

Ginny shook her head. "I feel like I'm making it up. It's been a lot to take in today.

"I don't doubt it," said Jack, and he directed some winds to lift Kaimund from the ground. "Now, why don't we get him to a more comfortable position and let's listen to your convoluted story? Jana?"

"I'm going to try to keep probing the Forest and see if I can get any answers from it," said Jana with a weak smile. "I know it's pushing everyone away, but surely there's *something* I can do!"

"Jan…" Jack frowned in concern.

"I'm the strongest Sensitive on this side of the Forest," said Jana, raising her chin. "And even if I can't get in contact with Mother and Elin, I need to try to contact Ela. You might know nothing about it, Jack, but Mother and Elinrose put in place multiple contingencies in case of emergencies. If they're sealing the Forest, then something has gone very wrong, and Ela's supposed to be on the other side. We're supposed to make contact as soon as possible, through the trees, and prevent the world from completely falling apart." Her shoulders fell, and she shook her head. "We've practiced this, but it's never been with a *truly* sealed Forest."

And with that, she turned and sauntered away.

"I'm going to follow her and … provide moral support. See who else I can help," said Jack, standing. "Take care of your young man, Aunt Ginny. He's looking better."

Ginny frowned as she was left alone, and she tightened her hold of Kaimund's hand, absentmindedly seeking his pulse.

Was his heartbeat quicker now? She wasn't sure.

Please, Austere. Please let him wake up…

"Ginny? Is that you? Oh, Ginny, you made it out of the Forest, with Kaimund, too! Thank Austere!"

She looked up to see Princess Maia rushing towards her, disheveled and out of breath.

"I made it out too, yes," she continued, throwing herself onto the grass beside Ginny. "My path converged with Lilly's and her family. I didn't have time to explain anything to them, but we're here now, and we found Jack and Jana – they found you, didn't they? Oh, but it looks like Jana already tried to help Kaimund, and he looks better! Oh, but she's a sight, and I can bearly look at either of them. Hans has ruined everything!"

Ginny swallowed. "Do … do you think the Gardener and Emmazel are all right? The look on Jana's face … she knows something. She said that what happened was part of protocols that they and Ela have practiced?"

"I don't know anything," said Princess Maia, her smile fading. "I've … I've always tried to ignore politics as best as I could, and now … now…"

Ginny wanted to reassure her friend, tell her that none of this was her fault … but the words stuck in her throat. All she could think now was that Kaimund was still unresponsive because of Princess Maia's ice.

"I don't think I can look at him, either," said Princess Maia, after a moment more, as she stood and shook her head. "Everything else, I can blame on Hans, but Kaimund is on my conscience and … and … and he trusted me. He trusted me, and I hurt him, and I…"

She fled without another word.

⁓

The world was undeniably broken. No one could enter the Forest, and anyone within it had been expelled, on one side or the other. Jana did establish communication with Ela, late that evening, and she confirmed that there was an exodus on her side as well.

At some point the next morning, Ela reported that Will and Robert had emerged on her side with Calla, and then Night was found a few hours later. There was no sign of either the Gardener, Emmazel, or Prince Hans. Will and Robert's report was incoherent, while Night said that all three still lived but were locked in a power struggle. Calla, it seemed, had no memories at all, and was no help to making sense of the situation.

Time would tell who would win, but the Forest was unsafe until Emmazel and the Gardener won.

"We don't know why Mother and Elin sent your sisters and my father to Ela's side," Jana said, shaking her head. "But it was chaotic, and they were directing a lot of escapes while locked in battle. I'm sorry."

"I'm sorry for you, too," said Ginny with a small smile. "You just lost your parents."

"I still have both my sisters and my brother," said Jana, shrugging. "You just lost the only family you had. I'm more worried about my father than myself. He … went through a lot before he married our mother; he didn't get to raise Lilly and was barely in Heather's life. Being separated from all of us is going to be hard for him."

"Hopefully, your mother and the Gardener will win soon," said Ginny.

But Jana just shook her head. "They've gone quiet. The whole battle. I don't think they're dead – I still feel their magic threaded through the Forest, but I don't hear *them* at all. I think they're trapped in some form of stalemate, and that scares me. There's no telling how long it will last, or if they can even break it on their own."

Ginny sighed.

"Ela and I will keep talking as best we can. Her Uncle Barend will make sure that they have a home on the edge of the Forest, and Jack and I will establish something here with Lilly. I don't know what good this will do, but it will prevent the complete cutoff that existed under my grandmother's reign, especially on this side."

"And the pass between the North Country and Snowfield Palace should be nearly finished," said Ginny. "The Forest will still cut us off from Binfield, Ember, and Farra, but Howsill and North will at least have each other, this time. The North princesses *will* be able to go home."

"Elin wanted that pass so badly for a reason," said Jana. "It's just terrible that it's already necessary, and not still the far-off maybe someday. Speaking of Snowfield, I think you need to return there with Kaimund. I've done what I can for him, and I know you have too, but he needs a Cinder's heat, so he might as well go home where Giana can take care of him."

Ginny nodded. "But you do think he'll recover?"

"Once he gets some heat in him, yes," said Jana, nodding. "Now, Maia will accompany you, of course, and be gentle with her. I've gotten as much of the story out of her as I think she's able to tell, so try to not push her for anything more. Her brother betrayed everything our family stands for and made her do things against a Frost's code, and it's left her a broken shadow of herself. I hope she finds peace again, but it may be a while." She shook her head. "I don't think she'll ever be the same."

"Good. As long as … as long as someone knows what happened." Ginny sighed, wondering if she dared ask for details or if that was something better left to people who could do things about it.

"Jack and I do plan to visit Snowfield before the pass is built to appraise Mayblossom of the situation. And to make sure we stay in contact with you. You're family, and I think we're the only family you now have on this side of the Forest." Jana reached for Ginny's hand and squeezed it. "If you don't want to stay with the Bethims or can't, you can come to stay with us."

"Thank you."

"Stay safe, Ginny. Take care of them."

A carriage was found, and the three of them were put inside it. Kaimund lay unconscious on the floor, and then Ginny and Princess Maia sat on either side, knees pulled up to their chests.

"I keep wondering if he would have done this if you had just allowed him to court you," said the princess after a long silence. "I don't blame you for rejecting him – not knowing his reputation, and especially knowing what he's done – but … he was better, while trying to earn your love. He really was. I never saw him serious about a girl – never saw him give a woman a second thought once she left his presence – but he chased you."

Ginny took a long, slow breath. "I never would have been enough for him. I know you want Prince Hans to have had a chance, because he's your brother, but I only interested him because I rejected him. He'd never *had* to pursue a woman before, and he would have lost interest as soon as I returned his affection."

"Perhaps so." Princess Maia sighed heavily and laid her head against her knees again. "I still can't help but wonder."

"Kaimund will be all right just as soon as we get him to Princess Giana," said Ginny. "And whatever part you played in this, it was against your will, wasn't it? And Emmazel and the Gardener will win in the end. They have to."

"I pray they will," said Princess Maia.

More silence reigned, and Princess Maia finally shook her head. "I wish more than anything that I'd seen through him years ago. But admitting that something was wrong with him felt like it would be admitting that something was wrong with my parents and how they raised him. And I didn't want to think badly of them. But this magic he has? It's terrible, and I couldn't do anything about it."

"No, you couldn't," said Ginny.

"He made me an accomplice against my will!"

"You're free now," said Ginny, giving Princess Maia the best smile she could, even if she didn't feel it. "And at least he never had a chance to be king. We can be thankful for that."

"I suppose we can," said Princess Maia. "It feels like an awful thing to be thankful for, though. He's my brother, after all."

"I'm sorry."

"But did I hear right?" Princess Maia sat up straight with a more cheerful voice. "About you and Will? That you're actually Aunt Emmazel's half-sisters? Oh, but you *can't* think of yourself as a nobody now, can you? Not if you're part of our family."

Ginny chewed her lip. "I'm her half-sister, but our father was … hardly the important parent—"

"Your father was the only parent Aunt Emmazel knew," Princess Maia countered. "Look, I know it's a mess, but *he's* the important parent if you ask me, and we don't count by halves in our family. Stop deprecating yourself, Ginny, and realize that you *do* belong in this world. At the end of the day, we're all equal in the eyes of Austere, and you are no less worthy of … of *anything* than I am."

Ginny laid her head against her knees and squeezed her eyes shut. "But…"

"But *nothing*. You love Kaimund. That's obvious to anyone with a pair of eyes in their head. He's been courting me, and I know you're willing to step aside for me, but … he deserves to be loved the way you love him, because he is a good man, even if he's not the man for me."

"Kaimund will only ever see me as a little sister."

"*Right now*, he only sees you as invisible," Princess Maia countered. "And it's devastated him to lose you. I think he just needs to know that you're there and that he *can* look your way. I think once he does, he won't be able to look away."

Ginny didn't answer but stared frowning down at Kaimund, still unconscious, and prayed that he would wake. The whole conversation was pointless if he didn't.

27

The news hadn't traveled ahead of them, and it threw all of Snowfield Palace into an uproar when the carriage rolled up the drive, and the unconscious Kaimund was carried up to his room.

Ginny and Princess Maia hung back to be pelted with questions, and neither was entirely in the spirit to give answers.

But it was necessary to answer, and so, between the two of them, they did as best they could.

"Kaimund wasn't supposed to be involved," Princess Maia declared. "He was in the garden when we snuck into it, to use the hazel tree. He tried to stop us, and Hans said that either I had to subdue him or he would do it himself. I'd already seen what he'd done to Rina and Calla, so…" She shook her head.

"And why were Rina and Calla involved?" Lord Bethim demanded.

"Because they were easy targets," said the princess. "Rina was unhappy in her marriage, and Calla was unhappy with her singledom. In their unhappiness, they were vulnerable, and Hans played them against each other like it was an art." She shook her head. "They were lost before I realized what had happened, and then…"

"Rina? Unhappy!" Lady Nora scoffed. "That girl should have been grateful for the husband she had! I worked hard to secure that match."

Ginny sighed.

"It takes more than good connections to make a happy marriage," said Princess Maia, shaking her head. "And my brother has left many a broken heart in his wake. It's just never been that bad. And now she's gone, her years all stolen in a moment."

"Terrible, terrible," said Princess Giana, shaking her head. "Poor Mayblossom – so close to her time, and to lose the support of her favorite aunt in this circumstance. Someone needs to tell her what has happened, and I fear such a shock won't be good for her. But it can't be avoided. She knows something has happened. We can't use the hazel tree to reach the Forest."

"Poor Rina, poor Rina," Lady Nora was muttering as she paced up and down the room. "She was so well settled, only to throw it all away, and now! Oh, poor Rina."

"Poor Calla, too," Ginny whispered, though no one noted her. At least Calla lived, even if … well, Princess Maia had yet to say exactly what had happened to the younger Bethim sister, only that it was unnatural. Ela's report had only said that she lacked all memories – not just of the last few weeks, but of her whole life – and that Will and Robert would be taking care of her.

"I should go see how Yarro is doing with those cuffs for Kaimund and if he's ready for me to add my fire to them," said Princess Giana, standing suddenly. "And then I think I'll go check on Mayblossom and see if I can gently break the news to her. The poor girl. Elinrose was like a mother to her, and with Hans' betrayal, too!"

She shook her head as she left the room. Ginny quickly jumped up and followed her. She didn't think that she could do anything to help, but … she needed to see how Kaimund was doing. And if she escaped, it meant that she didn't have to answer any more questions.

Princess Giana cast a smile over her shoulder as she noticed Ginny. "Worried about him, are you? Of course you are. Come along. I could tell you hated letting him out of your sight, so let's see how he's doing."

Ginny gave a small nod.

"I also hear that we need to welcome you to the family," Princess Giana continued. "Emmazel's half-sister. That makes you my sister-in-law's cousin. Also my older half-brother's, but he…" She shook her head. "So, I'm happy to call you a cousin myself, if you'll let me. Family is the more the merrier, if you ask me, and you seem to come from the good part of the family."

"Oh," Ginny whispered. "I … if you want to, I don't think I can stop you. Thank you?"

Princess Giana laughed. "The timid part, to be certain! Ah, I'll have to cure you of it, but then again, it's part of your charm. And here we are."

Ginny sucked in a sharp breath as they stepped into Kaimund's bedroom. She'd never been in his room before. It was … a nice room.

Since he was unconscious, it wasn't inappropriate for her to be here, right? She was just here to make sure that he was all right.

Lord Yarro stood at his bedside, fiddling with Kaimund's wrist, and he looked up with a smile as they entered. "These are just about ready for you, dear," he said. "This should get some warmth into him."

"Should … should I continue trying to draw the cold *out* of him?" Ginny asked, wrapping her arms around herself.

Lord Yarro gave her a raised eyebrow. "That would be a good idea. These cuffs are made the same way as the shoes that Frosts and Cinders wear to keep their powers under control, but they are generally expelling heat or cold, forcing it into the glass. If you can help cycle the cold out of him, that would help."

Ginny nodded as Princess Giana stepped forward and wrapped her hand around first one glass cuff and then the other. They heated, and then she stepped back.

"Now I must break the news to Mayblossom – it would be

best if it came from Maia, I know, but I don't think she's in a state to deliver it. I'll come back and heat these again if I need to, but that's hopefully enough," the princess said, stepping back, and then she nodded at Ginny. "I'll leave him in your capable hands. I don't think he can be in better."

"No, I don't think he can," said Lord Yarro. He took Princess Giana's hand and led her out of the room, leaving Ginny quite alone. Well, not completely alone. Kaimund was there, in the bed. Asleep. Still a little frozen.

Sighing, she sat down at his bedside and took his hand, taking a sharp gasp as she felt the ice being forced into her.

"Oh, please wake up soon," she whispered. "You … your father needs you. I know everything has gone wrong now, and I can't imagine how you will feel when you wake up and find out what happened to your sisters and … everything. The Forest is … how could Prince Hans do what he did?"

Ginny frowned, raising Kaimund's hand to press it to her cheek. Lady Nora would be horrified if she walked in and found them like this, but if it meant he would wake up, then it would all be worth it.

"Everything has changed, Kai, and there's no way to go back."

And, admitting that, the numbness of her heart broke, and tears sprung to her eyes, freezing on her cheeks. She didn't stop them, though she tried to wipe them away with her free hand. They just kept coming as she cried for everything and everyone who Prince Hans had hurt or destroyed in this madness.

"Is that you, Ginny?"

She nearly choked on her tears at Kaimund's voice.

"Or am I dreaming again, and you're still far away, hiding from me?" His voice was a soft whisper. "This feels like a dream. I feel like I've been in a nightmare I couldn't escape. A cold, dark nightmare."

"I'm here," she whispered, tightening her hold of his hand. "But this last week *has* been a nightmare, especially for you."

"It's not a nightmare anymore if you're here." Kaimund let out a puffing breath of a laugh. "Promise me you won't run away again, Ginny. I don't think I could take it if you do."

Ginny swallowed. "I … I don't have any plans of leaving, not right now. Not after everything that happened. Though … I need to make sure the girls are all right since Will is trapped on the other side of the Forest, I'm all they have now."

"You're a good girl, Ginny." Kaimund gave a sigh. "Why am I so cold?"

"Because you've had a whole bunch of ice in you," Ginny answered. "To tell the truth, we weren't sure if you would recover, but if you're awake now, I think that's good. You're talking."

"Ice…" Kaimund repeated, and his hand tightened around hers as he shifted uncomfortably. "Maia … she … she used her ice on me, didn't she? How could she do that? Frosts don't use their ice on people unless in self-defense."

"She didn't want to." Ginny shook her head. "I'm so sorry, Kai. But, at least, I think she did it to protect you? A lot has happened, and I think we should wait for you to recover a bit more before we tell you everything. It's bad, I won't lie, but please don't let your imagination run ahead of you with worry. There's nothing else that can be done to fix things, not that either of us can do. Just, please focus on getting better."

"Anything you say, Ginny," said Kaimund with a contented sigh. "I've been so lost without you. Do you know that?"

Ginny released a relieved breath of her own. "Just, please get better."

~

Princess Giana had been right to worry about Princess Mayblossom. For no sooner did she learn the fate of her aunt, than the shock sent her into labor, but, thanks be to Austere, she delivered a healthy baby boy twelve hours later. Ginny finally pried herself away from Kaimund's bedside to visit his aunt.

"I survived," Princess Mayblossom announced as Ginny stepped into the room. "Now, this doesn't mean I won't be taken by a wasting disease in the next few days, but I've made it this far.”

“Jana sent potions that will help you recover,” said Ginny. “Said that since the baby could come any day now, you needed them, just in case. There’s more to help your anxiety, too.”

“Good girl, Jana,” said Princess Mayblossom. “Poor thing. Losing her mother like that. How could Hans do that to all of us?”

Ginny sighed and shrugged. “To be fair, I suspect that it wasn’t personal. I think … I think he just wanted to prove that he could. I think it was all a quest for power.”

“Perhaps,” said Princess Mayblossom. “I won’t argue. Hans always struggled with compassion and empathy. Father thought that he would grow out of it, and Mama Faia … she’s going to blame herself for it, isn’t she? She’s going to think that her frozen heart made Hans the way he is.”

“Is it?” Ginny took another step forward, hugging her arms around herself.

“I doubt it,” said Princess Mayblossom. “Magic doesn’t make people bad. Aunt Elin cured Mama Faia’s broken heart, and Hans was just … broken. Maybe there’s a connection, but it’s not her fault. It’s not Father’s fault. It’s … Hans.”

“There’s nothing we can do now,” said Ginny.

“Nothing except rebuild as best we can,” said Princess Mayblossom. “The pass to the North Country is nearly finished. As soon as I’ve recovered and we can leave, Maia and I will. Unless I die, of course.”

“You’re not going to die.”

“So they tell me.” Princess Mayblossom gave a small laugh. “And I suppose I need to recover. If Hans has … if he’s gone, I’ll be the crown princess again, and Father will need me at his side. And then this little man will one day be king. Oh, but if you would have told me this is where I would be now, just a year ago! I never would have believed you.”

“I … I concur with that,” said Ginny.

“Do you want to hold him?” Princess Mayblossom asked, lifting the baby up to offer him to Ginny. “And don’t worry about your cold – he’ll get enough of that from his aunt and grandmother, and he'll just need to get used to it. I'll wrap him in an extra blanket, though."

"I think you're going to make a wonderful queen and an amazing mother," said Ginny, as she accepted the bundle, frowning down at the squishy little face. "I … I don't think Hans would have ever been good for the North Country. It needs you."

"Ah, but no one ever wants to hear that their baby brother did the sort of things that Hans did." Princess Mayblossom sighed and shook her head. "And poor Maia – having to witness it! She looked up to him, you know, even despite his flaws. I don't know if she'll ever recover from what happened this last week."

"We can pray to Austere that she will," said Ginny, handing the baby back to the princess. "We all can. And at least things won't entirely go back to how they were under the Mistress's reign. We have the pass to the North Country, and Ela and Jana will keep up communication between both sides of the Forest."

"Yes," said Princess Mayblossom. "Aunt Elin made sure that the problems of the past wouldn't be repeated – and it's just like her to do that. Now, keep that chin up – Snowfield Palace will need your steadying presence in the days to come. No running away this time, no matter how you want to do it. You have Maia and me until the pass is finished, though I don't know what Giana and Yarro will choose to do once they're done. I doubt they've let themselves think about it, yet. So many people have lost their homes, or have been trapped on the wrong side, haven't they?"

"I'm going to let you rest," said Ginny, giving Princess Mayblossom a small smile. "Take care of yourself, and don't think about dying. We've … we've lost enough already."

28 Lady Nora took the loss of her nephew and favored nieces hard, and she melted into a mere shadow of herself. She blamed herself for Rina's death and the accusations that Lord Reynard threw at the Bethims, and her sharp eye and voice were gone. Two weeks later, when the pass was ready, and the North Princesses returned home with Lord Graham, she also left, going to stay with her own family. Lady Bethim's nerves had been completely destroyed by the loss of her daughters, leaving Ginny to step into the role of the mistress of the household. The shift was so natural no one even thought of it. The housekeeper came to Ginny to make decisions, and she made them.

Lord Bethim had even allowed her to send for any of the girls who remained in Will's house, to give them a better home, and Kaimund went himself to fetch them. Half of the girls were gone when he arrived, but he brought those who remained back to Snowfield Palace, where employment and education was provided for them. The boys happily apprenticed themselves as stablehands, and Suzy soon took Ginny's place as Lady Bethim's favored companion.

In the wake of everything that had happened, Ginny could honestly say that their new life was good. If only…

"You can't imagine how good it is to be able to see you

again, Ginny-dear."

Ginny gave a sharp gasp and spun around from the flowers she was arranging to see Kaimund standing in the doorway with a small cake in his hand.

"I—" She swallowed, frowning. "What is that?"

"A birthday cake," he said, glancing down at it. "I know you don't know your own birthday, but I asked Will if she remembered it, when she was here, back when we thought she was your brother. It's today, so I thought you deserved to have it celebrated properly for once in your life. And twenty is a pretty important birthday – you've made it through two whole decades."

A smile flickered on and off of Ginny's face as she stared at him, her heart speeding. "Oh. Thank you."

"I know you don't like being the center of attention," he continued, setting the cake down on the table. "So I'm not making a fuss of it, but I still want you to know that you're remembered." He gave a slow sigh and placed a hand against her cheek, grinning down at her. "You're a vital part of life here in Snowfield Palace, and I'm so happy that you've recognized it."

Ginny's smile continued to falter as she stared up into Kaimund's broken gray eyes. There seemed to be no cure for the magic he'd absorbed from the mirror, but he was slowly adjusting to how he now saw the world. And at some point, since she had discovered the truth about her father and had fallen into her new role in Snowfield, her view of herself had shifted, and she was no longer invisible.

"Poor Maia, though," he said as he stepped away from her and pulled out a chair for her at the table. "Knowing that it was Hans who made her do what she did, I don't hold anything against her … but she sees herself as a monster now, and … and I just pray that she'll one day find healing again."

Ginny swallowed. "I think she did care for you, in her way. I know … I know she pushed you away, but I think, in time, if her brother hadn't come between the two of you, and perhaps if you weren't her sister's nephew and so far away from the rest of her family…"

"I kept telling myself that, too," he said, shaking his head. "But you know, now that she's gone, I just can't find it in me to … *care* isn't the right word. Because I do care. She left with a heart filled with guilt, and her brother betrayed her. Who wouldn't care if a friend leaves like that?"

"They would have to be as heartless as her brother, I suppose," said Ginny, shrugging.

"They would," Kaimund agreed.

"What kind of cake is that?" Ginny asked, not sure if she liked that the conversation had drifted to Princess Maia. He might be calling her only a friend now, and she might agree that the princess deserved all the sympathy they could give her, but it still hurt to discuss her with Kaimund.

"Um … I'm not sure, actually," said Kaimund, tilting his head to the side as he stared at it. "I just told the cook that I needed a cake for you, and this is what she gave me. Let's cut it open and see, yes?"

Ginny nodded and took the serving knife to slice into the cake. A sharp scent of peaches wafted out of it – it was still warm. She gave half to Kaimund and kept the other for herself

He smiled as he took his, but his expression turned thoughtful as they ate in silence. It was a good cake, probably one that had been meant for dessert that night, but it was a bit more special to eat it now, alone with him.

"She's gone, and I don't think either of us will be able to look at each other again the same way," Kaimund continued, putting down his fork about halfway through. "And with my sisters gone, my father has been making stronger and stronger hints for me to marry. I don't know how to start, and after my failure with Maia, I don't know – is something wrong with me? Even as the heir of Snowfield Palace, I've never had any form of success…"

Ginny gave a strangled squeak, her bite of cake suddenly turning dry and tasteless in her mouth.

"So, tell me, Ginny – you're a young woman. What am I doing wrong? What do I need to change to attract a wife?"

She swallowed and set down her fork, looking away from him. "Oh, Kaimund…"

"Come now, Ginny. Am I that hopeless? Surely there must be something that I can do or change…"

"I … I don't know … I…" Ginny pressed the heel of her hand to her forehead in distress. "I don't think I'm the best person for you to ask. I don't know…"

"Ginny, you're fading again," said Kaimund, taking her hand suddenly. "And don't tell me that you can't help me – I know you see me as an older brother, but you're still a woman, and you can tell me how women think, and there's no one I trust more than I trust you…" He squeezed her hand. "I'm sorry. If it distresses you too much to think about me like this, I'm sorry. I'll … I should…"

She squeezed her eyes shut, the word "brother" tearing through her painfully. How could he think that she only saw him as a brother … how could he think otherwise?

"I don't think you need to change anything at all," she finally said. "I think you're perfect, just the way you are."

He gave a low chuckle as he relaxed. "Ah, Ginny, you would think that, wouldn't you? Alas, but I'm as imperfect and flawed as any man."

"I know…" It was hard to think with her hand in his. "You're leagues better than Hans, I know that."

"Oh, but it's hardly fair to compare me to him, now is it?" said Kaimund. "We both know I would never stoop to his level. Even if I had the same twisted magic as he does."

"But he was charming enough that every young woman practically fell over him! Your own sisters *fought* over him." she countered. "What I mean is, it's hard to know a man's true value based only on the facade he gives the world. I think you would … I think whatever young woman you marry will be lucky to have you exactly as you are, just maybe not Princess Maia."

Kaimund swallowed, nodding slowly. "If you think so, Ginny. But it doesn't help me find a wife fast enough to please my father. You would think he would be more cautious about marriage after what happened to Rina, but here we are. Then, again, I think he's feeling uncertain about his legacy."

Ginny nodded. "Don't … don't change yourself. If a girl doesn't love you exactly the way you are, then you're not going to be happy."

"Wise words," said Kaimund. "I knew I came to you for advice for a reason. Still…"

"Kaimund, I have been in love with you since I was nine years old," she blurted out. "*Any* young woman would be lucky to have you as her husband. You just have to find the young woman able to see that!"

She pulled back, going cold as she realized what she had just said, but Kaimund *still* had hold of her hand, and his grip only tightened as he stared at her. "You…" He pulled the word out as far as it would go. "Oh. I see. *Oh.*" He finished with a breathy laugh.

Ginny swallowed, pressing her free hand against her eyes as she was unable to look at him. He was laughing at her, the way she always knew he would, when he found out.

"Oh, Ginny," he finally whispered. "I've been so blind, haven't I? Long before the mirror changed how I saw the world, I never saw you, did I? Well, that settles it. I shall listen to your advice and marry you."

She straightened, turning to stare at him. "Kai, please, don't tease. I know it's silly, and I know it's practically…" She bit her lip and glanced away before she could add any more fuel to this mess. "You weren't supposed to ever know."

His smile faded, and he stared at her with all seriousness. "But is it the truth?"

She sucked in a sharp breath and glanced away again. "You weren't supposed to know," she repeated.

He gave a long sigh. "No wonder you were so upset when I was trying to court Maia. No wonder you left. I've been an abominable blind fool – but that ends today."

"Kaimund, you don't have to marry me *just* because I have this senseless crush on you," she said. "I was just … trying to convince you that you don't have to change yourself. I know you need to make a good alliance by marriage, marry someone of your own rank, and I—"

"You're the Gardener's aunt," said Kaimund. "I think you need to stop questioning your worth in this world, Gin. It makes you turn invisible, and I like being able to see you. Because you're the dearest person in the world to me, and I've never been more certain of anything in my life. Ginny, look at me – you are everything I could want in a wife, and I've been too blind to realize it all this time."

He stared at her, his expression so open and pure, but Ginny couldn't meet his eyes. She pushed her chair back and stood, though she couldn't escape the hold he had of her hand.

"But Princess Maia…"

"Oh, sweet Ginny," he continued, standing and wrapping a hand around her waist to keep her from going. "I think my interest in Maia was mostly the fact that she reminded me of you. Besides, she's been gone for two months now, and I've scarcely noticed. The day you walked out of my life, I was devastated. I can't lose you again, but I see now that you're not going to be able to sit calmly by as I court any young lady – and I don't think any of them will befriend you the way Maia did. No, the only answer is for me to marry you. And if my father makes a peep about alliances, I'll remind him that we already have his own brother married to the crown princess of the North Country."

"Kaimund, you can't make a rash decision like this based on … on my heart."

"I can and I should," he countered. "I can't let you out of my life again, after all. You've had my heart for a long, long time, but I was too blind to realize that. So, please forgive me for being a blind fool who has abused your heart for so long, and let me love you the way you deserve to be loved." He *finally* let go of her hand, only to hook a finger under her chin to force her to look up at him. "You can't make a declaration like that and then run when you find it's reciprocated."

She gave a small whimper, unable to do anything else. The knot of confusion in her heart was too twisted for her to make any sense of. This moment, right now, was everything she had ever wanted and everything she had dreaded. He wasn't hers. Why was he standing here offering himself to her with such overwhelming insistence?

"Don't promise what you can't give me," she finally said. "I know I'm just a little sister to you…"

But hadn't he just said that he thought she saw him as a brother?

"Ah," he said, a grin pulling at the corner of his mouth. "That's what all this is about. Well, why don't we just put that worry to rest?"

The kiss wasn't sudden. He gave her time to pull away or run, but she didn't. Her eyes slid closed as his lips met hers, and she gave a contented sigh, even as her legs threatened to give out from under her.

This couldn't be real.

Then he pulled away, still grinning. "Yes," he said. "I think I will be quite happy with you as my wife."

And even though she knew she should make more protests, that she should leave and let him think through this rationally, she was weak.

Pushing herself to her tiptoes, she wrapped her arms around his neck and kissed him again. Time lost meaning, and the world around them faded into nothing. It was just her and Kaimund, together, the way things should be.

"And just what is going on in here?"

She pulled away to find Lord Bethim standing in the doorway, frowning at them in confusion.

Kaimund's arms tightened around her waist, even as he turned to face his father. "I've found myself a wife like you wanted me to, sir. I hope you don't have any issues with her, because I have my heart quite set upon her."

Lord Bethim just stared, blinking, and then he shook his head. "Ah, well, she's a good girl, and it'll keep things from changing anymore now, will it? Perhaps it's for the best. Yes." And then he turned and continued down the hall.

"That settles that, then" Kaimund whispered against her

lips, and holding her tight again against him. "And you know my mother loves you as a daughter, already. So all that remains is for me to find a ring and make it official, right?"

"Oh!" Ginny squeaked, pulling back and removing a chain from underneath her dress, and he blinked at down at the ring it held. "It's the one you gave me as part of the whole … *thing*, with the mirror. Will insisted I keep it, because, well … it hardly matters now."

Her Frost blood kept her from blushing, but if she were otherwise, she was sure her cheeks would be bright red.

"Ah," he said, wrapping his hand around hers. "This would be perfect."

~

Ginny's nineteenth year had broken the world in two, but her twentieth had been a year of healing. While she desperately wished that she still had Will and so many others in her life, she was content with what she had.

No, more than content.

A smile curled her lips as she stepped into the garden alcove where Kaimund stood, showing their month-old daughter his roses. He spun around as he heard her approach, and his grin grew even broader as he saw her.

"I was just showing her where it all began," he declared. "I think she likes the roses just as much as her momma ever did."

Ginny smiled brighter as she stepped forward to take the baby from his arms. "Your father is looking for you."

Kaimund sighed, wrapped arms around Ginny's waist, and pressed a kiss to the top of her head. "Have I ever told you how beautiful you are?"

"Be careful, or I'll think that I need to reevaluate my view of myself," she answered, but her grin didn't falter.

"I'm going to remind you of your beauty every chance I get," he answered. "Because that's the way I want to see you. The most beautiful woman in all the world." He stood for a moment, fidgeting with her braid – since she was married now, she had given in to propriety and traded her two braids for a single one – and then gave a contented sigh. "Babies are fascinating, do you know that? They don't know enough yet to see themselves as anything. They just exist."

Ginny hummed an answer as she relished his hold and stared down into their daughter's clear blue eyes. They worried that Kaimund's eyesight might be inheritable, but right now, Ginny's Frost blood seemed more dominant.

"Your father says there's business for you to attend to, so you can't hide in the garden all day."

Kaimund sighed. "Ah, very well. I'll blindfold myself again, and you can lead the way."

"Naturally."

He'd taken to wearing a blindfold just a few months before, claiming that he trusted her eyes far more than his own. Yet he always took it off to talk to her, which sent secret chills of delight through her. The fact that he trusted her to guide him through the world and tell him how people *really* appeared…

Oh, but this last year had been so strangely wonderful.

Maybe the speed with which they'd married – barely a month after he'd made up his mind to do it – had been borderline scandalous, but it had been a small, private affair, only family really, and few outsiders had known until the birth of their daughter this month, leaving them to speculate when it had happened and how long the engagement had been. Jana and Jack had been there with their sisters, and Princess Mayblossom and Sir Graham, of course, with their son, and also Ginny's oldest sister, Mayblossom's step-grandmother, Queen Foxglove, but that was all. An invitation had been sent to Lady Nora, but she never responded.

Only the missing faces had marred the day.

Will and Robert were doing well; Ginny knew that. They'd built themselves a home on the other side of the Forest and, according to a note Jana sent, had welcomed a son into the world just a week before Ginny and Kaimund's daughter. But the world would still be so much a better place when the rift was healed.

And they, like everyone else, still held out hope that

Emmazel and the Gardener would one day win the battle with Hans, and then everything would go back to the way they had been before.

But they needed to focus on what they had. And Ginny, for one, was exceedingly thankful for what she had. As her husband replaced his blindfold, she took his arm and guided him carefully through the garden paths.

"You know, I had a thought just now," he said. "You're Emmazel's younger sister, right?"

"So we assume," she said, biting her lip. "We're a lot more sure about Will, but the logical assumption would be that I am as well."

"Exactly. Which means that you're the Gardener's aunt."

"Assumedly."

"And she's my Aunt Mayblossom's aunt."

"Where are you going with this?"

"Well, that makes you my great-great-great ... or so, aunt, doesn't it?"

"Foxglove is Mayblossom's *step*-grandmother, and then Mayblossom is only your aunt by marriage," she pointed out. "There are a few missing links in the chain."

"I know," he said. "But I know that practically being my aunt was the dealbreaker for Maia, and I just thought you might want to be aware of the situation..."

"It's a little late for that, and I've never seen you as my nephew." Ginny shook her head. "Let's agree to never think about this again? Please."

"Whatever you say, Aunt Ginny."

"How did I never see that you were such a tease?"

"Maybe I never realized how easy it was to make you laugh and how much I enjoyed doing it." Kaimund reached over to pat her hand. "I love you, by the way."

She sighed. "I love you too."

Coming Soon ...

Thornrose Estate

When *Northanger Abbey* discovers *Beauty and the Beast*
Summer 2023

A Little Persuaded

When *The Little Mermaid* needs some *Persuasion*
Fall 2023

Acknowledgements

Thanks so much to everyone who help me brainstorm and create
this story! Again, especial thanks to Kelsey for encouraging the first
spark when it came to me.
A huge thank you to everyone who's read and given me feedback,
as I've written. Sarah, Patience, Rachel, Cat, and a few others.
And thank you to you, lovely reader. I hope you enjoyed reading
this story as much as I did writing it.

About the Author

Kendra E. Ardnek is the penname of Kendra Roden, a Christian author who makes her home in the Piney Woods of East Texas with her herd of giraffes and clutch of dragon babies, alongside her honor guard of nutcracker figurines. When not writing, you can usually find her sitting in a box, because she might actually be a cat, and she's frequently been known to act before she thinks.

www.ingramcontent.com/pod-product-compliance
Lightning Source LLC
Chambersburg PA
CBHW020322160726
47992CB00004B/1651